THE TROUBLE WITH
THIN ICE

THE TROUBLE WITH

THIN ICE

CAMILLA T. CRESPI

HarperCollins*Publishers*

HarperCollins books may be purchased for educational, business, or sales promotional use. For information please write: Special Markets Department, HarperCollins Publishers, Inc., 10 East 53rd Street, New York, NY 10022.

FIRST EDITION

Designed by George J. McKeon

Library of Congress Cataloging-in-Publication Data

Crespi, Camilla T.
   The trouble with thin ice / Camilla T. Crespi.—1st ed.
      p.   cm.
   ISBN 0-06-017726-8
   1. Women detectives—Connecticut—Fiction.   I. Title.
PS3553.R435T76   1994
813'.54—dc20   93-23031

94 95 96 97 98 ❖/HC 10 9 8 7 6 5 4 3 2 1

For Stuart, who made it possible

I would like to thank Larry Ashmead, my agent Ellen Geiger, Judith Keller of Tricepts Productions, Dr. Barbara Lane, Dr. Joseph Lane, Aline and Seth Lawrence, Geoffrey Picket, Esq., and Captain John Roche of the Ridgefield Police Department.

CAST OF CHARACTERS
IN ORDER OF APPEARANCE

Simona Griffo Transplanted Italian, who finds herself skating on more than ice.

Stan Greenhouse New York City homicide detective, torn between loves.

Willy Greenhouse Stan's fourteen-year-old son, who likes the pasta but is wary of the cook.

Jean Shaw Owner of the Sleepy Hollow Inn, who hands out bad food and a warm soul.

Chuck Dobson Only heir of the Dobson clan, looking for his way.

Elisabeth Dobson Chuck's aunt and owner of the much-desired RockPerch house.

Joe Pertini Fieldston cop, whose sweetness is no match for his boss or his girlfriend.

Copper George Fieldston's police chief, who'd like to blink this murder off his log.

Kesho Larson Black bride-to-be, whose sudden reappearance spotlights the past.

Richard Mentani White groom-to-be, who has his own reasons for being in town.

Charles Dobson Chuck's father, who thinks he has a God-given right to privilege.

Myrna Dobson Chuck's mother, an expert on saving money and memories.

Edith Holmes Town snoop, who has her own ideas on who murdered whom.

Henry Holmes Edith's ear-worn husband, who insists she has good heart.

Nell Bishop Town librarian, who has her own claim on RockPerch.

Roxanne Santinelli Joe's girlfriend, who doesn't like stereotypes.

Mrs. Santinelli Roxanne's mother, who is p.c. only in her cooking.

Plus

An assortment of skaters, mothers, dead husbands, ex-wives, a cat, and a forgotten ghost.

CHAPTER

1

Where did you throw my pajamas?" I surfaced from a whirlpool of sheets and quilts on the four-poster bed, hands searching. Greenhouse, naked under the sheets, kept busy with various parts of my body.

"Ouch." I was stalling for time.

"Yum!" was Greenhouse's reply.

We were on our first night of what was to be a week's vacation at the Sleepy Hollow Inn in Fieldston, Connecticut. It was also my first extended vacation with Greenhouse after two years of on and off dating and my first ever with Greenhouse & Son. Too many firsts for relaxation.

"Isn't it sacrilegious to make love on Christmas Eve?" I asked, as Greenhouse's fingers found a nipple. I squirmed. "In Rome, I'd be at midnight Mass."

"In Rome it's six o'clock in the morning," he mumbled back from somewhere around my stomach. "You'd be in bed."

"Not with you." A hot palm found my thigh.

"You talk too much."

"Aah!" My groin lurched, making the bed creak.

"He'll hear us," I whispered. His fourteen-year-old son was next door, in the room they were sharing.

"Willy's fast asleep." Two hands pulled me down until we were mouth to mouth.

"Merry Christmas." Greenhouse gave me a soft, damp kiss.

"*Buon Natale.*" I pushed against his lips for more, letting my lower half take over. I threw off the sheet. My skin was burning.

We let our hands and lips play, but the moment stolen from Willy's wary vigilance was too precious for us to linger. I lifted my hips and Greenhouse slipped in. Delighted, I clasped this lovable man with my arms and legs.

Something knocked.

"*Amore,*" I whispered.

"Da-a-a-d!" his son cried. The bedroom door was gaping open.

Arms and legs flailed. Greenhouse flashed off me and ran, naked butt quavering, to his son. I screwed my eyes closed, hid behind a storm of pillows, and wished for instant death.

After an eternity of humiliated immobility, I heard the door click shut. I gingerly opened my eyes to a room empty of men. Willy's disgust was still there though, in my ears, tingling over my undressed body, clinging to the vines of the flowered wallpaper of that ex-romantic room.

I pressed my ear against the wall behind the four-poster. Greenhouse's voice came through, too low for me to catch actual words. I imagined him sitting on the twin bed, facing his son. Saying what? Thanks to his divorce, he already had enough guilt to hamper their relationship for a lifetime. Would he tell Willy that sex with someone you love is good and wonderful? That's what I would have told a child of mine. But I have no children and I couldn't go in that bedroom and explain to Willy. I was a new character in the Greenhouse family saga, the outsider. Which is where I wanted to be right now. Outside in the snowy cold night, walking across land new to me. Away from the mess of this bed, from the prickly cinnamon smell of Christmas potpourri, away from my embarrassment.

I stretched wool tights over my legs and brimming hips, eased on a skirt and sweater and concluded the dressing with a skimpy black coat that didn't keep me warm but had the redeeming feature of thinning me out. I'm five-foot-four, hippy, top heavy, with ten extra pounds soldered to my middle. Vain, like all Italians, I won't wear blimpy down coats or clunky snow boots. Since I was going to take a long walk in the snow, sleek black rain boots would do just fine. I would probably freeze to death, which would relieve Greenhouse of any embarrassing explanations. Willy would be ecstatic.

As I passed the Greenhouse door, the floorboards creaked so badly I desperately hoped to be taken for some ghost of yesteryear.

Willy's voice came out loud and clear. "But what if she has AIDS?"

A well-chosen concern, I whispered to myself, not knowing whether to rush into that room to reassure him or to yell at Greenhouse, "Why the hell didn't you lock the door?" I headed for the kitchen and the back door instead. A cowardly ghost.

"You're up, too?" asked Jean Shaw, the owner of the inn, as my feet now squeaked on linoleum. Jean's 230 pounds—declared right after introductions that afternoon—stood swathed in a red bathrobe, glowing in the light of the open refrigerator door. Two curlers trapped the front part of her unruly bleached blond hair. Premi, her dark Siamese, curled across the back of her neck like a mink collar. The rest of the kitchen was dark.

"I'm restless," I mumbled.

"So's half the household." She smiled as she unwrapped a slice of orange cheese and folded it into her mouth. "That dinner did it." She reached for a casserole dish still half full of brown roast beef floating in gravy. "Hungry?"

After one bite of it at dinner, Willy had decreed, "Metamorphic rock." He was deep into ninth grade geology.

"No thanks," I said. "I couldn't eat a thing." Premi gave out a Siamese growl.

"I'm really sorry about the Dobsons," Jean said. "Sometimes they get a little crazy. They've been here since the first settlers. Their brains wore out." The refrigerator door closed. "Put them out of your head."

There was no way I was going to forget the Dobsons, with whom we had shared a terrible Christmas Eve dinner, but Willy and Greenhouse were uppermost on my mind. At that very moment, they were trying to get back into their roles of innocent son and all-knowing, respected dad. Where did I fit?

The back door smashed into me, bringing with it a rush of icy air.

"Have you seen Elisabeth?" I recognized the man's nasal voice from dinner.

The lights snapped on.

"Chuck, thank the Lord!" Jean said, an empty spoon coming out of her mouth. "I was getting worried."

"*Ciao,*" I said, rubbing the dent the doorknob had left in my hip.

"Is Elisabeth here?" Chuck asked Jean, tugging at the zipper of his blue down jacket instead of closing the door.

"Isn't she up at the house?"

"No." Chuck's palm pushed his wire-rimmed glasses against his nose. "I thought she might be looking for me." His face was narrow, bony, raw with cold and intensely unhappy. In his early thirties, he was the youngest of the Dobsons.

"Your aunt Elisabeth is probably on one of her night

roams," Jean said. "My Lord, take those boots off!" The snow covering Chuck's boots and jeans was sliding down to the impeccably clean yellow linoleum.

Jean dropped the croaking cat on the kitchen table and grabbed a mop. I stood in the polar draft and wondered if I was ready to freeze to death for Greenhouse & Son.

"I don't understand how she could do this to me!" Chuck slammed the door with an angry backward kick, finally shutting off the icy air.

"What did she do?" I asked. "Push you into the snow?"

Chuck stared from behind his glasses, seeing me for the first time. "I fell." The mop slithered past our feet.

"You met Simona Griffo at dinner, remember?" Jean said loudly, giving us both a quick smile.

Chuck nodded.

Jean glanced at the cuckoo clock. "Well, it's twenty past midnight. Merry Christmas to one and all."

"Buon Natale."

Chuck looked dour.

"Italian makes me want to burst out in song," Jean said. She was now piling a plate with beef slices, Premi plastered to her ankles.

"Simona's going out on a roam, too. I guess you New Yorkers don't get a chance to do that much." On another plate she dropped spoonfuls of gravy. "You'd get a knife stuck in your chest, just like that poor kid from Utah."

"In Greenwich Village, I walk around at night all the time," I said, immediately defensive about my new American home.

"Now you've got terrorists to worry about too."

"I got used to that in Rome."

Her look was skeptical as she bent down to give Premi his gravy. "Well, there's nothing dangerous out here except maybe a patch of ice."

Chuck jerked his head. "And my father." Premi took cautious licks.

"Why don't you go to bed, honey," Jean said, now handing Chuck the plate filled with beef slices. "And eat something. It'll help you sleep." He'd left home two years ago to come live at the inn. After having met his parents, I wondered what had taken him so long.

"Good night." Jean gave his arm a pat. "Be careful how you open doors."

Chuck turned his unhappy face to me. "I didn't see you."

Willy's "Da-a-a-d!" came screaming back into my head. "That's just fine with me," I said, walking out into the Ice Age.

"Simona!" Jean's voice stopped me just as I was closing the door behind me.

"It's only a half moon," she said. "You'll need this." A sturdy red arm shot out the door, dangling an equally sturdy flashlight.

"Thanks." The flashlight changed hands.

"Don't stay out long. It's one of the coldest Connecticut winters in years."

"If you see Elisabeth . . . "

"Watch out for ice!" A phone started ringing and the door to the inn slammed shut.

CHAPTER

2

I chose the steepest slope and followed a clearing wide enough for snow to pick up the moonlight. There was a spattering of stars, no clouds. I jogged my arms to keep warm, the flashlight a welcome weight. I liked this silvery dark; the snow-muffled silence was reassuring. A true New England Christmas scene, I thought, feeling lucky it had snowed heavily here two days before. New York had been covered by three inches that got churned into sooty mush in a matter of hours without disrupting the frenzied pace of the city. I dug my chin into my coat collar to keep it from turning into an icicle and thought of the stark difference between this land and Rome, from where I had come four years ago after my marriage fell into the Tiber.

Snow falls in Rome maybe once every ten years. Two inches of the stuff is enough to break tree branches, exhaust the city's supply of boots, and cause traffic jams even more paralyzing than usual. At work, for those who've been brave enough to make it in, "Let's check the snow," becomes another excuse for a quick espresso at the corner bar, the half-inch deep black brew "corrected" with Sambuca or grappa. In my parents' building, the old portiere, a World War II resistance fighter, would be shaking his head, saying snow was just another German insult.

As I climbed now, I wondered on whose private property I was trespassing. One of the Dobsons for sure. They owned the eighty acres surrounding Jean's meager two and lived in two homes on either side of the lake. My light raked over boulders, across thick, snow-coated pines, between bare birches and straggly, bone-thin trees fighting for space and light, until it met a high wall of drooping rhododendron. It was a moment frozen in time, I thought. And frozen in temperature, I realized, breaking into a stomp-the-earth dance. My feet were going to need microwaves on HIGH to get back to normal.

The vacation—all twelve hours of it—had been a fiasco so far. When Kesho, an African-American friend of Greenhouse's, invited him and Willy to her New Year's Eve wedding at the Sleepy Hollow Inn, he decided the time was ripe for Willy and me to spend some "real" time together, ignoring my objection that we ourselves hadn't spent more than a weekend together. I'd loved the idea anyway, full of romantic thoughts of being part of the Greenhouse "inner circle," my need to belong to someone else getting the best of me.

Willy, who in the eleven months since I'd met him accepted me as long as I fed him pasta carbonara in his father's apartment and left after dinner, made his feelings clear from the start of the trip. As Greenhouse piled our luggage in the car trunk in front of his building on West Seventy-seventh Street, Willy insisted that if he didn't sit in the front seat with Dad he'd throw up. I smiled, slipped into the back seat, and off we zipped to the West Side Highway, where all of Manhattan and New Jersey had decided to greet the holiday season by kissing bumpers and honking horns. The normally one-and-a-half-hour drive to Fieldston took three, during which time Willy, claiming his Walkman didn't work, sang along to a tape of Guns 'n' Roses turned up to blast-Dad's-girlfriend-out-of-the-car volume while Greenhouse's head got an obtuse slant to it, and I pretended to be a deaf corpse. Not once in the three hours did either of them look at the back seat to see if I was still breathing.

A branch cracked and I heard the soft thud of a snow clump falling. Then a repeated, hurried crunch. I swung my flashlight around to the sound, hoping to catch a deer loping between the trees. All I got was a rock tumbling down the slope and hitting a boulder with a dull flat sound that was instantly swallowed by white frosty silence. I stomped my feet to keep the blood moving, maybe even to express my disappointment, and swung the flashlight, wondering which way to go next. An opening in the pine trees let me see the lake, four acres of frozen hollow sitting in the middle of the wooded Dobson land. Goose Lake, the locals called it, because of the Canada geese that came in the spring. Its official name was Ramapoo Lake, after the migrant Indian tribe that had camped here every year even after the first English settlements. From this vantage, the land looked as it must have almost three centuries ago. Suddenly New York seemed as far away as Rome—both barbaric civilizations compared to this quiet, elegant wilderness.

I moved the flashlight high, above the rhododendron on my left, breaking the beam over the Frank Lloyd Wright house that leaned over the lake, its eaves reaching out like warning hands. There was something self-congratulatory and arrogant about the way the house possessed the rocky brow of the hill, I'd thought this afternoon on the lake, gazing at it for the first time with Kesho.

"Isn't it gorgeous?" the bride-to-be had said, following my look. "It's called RockPerch and Richard and I are buying it. We're signing the contract the day after tomorrow." They were hoping to close by Valentine's Day, but I shouldn't say anything. Elisabeth Dobson, the owner, wanted the sale to be kept a secret.

"Why is it a secret?" I asked, suspecting the answer. During a short tour of Fieldston I hadn't seen a single African-American.

"Because I'm black and a few other things." She had not explained the "other things."

Just a few hours later, in Jean's red cabbage rose dining room festooned with Christmas garlands and too many red bows, Elisabeth suddenly gave up her "secret" and announced to her Dobson in-laws the upcoming sale of RockPerch. What followed was *un macello*—"a slaughter" being what my mother likes to label even mild family arguments. The Dobsons were mild only in the volume of their voices. Their prejudice loomed large and ugly in their terse spurts of anger. Chuck's father was the first.

"I never thought I'd see the day," Charles Dobson said, calmly using his full red wine glass to catch reflections from the brass chandelier. "I never thought I'd see the day when Dobson land would fall into the hands of servants' seed."

With Greenhouse quickly pressing a restraining hand on my thigh, I marveled at Kesho's composure. Only her earrings—large clusters of red and green plastic discs—had trembled.

I switched off the flashlight now and started walking down between the maple, oak, and pine trees. It was too cold, the memory too uncomfortable, to just stand. Rock-Perch sprawled over its mammoth ledge, now only an inked-out darkness against the lighter dark of the sky.

A few feet from the edge of the lake, I swept my light one last time over the sloping circle of trees in a romantic good-bye gesture to what was, in the fantasy of the moment, the primordial frozen wilderness. I am true to my country in my operatic range of emotions. Beauty thrills me and makes me cry as much as sadness.

A movement caught my eye. Two hundred feet ahead of me, near the small island of rushes girdled by the frozen lake, something or someone was moving. For a moment, in the weakening white shaft of my flashlight, I thought a sheaf of dull brown rushes was detaching itself from the island. Then I saw the white flash of tail and the head, small and delicate, turn toward the light. *Un cerbiatto!* Bambi incarnate. I gasped, my only sighting of a fawn having been at the zoo. He flicked enormous ears, his legs trembling, and suddenly the memory of that terrible forest fire came back to me. I stroked the flashlight's beam over the rushes, hoping to find Mom. I had howled through most of *Bambi*.

I gasped again, louder this time, when my light hit the fawn again. He was backing away. The white flash of tail made a sudden downward arc. The fawn crumbled, his hindquarters disappearing.

I ran and slid to him, the flashlight zigzagging white streaks against the trees and the sky, in concert with the movements of my arm. The fawn thrashed against the rushes trying to find a foothold while I imitated the skating gestures I'd seen that afternoon, sliding one foot, then the other, praying I wouldn't break an ankle before getting to him.

I crashed on my back, got up, took a few more steps and slipped onto my knees, dropping the flashlight. I crawled on gloved hands and knees, the fawn still clearly in sight at one edge of the flashlight's low shaft of light. He reached his head and neck up toward the half moon as if he could stretch himself out of that hole. Shifting his weight from one elbow to the other, he tried to nail his front hooves into the ice. He was waist high in water. The lake cracked.

"Don't get near the island," Kesho had warned me earlier that afternoon. "The ice is too thin." What if I go under too, I thought, cursing myself for not losing those extra ten pounds. I lunged on my stomach toward the fawn. He reared his head in fright. I grabbed a hoof that cut through my glove and then slipped away from me. Lifting myself up on my knees, I lunged again, grabbing his neck. Ice splintered under me but did not open. With my head pressed against his warm fur, smelling his musty sweat, I made soothing sounds that reassured neither of us. I pulled. His hind legs, deep in water, were too long for me to drag him out. I needed to lift him out, but I couldn't get any closer to the edge of the ice without falling in too. How? He weighed forty to fifty pounds, but my biceps had worked themselves up to a cumulative ten pounds tops.

The fawn was now perfectly still, probably frightened into immobility. Or was he aware I was trying to help? I got more crackling sounds as I gently let go of his neck and inched slowly three more feet to the edge of the ice, out of range of the fallen flashlight. I stretched my hand to the island, deep into the rushes, testing for solid ground. Freezing, icy mush seeped through my glove. I grabbed reeds and pulled to see if they would hold. I was left with a bouquet in my hand.

Then I made out the tree, seven or eight feet inland, with a branch curving temptingly toward me. Standing a couple of feet back on safe ice, I could just reach it on tip-toe, but it was too high and far to one side for me to hold on and grab the fawn at the same time. Encouraging the fawn with a banter of baby words—*cicciolino, bello di mamma, bombolotto mio, pippolo*—I took off my coat, stretched to tie a sleeve to the branch and tugged with my 135 pounds. The branch creaked but miraculously held. I inched away, back into the shaft of light, pulling the coat toward the fawn. He was thrashing again, his eyes popping, the mouth open, too terrified to cry out. "*Calma, bello, calma,*" I whispered, close to him now. He had slipped in deeper, looking, in a moment of stillness, like a trophy hanging from an icy white wall.

I clenched my fist around the untied coat sleeve, bent down and plunged my free arm under the water, catching a hind leg so thin I let go for fear of breaking it. I reached down again, following the ridge of his back, aiming for that white flash that had allowed me to spot him in the first place. I wrapped my fingers tight around his tail even though I could hardly feel them from the cold.

"Che Dio ce la mandi buona," I said, tugging with all my weight, my other hand working itself up my coat, shortening the distance. "May God send it good," the "it" being luck. I was petrified I would lose my grip and fall down after him. My arm sockets burned, my hands were frozen pain, and my head boomed with cracking, tearing, breaking sounds. The tree, the ice, my coat, my arm—they were all going to crash. Thank God he wasn't full grown!

The fawn's forelegs scrambled on the ice as he heaved himself forward by sheer force of will. One thigh came out of the water and I gave one last upward tug, then thrust my weight to one side to lift him up and out. The branch cracked. I let go of my coat and threw myself backward, taking the fawn's behind with me. Suddenly I was flat on solid ice and my *cerbiatto* was home free. I watched those long twigs he had for legs unfold as he picked himself up and gave that puff of a tail a good shake. Tears iced down my cheeks.

"Hey, how about a *grazie!*"

The fawn skittered away onto firm land.

"You're welcome," I yelled at that lovely white sopping wet tail before it disappeared up into the woods. Let the Dobsons hear me, what did I care? I'd won the war.

This hero stood up cautiously, the only creaks now coming from my arm muscles. My stomach was frozen tight, the only time it was flat in thirty-seven years of lifetime, and my coat dangled in front of me, still attached to the branch, the loose sleeve dipping into water. If it hadn't been so cold, I would have liked to leave it there as a commemorative flag to my strength. Actually it was those extra ten pounds that had done the trick, I told myself, to excuse the reward eating I planned to do as soon as I got back to the inn. With Jean asleep I could sneak in some cooking. Maybe I'd try venison to teach that ungrateful fawn a thing or two.

I leaned over to untie the sleeve. The coat fell over a small bush at the very edge of the island. I reached and pulled. The branches bent forward, then snapped back, dropping a light something on my foot. I kicked the "something" toward the beam of the weakening flashlight and stared at a cluster of red and green plastic discs. One of Kesho's earrings—the ones that had trembled during that terrible dinner. What was it doing out in the middle of the lake? I turned back and carefully stepped around the ice hole to get my coat. Then I screamed.

CHAPTER

3

N o one heard my scream. Once again I lay down on the fragile ice and yanked, this time at a long, graceful hand that had bobbed up where the fawn had almost drowned. A woman's white hand.

"Vieni fuori!" I begged, pulling at that wrist, reaching down for her elbow. "God help me!" I cried, remembering in my panic about a boy who had stayed under water for more than twenty minutes—a death-inducing eternity. He had lived. I wanted this woman to live too, but I couldn't get her. I was too tired; she was stuck under the ice; she was too heavy; I was numb with cold. Holding on to that frozen hand, I yelled my head off for help. Lights suddenly streaked up trees on one side of the lake. A male voice yelled back and what seemed hours later Chuck came sliding across the ice.

Flat on our stomachs, we pummeled ice with our fists and pulled. Her head appeared, covered with long hair black with water, then sharp, thin shoulders. We had to wait for the police to get the rest of her out.

Elisabeth Dobson had wrapped rocks in her skirt, holding them in place with a wide ribbon belt. That's what made her so heavy. While one patrolman tried mouth-to-mouth resuscitation, the other shined a flashlight in my face and asked me how I had found her. Chuck ran to tell his parents.

"Her skirt's made of velvet," I told the patrolman, as the important bearer of news. "The color of pines. You know, for Christmas." I wiped my nose, from the cold, from the tears, wishing I could see this man's face, anyone's face. A breathing face.

"Hey, what's this?" my patrolman asked, his flashlight picking up the withered, darkening yellow streak of my own flashlight, lying where I had dropped it years ago. Kesho's earring sat on the streak of light like a scaly lump of dirt. I'd forgotten all about it. The cop scuffed over to the earring and scooped it up. "This yours?"

"No." I couldn't even begin to think how the earring had gotten on the island. I just hoped Kesho was fast asleep with Richard wrapped around her.

"No good, Joe," the resuscitation man announced with a shake of his head. "She's gone." My throat closed.

"See if she's wearing the match to this." Joe shined his light on Kesho's earring. "Looks more like some tree ornament than an earring."

"Paco Rabanne," I offered to distract us all on that morning meant to commemorate a birth.

"Who?"

"A designer famous in the late sixties. He used plastic discs to make jewelry and clothes. My mother used to have a shoe box full of those earrings in all colors. When they went out of fashion, she sewed the discs on my sweaters. For a while I thought I was very chic."

"You OK?"

"No, I'm not OK. I want to go home." I had no idea what I meant by home. The Sleepy Hollow? My studio in the Village? Rome?

"Take it easy on yourself," Joe said. "She's probably been dead for hours."

"I guess." Not that many hours. I'd walked out on Elisabeth and the rest of the Dobsons around nine o'clock. Joe's watch now read 1:00 A.M. I'd probably met up with the fawn at 12:35, maybe 12:40, so that made it three and a half hours at the most. That taxing calculation cleared my brain a little. I looked up at what I could see of Joe's face, his flashlight now aimed at his thick boots. All I got was a square chin, a small head, and lots of intriguing shadow.

"Those look warm," I said, dropping my glance.

"Sure are." He snapped the catch of his watch a couple of times.

The ambulance arrived from nearby Danbury, without the wrenching wail that sweeps New York streets. There was no point to sirens here in Fieldston; no traffic to fight at this time of morning; too many children straining to hear sleigh bells and a "Heigh ho." Besides, silence was fitting.

Charles Dobson and his wife, Myrna, made it down the hill from the other side of the lake just as the ambulance stopped. Chuck followed at a reluctant pace. The family patriarch barely glanced at the dark shape of Elisabeth lying on the ice, her velvet green skirt a dark stain, then began snapping questions at the two patrolmen, immediately possessing the scene. Myrna, half hidden in a brown parka, stared at the gurney making its way across the lake as if it were coming for her. Joe told me to go back to the inn. As I passed Chuck, I heard him sob.

"So what were you doing on Goose Lake in the middle of the night?" the police chief asked me an hour later, after he'd wiped his boots on the kitchen mat to Jean's satisfaction.

Jean handed us two mugs of instant hot chocolate. She was still in her red bathrobe, but now her lips were a

matching red, her cheeks were rouged, and her two
curlers had disappeared. Chuck had woken her up with
the news, and after Patrolman Joe Pertini, still snapping
his watch, had come by to let me know the police chief
was on his way, she and Premi had kept me company in
the kitchen. I let Greenhouse and Willy sleep. They'd had
enough bad news from me to hold them for a while.

"This girl needs rest," Jean said, getting ready to sit
down by her round table.

"No sense in you missing yours, Jeanie," the chief said,
after thanking her. "And take that cat with you. She gives
me the creeps."

"Premi's a he." Jean picked up the Siamese, who gave a
parting yowl. "If he'd been female, you'd have loved him."

"I like my cats good-looking," he said, laughing long
and loud as Jean scuttled out of the kitchen. He took one
look at my face and stopped.

"Odd thing to do on Christmas morning," Copper
George said, sitting down on a wooden armchair by the
round kitchen table. That's what Jean had called him as
he'd first walked in, hulking, into the kitchen—Copper
George. I sat down on the ruffled, checked pillow of the
chair opposite and wondered if the nickname had stuck
because of his red hair or his profession.

"Odd what?" I asked, thinking the Dobsons had to be
really important for the chief of police to show up at two
o'clock on—as he himself had stressed—Christmas morning. Under shock my mind tends to wander to the trivial.
Greenhouse thinks I'm under shock a lot.

Copper George asked again, "So what were you doing
there in the middle of the night?"

"Waiting for Santa Claus," I said, angry that this man
had laughed. I gulped down too-sweet chocolate, the calo-
ries instantly lulling me. All right, he's a policeman, I told
myself. He's used to death. I'd seen a few deaths myself.
The last ones, on Guadeloupe, had been gruesome enough

to make me shed ten horrified pounds in a week. Not a diet I recommend.

"I played Santa to a bunch of wide-eyed kids over at town hall all afternoon." He seemed to have enjoyed his role. "If it'll make you talk I'll get right back into my Santa suit." He smiled encouragement.

I started to explain about not being able to sleep and needing a walk.

"You've got some kind of accent," he interrupted.

"I'm Italian."

"We got thousands of those in Connecticut. Every block's got a pizza parlor, seems like. One of them's even after my job." He peered at me as if it were my fault. Next I expected to hear how he'd gone to Rome and been robbed. I got that a lot in New York. I fought back with the story of how my Village studio was robbed *and* vandalized.

"Well, on this walk I found a fawn drowning in the lake," I said to get on with things. "In the hole Elisabeth had drowned herself in. I fished him out."

"A fawn?" he said, tilting his chin down, as if to see me better. He was somewhere in his late fifties, with a thick head of red-gray hair and a strong, large face with brown eyes half wrapped in wrinkles, a spreading nose, and full, sensuous lips. He was not my idea of a ladies' man, even though his eyes made me think of chocolate-covered almonds. That was just hunger.

"You should have let that thing drown." Copper George took a loud sip from his mug and leaned back against the chair. "You better check yourself for ticks."

"The hole in the ice wasn't that big," I said. Lyme disease seemed irrelevant at the moment. "The fawn only fell in halfway. I know she was very thin, but still, she'd have to cram herself down into that freezing . . ." I took another sip to warm up and lull my mind. "What a desperate way to commit suicide."

"You knew Elisabeth?"

"I met her this afternoon up at her house. She was kind enough to let me use her bathroom." A sad, odd woman.

"Walter was declared dead last year, but I know he's alive," Elisabeth Dobson had told me in a constricted voice, sitting perfectly still against a ten-foot band of windows overlooking the rocky, snow-covered hill dropping into Goose Lake. I'd started the conversation with "who's that handsome man in the painting?" feeling I owed her more than a toilet flush.

We were in what I took to be a man's study. Above a ledge of gray rock, cypress shelves were half-filled with books on modern architecture and biographies of famous men—Truman, Roosevelt, Lincoln, Wright, I. M. Pei among others. Even *Mussolini's Roman Empire* by Denis Mack Smith. In front of the rock ledge, a rectangle of concrete, covered by a thick slab of overlapping oak, served as a desk. There was nothing on the desk except a small enamel and gilt clock abandoned by some ancestor, a black cordless phone, and a silver pen and pencil set, lying in its open box.

"My last gift to Walter," Elisabeth said, following my gaze. The room was furnished only with the desk and a set of four dark square armchairs very similar to ones I had seen in the Frank Lloyd Wright room at the Metropolitan Museum. On the other side of the vast room, above layers of gray rock recessed on one side to fit a fireplace, hung the lifeless, awkward painting that had prompted her strange reply.

"Walter Dobson, younger son," Elisabeth said with her strange, raw voice that spoke of a perennial sore throat. "My nephew Chuck did the painting." Her cheeks puckered in a smile, giving her a crinkled-paper look. She was in her mid-fifties. "It's ghastly. So was Walter in the end. But he was powerful-looking, wasn't he?"

A big man, made bigger by a black cape, one end thrown theatrically over a shoulder. Undeniably handsome and probably well-aware of it. And yes, powerful-looking. I nodded my agreement.

"Kesho's fiancé looks powerful, too," she said, her voice rising as we both turned to gaze down at the lake. Kesho and Richard danced on skates, side by side, her darkness shining against the hard whiteness of the ice, his thick frame suddenly graceful.

"It's a warning sign," Elisabeth added.

"Napoleon looked like a wimp." I gazed up at the low ceiling, a mixture of dark wood planks and sheets of glass lunging dramatically at sharp angles toward the sky and the treetops. The house blended beautifully with the woods and dramatic outcroppings of rocks outside, but I found its starkness unwelcoming. I remember thinking that if I had that kind of money, I'd go for a cozy Renaissance palazzo. I was also uncomfortable with this once-pretty, painfully thin woman. Besides, she hadn't even put out a tree, a wreath, a poinsettia, a Christmas cactus. Or asked me to sit down.

"I know Walter's alive," she continued. "It's his way of making me suffer. He's very good at that, my husband is." She moved her head and neck in a wilting movement, smiling at me as if I knew what suffering was all about. It was her voice, wobbly and hoarse, that knew about suffering. All that was wrong with her life had lodged itself in her throat.

"I'm divorced," I said, hoping that would help. Two hundred feet below me, Greenhouse, muffled in a kelly green scarf and hat, raced Willy toward the island of rushes and straggly trees. I waved at them. Kesho saw me and urged me with broad gestures to join them.

"How lucky you are to be divorced," Elisabeth said. "At least you know where you stand. What am I? A deserted wife or a widow?" The circles around her small eyes looked as if they'd been smudged with taupe eye shadow to make the blue stand out. Her hair was fading brown, long strands curling down over high cheekbones. The rest of her was covered in the same dull color—a long shapeless sweater drooped over a wool skirt that came down to her ankles.

"You're a who, not a what," I said. I'd had to remind myself of that in the past, when the "divorced" label felt like a dog tag shoved between my teeth. "I dumped my married name. That helped." And get rid of that portrait, I wanted to add. Instead I shifted weight and slung my borrowed ice skates over my shoulder, itching to get back to the lake. Rome doesn't even supply ice for a Coke, so I wasn't going to be Dorothy Hamill down there, but I could at least look the part. Elisabeth Dobson let me go with a resigned wave of her long hand.

"I hope their marriage is happier than mine," she had said, the voice begging to be soothed.

"Last time I saw her was last night at dinner," I said now to Copper George, who sat so still he might have been asleep if it weren't for his eyes. He blinked a lot.

"You were part of the Dobson Christmas Eve dinner here at the inn?" Copper George sat up. "That's a privilege I've had only a few times." He scowled. "You know them well then?"

"No." I sighed and told him about being invited to Kesho's and Richard's wedding, how Kesho had known Greenhouse since she was a teenager, how Elisabeth had invited Kesho and Richard to the dinner, including us at Kesho's request.

"Last I heard, Charles Dobson likes to do the inviting, although he does have a weakness for Lizzie." He scrubbed his chin. "But then what man doesn't."

"Mr. Dobson didn't know about it. Elisabeth wanted to surprise him."

Copper George laughed. "He must have loved that. Black rap and egg nog."

"She did commit suicide, didn't she?" At dinner, Charles Dobson had accused his sister-in-law of having an "unsound mind."

"What makes you think she'd do that?" He had dressed in a hurry. Underneath his red knit wool tie, his shirt was unbuttoned.

"The alternative is scarier." He hadn't mentioned the earring yet. I barely knew Kesho, but both Greenhouse and Willy thought she was great, which was enough for me not to want her in any trouble. "So what was it?"

Copper George dropped his elbows on the table, a distracted look on his face. "I once knew a black squirt of trouble by the name of Kesho." He had not brushed his teeth. "She left Fieldston more than twenty years ago."

"I'm here for a comeback." Kesho cut the kitchen air with long, determined strides, wearing bright green sweats with a sequined squirrel and RUFFY sewn across her chest.

Her having lived here before was a surprise to me, but then that night, what wasn't? I stole a glance at the window, half expecting to see Rudolph's red nose streaking across the sky.

"Hey, you look almost good," Copper George said, giving her the once over.

"A squirt no more. There's five feet eight inches, 130 pounds of black me now and you might as well hear how I see it." Kesho had hair cropped tight over her head like a cap, a dark oak complexion and a wide smiling face with puffy cheeks that at thirty-four made her still look like a teenager. Her expression was different now, pulled out of shape by anger.

"That was no suicide. Elisabeth was killed."

I cringed. Copper George stopped blinking.

"What makes you think she was murdered?" His voice was barely audible.

"She was going to sell me RockPerch."

"Like hell she was." He didn't believe her.

"We were handing her a three-hundred-thousand-dollar deposit on Monday."

Now he sat up. "You were going to pay three million for that place!"

Three hundred thousand dollars would last me two lifetimes at least. Three million sounded like the price of cigarettes in Brazil.

"That was her price."

"Struck it rich with your white man?"

I pounced. "She writes highly successful books!"

"You must have wanted the place real bad." Copper George reached into the breast pocket of his worn tweed jacket.

"It's not an unreasonable price," I said. "The house was designed by Wright, has all his original furniture, plus forty acres of prime Connecticut real estate, only an hour and a half from New York."

That didn't stop him, as if anything would. A smell of tobacco came wafting out of his pocket as he extracted Kesho's earring. "Recognize this?" he asked.

"My mother used to have earrings like that," I started. Kesho cut me off.

"It's mine," she said, a hand going to an earlobe even though both lobes were naked. "Where'd you find it?"

"Who cares?" I tossed in, still rooting for the suicide theory.

Copper George nodded at me. "I'll catch you again in a few hours."

"Is Kesho right?" I stood up. "Was Elisabeth killed?"

Copper George flicked eyes from me to Kesho and

back again to me with a spatter of blinks. "That's what the ME claims." He looked angry, as if murder were a personal insult.

"Want me to get Richard?" I asked Kesho.

"Let him sleep," she said. Her face was resigned now.

I walked away. "Tell me about the dinner first," Copper George said. "I hear you got called some names." I closed the kitchen door behind me.

CHAPTER

4

Christmas Eve dinner had started out fine. Kesho, Richard, Greenhouse, and I gathered in Jean's large living room which was filled with badly made Shaker-style tables, an ornate Victorian red plush sofa and various-sized armchairs plucked from thrift shops across Fairfield County. In front of the bay window a fake pink pine was laden with lace bows, transparent glass balls and an assortment of miniature porcelain-faced dolls.

There were enough lamps to light up Times Square but only three were lit, giving the room a dim, firelight glow. The fireplace was filled with logs but hadn't worked "since Bill had his heart attack and died right there, staring at the flames." Jean pointed to where Greenhouse was sitting, a dark green armchair festooned with crocheted white cotton doilies. My lover, a courageous homicide detective belonging to New York's finest, will naturally converge on anything green—with the exception of brussels sprouts—probably thinking it's a way of upholding the family name. However, as soon as Jean turned her back, he quietly rose from that death-encompassing armchair. He saw me smile.

"Too close to the fire," he announced with that deadpan face that always gives me naughty urges. "You look great," he added, as a distracting ploy. "New?" He was referring to my silk dress, green of course, which he'd already seen at least eight times and was going to keep on seeing, since my job in the creative department of an advertising agency paid for my New York City rent, a healthy supply of DeCecco pasta and plum tomatoes, but little else.

"Never worn," I answered, deciding that I really loved this man.

"I like your dress, too," he quickly said to Jean, who was now arching penciled eyebrows at the armchair Greenhouse had abandoned.

"It was Bill's favorite too," she said, taken in by Greenhouse's grin-and-twinkling-eye bit. Jean was wearing a blue-and-pink flowered dress that almost matched the wallpaper and loudly accentuated her large size. I liked her gumption, her individuality. I was getting tired of obsessing about weight with the rest of America, I decided, dropping two half-frozen mushroom-in-soggy-pastry-shell canapés down my throat.

All right, I was a little on edge. From the den Willy blasted us with the unseasonal sounds of cymbals and electric guitars. I'd suggested *Miracle on 34th Street* and gotten "You cooking dinner?" in reply as he switched to MTV.

"Are you sure you're ready for this?" Jean said.

No, I'm not, I'd have said had she been talking to me. She was squinting at Kesho, who was stunning in a curry yellow satin sheath from the twenties and silver platform heels. She had a swimmer's strong shoulders and arms sculpted by muscles. Her bare back, straight as a plank, ended with an ass I would have killed for.

I've got curves too, but mine look like punching bags. I'm all-right-looking when I'm in a good mood: dark brown hair that, on humid days, curls nicely around my neck and now in the heat of Jean's living room, sagged to my shoulders in clumps; a long Roman nose, the only straight feature I've got; brown eyes, olivey skin—a face that might launch a sail across the bathtub. The body, as I said, should be a Don King special.

"Ready for what, Jean?" Kesho leaned against a muscled, chunky Richard clothed in an oversized rust cashmere sweater and baggy brown pants that flopped over his tasseled loafers. "My marriage to an Italian-American who doesn't even tan well, or dinner with the Dreadful Dobsons?"

I didn't pick up that she must have known them a long time. Willy was on my mind.

"I don't know why I let you railroad me into this good neighbor crap, Rich."

"Now Kesho, it's going to be tough enough as it is." Jean got a pinched look on that round happy face. It was hard to tell her age. Somewhere in her fifties, I thought, given the white roots of her blonde hair and the sag of her throat.

"Why tough?" I asked.

"It'll be fine," Richard said, his chiseled cheeks emanating wafts of Calvin Klein, while his hand played with a handwoven red and ocher cloth folded over Kesho's shoulder. "We're going to live here, remember?" His long black hair was held with a silver clasp at the back of his neck. Sexy.

"Why don't you grow your hair," I whispered to Greenhouse. He gave me a horrified look.

Jean seemed worried. "Kesho, you're not going to lose your temper, are you?"

"Why me?" Kesho popped a canapé in her mouth. "Ask the Dreads." The Dobsons had just walked in through the holly-wreathed double doors.

In his mid-sixties, Charles Dobson was not as tall or as powerful looking as the portrait of his brother. Strength seemed concentrated in a barrel chest that pressed open his weathered blue blazer. His dour, jowly face hadn't mustered a smile in decades. The sight of our motley group worked no magic.

"I wasn't told there'd be guests," he said, his watery blue eyes finding the reindeer cluttered on the mantelpiece more cheering.

Jean looked chagrined. "Elisabeth—" she started to say. Richard hurried over to introduce himself. We did the same, except for Kesho. We shook hands. Kesho offered a tight-lipped smile.

Myrna Dobson grabbed some eggnog and clutched the cup with both bony, freckled hands, acknowledging everyone with nods of her small pointed chin. Richard began talking to Charles about the restaurants he owned in the city. Myrna asked me something I didn't catch. I was too busy watching Greenhouse try out a feeble joke on Kesho who stayed grim-faced. Jean slipped mushrooms into her mouth, her cheeks now redder than Rudolph's flickering nose.

What was going on?

"Anytime you're in the city, just let me know," Richard said. "West Side, East Side, Soho, take your pick of my restaurants." He handed over a card. "It'll be on us."

Myrna muttered something again after a gulp of eggnog.

"Excuse me?" I said.

"It's only for dinner," she said. "We'll all get over it."

"Get over what?" I asked.

Charles straightened up to relieve those buttons that looked as if they might pop any minute. "We never eat out. Besides, Myrna thinks going into the city is a waste of gas."

We should have all left right then when the insult was hurled only at Manhattan. Instead we all shuffled our feet. I did my diplomatic bit, which I've hated since the age of four when my diplomat father started parading me, dressed in baby cute, at every cocktail party the Italian Consulate gave.

"Jean tells me you publish a monthly newsletter that's very successful." I smiled at Myrna.

"*Prudent Times*. I give tips on how to save money."

"Eat pasta, for one," I said, thinking *Stingy Times* was more like it. She looked stingy. Short, slim-hipped, thin, with short salt-and-pepper hair scraped back from her forehead. There was no makeup on her mildly wrinkled face except for a quavering line of lipstick on thin lips. She had brittle legs ending in the incredibly narrow feet—shod in vintage Ferragamos—that so many rich American women seem to have. The dark blue knit suit she was wearing even had a few moth bites on one sleeve. But there was nothing stingy about her bust, which pushed against her knit suit in imitation of her husband's chest. Nor did the double row of glowing Barbara Bush pearls choking her neck fit that stereotype. Myrna's, I would have sworn, were real. The emerald clasp alone had to be worth six years of my salary.

"I should subscribe," I said, fingering the sweet strand of cultured pearls proper Italian girls used to get on their eighteenth birthdays. So I was probably wrong about her stinginess. Making judgments in the first five minutes doesn't usually lead to a good score card on the I've-got-your-number game. "Is the newsletter expensive?" Maybe she was even nice.

"Chuck will give you a card." Then silence.

"Kesho and Richard are getting married here at the inn," I threw in for a reaction. "On New Year's Eve." Myrna's eggnog cup, empty by now, did a Dow Jones panic dip.

"Why here?" she asked. Her face, pruned long ago of any excessive emotion, managed a sort of pained disdain.

In Rome she'd be unkindly called *stitica*—constipated.

"Why here?" Myrna asked again.

I knew the simple answer—they were buying Elisabeth's place—but I couldn't tell her that. Why Connecticut, why Fieldston, why RockPerch? That I didn't know. From the den, a salsa version of "The Little Drummer Boy" volleyed into the room.

"Kesho is the author of a successful children's book series," I said, repeating what Greenhouse had told me. "*It's Ruff,* all about a squirrel who's been kicked out of his tree in Central Park and is now homeless. His name's Ruffy."

"God!" Myrna ladled more eggnog in her cup from the glass punch bowl at her side.

"She probably needs a quiet place to write." The Dobsons sure weren't going to drop in for a chit chat.

"That's ridiculous!" Myrna said.

"It's not quiet here?"

Kesho, behind Myrna, headed for the den.

"Why should children worry about the homeless?" Myrna asked after a gulp.

Elisabeth walked in with Chuck before I could think of some vacuous answer like "Somebody has to." Actually Elisabeth did a slow float across the now decidedly chilly room, in the same tawny skirt and sweater she had worn that afternoon. Chuck stood by the door, pushing his straggly hair back and looking morose. From the den came the very welcome sound of "Silent Night."

"Lizzie, finally!" Charles's chest did a pigeon puff at the sight of his sister-in-law. "I've been talking to your guests." To his son, he nodded. "Quite a surprise."

"Virgin ears for you, Charles. You should thank me." Elisabeth smiled around the room as if in apology.

The atmosphere changed with Chuck and Elisabeth's arrival. Myrna seemed to curl within herself like a wounded worm, while Charles got loud and proprietary, regaling Richard and Greenhouse with details of how a Samuel Dobson had been one of the twenty founders of

Fieldston in 1709, how the Dobsons had prospered ever since, netting acres and more acres.

"We were each given fifteen acres by Queen Anne herself, land rich in lumber, game, fish," Charles said, sweeping big, blue, suddenly vibrant eyes across our faces, "in recognition of our valorous service against the Wampanoags in the Great Swamp Fight." It was as if, having all the Dobsons around him, he could play out his favorite role as patriarch, showing off the family fame. All this in a droning voice that would have prompted me to change restaurant tables instantly.

"Who's 'we'?" Willy asked. Kesho had dragged him into the living room. They held hands, instant allies against Mr. Charles Dobson. "You weren't there for the fight so why do you say 'we'?" I could have kissed him if all touching hadn't been decreed out of bounds from the beginning of our relationship.

"It's the 'Direful Swamp Fight' Mr. Dobson," Kesho said. "There was nothing great about it."

"The Wampanoags got totally dissed," Willy added in disgust.

"Direful indeed." Charles laughed, a soft laugh of complete confidence. He turned to us. "They caught this chief who called himself King Philip and executed him."

Willy muttered, "What a dweeb."

Charles didn't hear. He was already into the family property surrounding and including the lake, talking about the family home, a large nineteenth-century brick colonial "like they have down in Virginia."

"Across the lake from us," he said, "we've got the Frank Lloyd Wright house. I don't like it much but there it is, built back in 1933 by an Italian."

"Simona's Italian," Jean offered.

"So's Richard," I added.

Richard waved my assertion away. "Diluted. Third generation."

Charles ignored us. "The place belonged to my brother, now to Elisabeth, his widow." The word *widow* sat on his tongue a fraction longer than necessary.

"We four are what's left of the Dobsons," he said, looking at Chuck, his son, who was handing Myrna another cup of eggnog. His expression wasn't happy.

CHAPTER

5

Jean announced dinner and seated us in a cold, damp room with the cabbage-rose wallpaper peeling from the corners. Charles commanded one end of the table, with Elisabeth and me on either side. Myrna, at the other end, sat between Richard and Greenhouse. Jean placed Kesho in friendly territory, between Willy and Greenhouse. Chuck sat next to me.

The mahogany table was elegantly dressed. In the center, surrounded by four silver candlesticks topped by red candles, a silver basket brimmed with Christmas balls and holly. Fine china plates gleamed from white embroidered place mats. A little too elegant, I remember thinking, preferring the comforting hodgepodge of the rest of Jean's inn.

Myrna caught my once-over glance. "I set the table myself this morning with our own things."

That meant she knew there'd be guests for dinner. I wondered why she hadn't told her husband.

"God forbid our family should cut their lip on a chipped plate." Chuck leaned over his butternut squash soup, clanging a spoon against his plate, the noise seemingly giving him some perverse satisfaction. "Christmas

Eve dinner at the inn is another one of our 'traditions,' along with making everyone miserable."

"A venerable one," Charles said, snapping out his napkin. "The only payment my father exacted from his minister upon donating these two acres on which to build his home." Between discreet sips of soup, Charles continued to fill our ears with news of his company, Dobson Realtors, founded in 1832 and successful ever since. Willy refused to taste the soup. I spooned slowly and silently, thinking Maalox might taste better. Chuck slurped. Elisabeth nervously rolled bread crumbs into pellets.

"The place was never meant to be an inn," Myrna said at one point, when Jean disappeared into the kitchen.

"Richard," Charles said, while frowning at his wife. "As you will see tomorrow at our annual ice skating party, you'll find our townsfolk very friendly. The town is the most beautiful in the state."

"I know," Richard said. "For ten years I had a little place in Ridgefield. This whole area is pretty wonderful."

"No sign of poverty," I threw in to put life back into my mouth. "Lovely pristine houses. Electric candles in each window illuminating holiday goodwill." What I had seen of Connecticut so far was the American dream, now as fake as Disneyland. "Dollhouse America."

"You might find it hard to leave." Charles fixed his eyes on Richard, skipping the sight of me.

Chuck looked up from his plate, pushing his wire-framed glasses hard against his nose. "Read that to mean, 'you look rich, Richie, how about I sell you some creaky colonial I bought for a song?' "

"Chuck!" Charles barked.

"Sorry, pater. Correction, he didn't buy them for a song. In fact, he thought the eighties would never bottom out. So now he's stuck and hurting."

"Sweetheart," Elisabeth said. The word sounded like a

soft moan. She capped it with a smile that sent Chuck back to his soup.

"Well, it is a buyer's market," Charles said. "The perfect time."

Myrna tilted her bowl back on its plate soundlessly. "They're getting married," she said.

"Congratulations," Charles said, his blue eyes accepting me now. "All the more reason for a—"

Myrna dropped the bowl. "Not her."

"I'm the one marrying Richard," Kesho said. Her earrings trembled. "And we do plan to buy a house here."

Jean swung in from the kitchen, a platter in hand. The silence was so thick she stopped.

Charles finally said, "It's a grave responsibility."

Jean moved, placing the platter of sliced roast beef next to Myrna. "We're having the wedding here," Jean chirped. "Just a few guests." Her face looked greener than May grass.

"Buying a house can be a heavy burden on a young couple," Charles added, "especially in these recessionary times."

"I thought these are the best times," I countered, watching Jean offer the platter around the table. Too bad she wasn't serving the Christmas eel that's the traditional first course in my parents' house. "It's a buyer's market, right?" I'd know just where to stick it.

"I think marriage is of even greater gravity," Elisabeth said with her pained voice. She handed Charles the platter directly, without helping herself. "Especially a mixed marriage. I think of the children. What will they"—she raised her eyes to me—"who will they be?"

"They can be an ingredient in the American melting pot," Richard said.

"*Più si mette, più è buono,*" I offered, taking a hefty helping of beef and mashed potatoes. "A saying from home. The more variety you put in, the better it is." Actually it was something my father always said when advising my mother on the making of minestrone, but the Dreadful Dobsons needn't know.

"I don't intend to sit here and romanticize about interracial marriage," Kesho said. "We're getting married. That's that."

"But won't it be difficult?" Elisabeth asked.

"If you can survive the Dobsons, you can survive anything." Chuck lifted his fork and with a stolen glance at Elisabeth, stuffed his mouth with beef, as though stopping himself from saying more.

Myrna clutched the stem of her wine glass. Charles looked stolid.

I gave up on the burlap beef. "Speaking of different heritages," I said, raising my voice as if I had to quiet a maddening crowd, "when my Venetian mother married my Roman father, her parents had a fit, but I got the best of it—Venetian risottos and Roman pastas."

"Willy's mother is Episcopalian," Greenhouse said, "and I'm Jewish."

"You are?" I had no idea.

It was then, while a thousand questions popped up in my head about Greenhouse and his heritage, that Elisabeth decided to break the news.

"Richard and Kesho are buying RockPerch. We're signing the agreement on Monday."

Myrna dropped her wine glass. Charles held his up and said that memorable line about selling the house to servants' seed. Jean hurried to get a mop. I wondered about New England restraint.

"I can do what I want now," Elisabeth said, her hand reaching over to cover Kesho's. "This young lady deserves that house."

Kesho jerked her hand away. "What's that supposed to mean?"

"You're selling RockPerch?" Chuck asked, the words

slow and heavy. "You can't do that!" Gravy clung to his chin.

"Oh, Kesho, I'm so sorry," Elisabeth said, a pained expression on her face.

"What are you sorry about?" Kesho's voice was blade thin.

"Baby, leave it alone," Richard warned.

I was lost.

"You have an unsound mind, Elisabeth," Charles announced, his face as mashed and yellow as the potatoes no one was eating. "This couple does not belong here."

"Charles, that kind of attitude is very old-fashioned," Richard said, in an amazingly placating voice. "Besides I don't come from the usual immigrant family. My grandfather wasn't some peasant immigrant. He was cultured, well-off, from Genoa."

I couldn't believe what I was hearing.

"I graduated from Yale," Richard said. "I do very well. Kesho is an extremely successful writer, artist. We're not—"

"Chill it, Rich!" Kesho stood up and tucked her chair back under the table. An incongruously well-mannered gesture for someone as angry as she was. And she was angry, her jaw squared tight, her large, all-encompassing eyes hot with emotion. Richard stood up reluctantly. I shot up, ready to join the Out parade.

Greenhouse tried to be reasonable, something he falls back on in emotionally charged moments. "Walking out doesn't do any good," he said. "We have to talk it over and clear up everyone's feelings."

"Not when you're angry, Dad," a wise Willy said.

"This is illogical," Greenhouse insisted, two red dots throbbing on his cheeks. "You're going to be neighbors."

Kesho passed behind Myrna on her way to the kitchen. Myrna's mouth relinquished the brim of a new wine glass long enough to say *"Thieving* servant's seed."

Kesho twisted her head around and as cool as snow

said, "Mama always said shit was white." With that she swung the kitchen door open. Jean stood on the threshold, holding a mop that would never get that room clean.

We walked out at that point, we being Greenhouse, Willy and me. "Your kitchen is cozier," I told Jean's crestfallen face as Richard asked Charles for an appointment to discuss the situation. "Goodwill to all men is the Christmas spirit," Richard added, as he too walked away after Charles didn't answer.

"I love you," Willy said, giving Kesho a hug that Greenhouse matched.

"I'm so sorry," I said, feeling awkward, chagrined, knowing I could never even imagine what Kesho was feeling.

"Thanks, all of you, but something's not right here. Three million dollars we're paying Elisabeth and all of a sudden I deserve that house? She's sorry? For what? Jean, you know?"

Jean shook her head.

"God, that woman better not change her mind," Richard said. He sounded more interested in the house than Kesho.

Kesho broke away from Willy's hug. "Rich, what was that 'she's a successful artist' shit? I'm not going to have you ass-licking to excuse the color of my skin, you hear me?"

"Couldn't you just have kept your mouth shut?" Richard asked.

"Hey, come on," Greenhouse said, "You're not going to get into a fight over the Dobsons, are you?"

"They're beyond repulsive," Willy said.

I had nothing to add.

CHAPTER

6

"Now Kesho and Richard don't have to worry about having the Dobsons as neighbors anymore," I told Greenhouse who had finally come to my room with a mortified, sleepy look. It was now six o'clock in the morning. I had just informed him of Elisabeth's death and the rest of the "'Twas the night before" events—such as my scanning my body inch by one-too-many-inch, looking for a dreaded deer tick and not being able to sleep even after the black spot on my hip turned out to be a mole. I'd twisted and kicked, making a list of all the things I hated as if they were hurdles I needed to jump over to get some sleep. Cinnamon came first. Then Christmas potpourri. Overcooked beef. Talcum powder potatoes. Ticks. Stupidity. Hate. Ignorance. Racism. Feeling helpless. Willy walking in on us. Death. Murder. Over and over again, until my exhausted mind hooked onto the innocence of cinnamon and Christmas potpourri, and relaxed. I drifted off for an hour or so, dreaming of being a fawn, half of me sinking. I had slept *con il sedere scoperto*, with my ass bare. That is, badly.

Now, after Greenhouse had given me a restorative hug, I was dumping all the Christmas potpourri into a plastic bag. The bedroom door had judiciously been left wide open.

"Did you talk to him?" I asked, as I shoved the bag in the back of the closet.

"The chief of police?" Greenhouse was sitting on a small pink chintz armchair, looking handsome and wonderfully out of place. He didn't have a movie star face or a fabulous build, but he had brown, friendly eyes that twinkled when he was in a good mood, which was most of the time, and a warm, kind face on which honesty sat like a second skin. I'd been bowled over in the first five minutes.

"I guess I'll go by headquarters and give the police my statement before I leave," he said.

"I meant Willy. Copper George isn't so convinced it is murder, by the way." My eyes widened, his words finally getting through. "What do you mean 'before I leave'?"

"My mother's broken her hip. The hospital called last night. I came to look for you, but Jean said you'd gone for a walk. I didn't want to leave Willy." He gestured toward the open door, looking embarrassed, uncomfortable. "Then I fell asleep."

"How awful for her!" I went over and gave him a hug. "For all of us," I added.

"I've got a 9:30 flight out," he said. His mother, a woman I had never met or even spoken to, lived in sunny Naples, Florida. "I should be back in three days at the most."

I rested my hand on the back of his neck, needing to feel his warm, soft skin. "What did you tell Willy?"

"I told him his grandma's going to be OK and that there's nothing wrong with making love and that he shouldn't barge in without knocking first."

"Stan! He did knock."

"I didn't hear him."

"You were too busy doing something else."

"I talked to him. He's OK."

"Did you tell him you love me?"

"And make it worse?"

"Grazie tante!"

"I can't tell him that, honey. He's going to think I want to marry you."

"God forbid!" I said. Not that I was ready for marriage as yet. I still had a few memories of the last time that I wanted to lose. But rejection never feels good, least of all that morning.

"The divorce has been real tough on him," Greenhouse said, giving my back awkward pats. "He's just beginning to make peace with it. Let's face it. You threaten him."

I knew that, but I hated hearing it. What I wanted most was to feel rooted. *"Natale con i tuoi, Pasqua con chi vuoi,"* I said. "Spend Christmas with your family, Easter with anyone you want."

"Another one of your Italian sayings, huh?"

"You're as close to family as I have in America." I felt precarious.

"I'll be back," Greenhouse said, catching my forlorn look.

"Are you really Jewish?"

I got a curt nod.

"Why didn't you tell me?"

"Does it make a difference?"

"Of course it does. How can you keep something that important from me?"

"It's not important to me." He was looking at me oddly. "I'm not religious."

"But it's more than a religion. There's the history, the culture, the Holocaust. How can it not be important?" Why was he looking at me so coldly? *"Oh, mio dio!* You think I'm anti-Semitic!"

"I wouldn't be here with you if I thought that."

"Then why didn't you tell me?" I didn't stop to think that we never discussed the larger themes of life.

"Why do you need to know everything about me?"

We had so little time together. Our conversations were mundane. Work, Willy, movies. We made lots of love. "I want to be close."

"We've been through this before, Simona. I've got to have space to move in."

I backed off physically. He had to think I was prejudiced and that hurt more than anything. "I don't care what religion or color you are," I said. "I love you. And when I love I can't stand even air to get between us." I raised my hand. "I don't mean Willy. I really don't." I just wanted to join in with them, not get between them.

Greenhouse's face softened. "Listen, we'll talk about this when I come back, *va ben?*"

"*Va bene.* How many times have I told you *bene* has an *e* at the end."

"Nag!" He came over and kissed me.

Three loud knocks on the open door interrupted him. Willy appeared. How do you look at a kid who's seen you naked, with his bare-assed dad between your legs? With a smile, I decided as I held on to Greenhouse this time, long enough for our embrace to appear a natural, good thing.

"Good morning, Willy! And Merry Christmas."

Willy avoided my eyes, hiding his own deep blue eyes under corn silk lashes. I released my grip and let Greenhouse slip away. "You're looking very handsome." Actually he looked awkward dressed up in gray flannels, blue button-down oxford shirt, a green tie sprinkled with reindeer and a blazer that showed too much shirt cuff. I was used to seeing him in sweatshirts and pants wobbling over his skinny hips. I got an urge to hug him.

"When are we going?" Willy said, shuffling enormous sneakered feet, that, like with puppies, promised greater height. The once-white Nikes looked like archaeological finds.

"Willy, we've been over this," Greenhouse said, standing up. "I can't take you to Florida. I've got to take care of Grandma." He turned to include me in his glance. "I was going to ask you to stay here, but now after Elisabeth's death, I'd rather you go back to New York and *both* stay in my apartment." There was something pleading about his expression, a first for Greenhouse.

"No way," Willy said, the weight of his hands plunging into his pockets.

"I'd love to, but why?" I asked. It turned out that Willy's mother was down on St. Martin's with her new boyfriend, and there were no relatives around to take Willy. I was apparently the "nearest of kin," if making love to someone over a period of time allowed me that definition.

"I got a better idea," Willy said, his freckled face locked in stubbornness. "I'm staying here with Kesho."

"Me too." There was a lot of talking and knowing that could get done between Willy and me without Greenhouse around to fight over. If Willy wanted to stay in Fieldston, I was going to make it easier for him. "We'll both stay."

Greenhouse looked torn between common sense and wanting to make up to his son.

I raised palms to the sky. "I'm not going to touch Elisabeth's murder, if that's what you're worried about."

"Promise?" That was Willy, also aware that his dad was very possessive about who should solve murders. Amateurs like me are an insult to the force.

"No, I won't promise. That's silly."

Daddy Greenhouse smiled.

"Come on!" A shadow of the same smile brushed Willy's face. "Cross your heart and hope to die."

I looked at both of these men, knowing I loved the older, wanting to love the younger if only he'd let me. Why did I feel that I was getting into trouble?

Greenhouse shook his head at Willy. "I don't think you should stay."

"We'll go ice skating," Willy said, testing the new deep notes in his voice, imitating his father's reasoning tones. "We'll go sledding, sleigh riding. Jean's going to let Simona cook and we'll eat lots of healthy pasta. I'll only have three Cokes a day. I promise. *Diet* Cokes." He looked over to me, focusing on my asexual chin. "We're not even going to *know* there's been a murder."

"That might be difficult," I said, hesitating. "Maybe going back to the city is the best idea." He was too young to be around death.

"Come on, promise," Willy insisted. "It's the only way Dad's going to let us stay here."

I glanced at Greenhouse who was giving me one of his lifeguard-not-on-duty looks. I shifted my gaze to Willy. This time his eyes didn't move away. He was clearly testing me.

"*Va bene*," I said. "I promise." I hate to flunk anything.

On our way to a quick breakfast, we exchanged the presents we'd laid out under Jean's fake tree. I gave Greenhouse a heavy forest green lamb's wool sweater that wasn't going to work in Florida. He promised he'd wear it tramping through the white Connecticut woods in "three days' time."

"The snow's going to be melted by then," said Jean as she hurried across the living room on red bedroom slippers. "Radio reversed itself. Yesterday they predicted iceberg weather. Now we're having forty degrees by noon." She pushed a button on her tape deck. Johnny Mathis started crooning "Let It Snow! Let It Snow! Let It Snow!" while Greenhouse nudged Willy to hand me a newspaper-wrapped present.

Two boxes of DeCecco rigatoni!

"How wonderful, Willy." Simona, the cook—that's my line.

"You always just make spaghetti," Willy accused. We obviously had a long way yet to go towards a truce, so I said nothing about spaghetti being the only pasta his father liked.

My present to Willy was a Rangers jacket that was so expensive it was clearly a bribe for his good graces. He tried to hide his thrill by dropping those eyes again, but his mouth quivered, giving him away.

Greenhouse flourished his big box of a present for me, smiling too much, his soft brown eyes somehow blurry as if they couldn't quite go along with the fake cheer. The box revealed a microwave oven that I didn't have room for in my minuscule kitchen. Last year he'd given me a vacuum cleaner which I displayed in a corner as pop art.

"Thanks," I said, smiling to rip point, hoping I was a better actor than either of the Greenhouses.

Then dad and son reached for their presents to each other. Feeling awkward, I pretended a need for the "necessary room," which I'd discovered was the settlers' euphemism for what I call the W. C., which here stood for wind chill factor. I felt awkward *and* confused.

I met Kesho in the hallway. The green sweats had been replaced by black leggings, an old tuxedo shirt and an oversized pink damask vest. In her hand, she held a plate of blueberry muffins that looked like they had been left behind by the sweep of the last glacier. Her face didn't look much better.

"Merry Christmas," I said, leaning over to kiss her.

She moved beyond my reach. "I'm in trouble."

"What kind of trouble?" I felt instantly guilty that I'd forgotten all about her.

"Copper George thinks I killed her."

The news astounded me. "Why?"

She grimaced. "The earring, the fact that I'm black."

"I can't believe this." I took a muffin and bit into it for support. It was surprisingly moist. "The earring next to her body doesn't prove anything. You could have lost it beforehand. Or she could have found it and was holding on to it when she was killed. And why would you want to kill her anyway? Did you know her from when you lived here?"

"That shit doesn't matter. It won't be the first time that man comes after me." Anger changed Kesho, made her a stronger, older woman who was now shutting me out as fiercely as she had welcomed me yesterday.

"Do you remember when you lost it?"

"No," she said, her shoulder sweeping past me into the dining room. I got the feeling she was lying.

"Why are you getting paranoid?" Richard stormed past me as Kesho slipped into a Windsor chair. His face made me want to reach for an extra sweater. Kesho crumbled a morsel of muffin into her mouth, her expression equaling his in temperature.

"The chief hasn't arrested you," he said, entering the dining room, "hasn't even mentioned the word *arrest*, so why are you sounding off about being the innocent victim?"

Kesho flashed her eyes at him. "Zip it with that paranoia shit. And we aren't living here. Elisabeth's dead, the Dobsons are going to inherit the house, and they sure aren't going to sell it to the *Jungle Fever* couple of the year."

I finally moved, to get beyond earshot. The century-old floor creaked. Richard whipped around and closed the glass-paneled doors to the dining room.

"Come on, where'd you go last night?" His lowered voice filtered through despite the closed doors. "And what's this *thieving servant* bit Myrna spit out?" His tone was so unfriendly I wondered if the sale of RockPerch was going to be the only event falling through this holiday season.

CHAPTER

7

Before driving off to the airport, Greenhouse stopped by the police station to give his statement of last night's events. Willy and I waited in the car, looking out at the huge yellow Victorian house sitting atop a sloping snow-covered lawn, with its double turrets and gingerbread details running along the eaves. It looked more like a proper girl's school than a police station, but then I was comparing it to the grim, utilitarian Manhattan stations. Willy drummed fingers against the dashboard. From the back seat I tried to start a conversation about the Rangers. I know nothing about hockey.

"Look, you don't have to do this," Willy said, suspending fingers in the air, his face staying set toward the house.

"Do what?" I clenched my hands, resisting an urge to clasp his shoulders and shout: let me into your life, damn it!

"Make small talk."

"I'm trying to get to know you, Willy."

"What for?"

"Well, you're Greenhouse's son, for one, and you know I ... " I hesitated, wanting to say "I love your father," finding that I couldn't, that somehow Willy's presence made *love* seem too big, too accountable a word. "I care for your father. He thinks the world of you, so you must be something pretty special."

Cavolo, why did I say that? "Must be" was a put down. "You are special, Willy." And why was my mouth so dry?

"You're just trying to horn in on us."

He was right, of course, but before I could get myself into further trouble with an inappropriate answer, Greenhouse swooped into the driver's seat.

"*Salve*, Greenhouse," I said, whipping a lot of cheer into my voice. "Did you meet Copper George?"

"In person."

"What did you think of him?" I wasn't sure I respected the man very much, mainly because of the way he'd treated Kesho. I expect all policemen to measure up to Greenhouse, and somehow feel embarrassed for him if they don't.

"He's got good taste in doughnuts. Cinnamon and powdered sugar."

"How many did you have?" Willy asked, wiping his father's chin with his fingers, a gesture of affection that made me happy and envious.

Greenhouse was silent as he maneuvered out of the congested traffic of the town.

"He sure doesn't like the murder theory," he said, once we turned onto 684. "But the ME's sticking to his guns, so the chief's had to concede."

"Why is the medical examiner so sure?" I leaned forward to communicate by rearview mirror. "Isn't murder by drowning hard to prove?"

"I bet they found an ice pick wound no bigger than a fingernail," Willy said. "Right in the middle of her heart."

"That's enough, son."

"Oh, come on, Dad. Lighten up."

Greenhouse's face went hard. "I mean it. This isn't a TV death. This is real and ugly, and I want you both in the city tonight. Have Christmas dinner with Kesho and Richard as planned, then back to the West Side."

Willy shook his head, his shoulder immediately hunching in defense. "I'm not staying with her. I mean it."

"I'm not going to take over your life," I butted in from the back seat. "I'll sleep on the sofa and be around to cook and make sure you're all right. I'm very easy, Willy, if you'll give me the chance."

Willy slapped his palm against the seat. "It's got nothing to do with you!"

"Then what is it?" Greenhouse asked, exasperated.

Willy kept up his slapping, the soft sound belying the frustration the gesture implied. "Kesho," he finally said. "We've been her real good friends, and now you're just dumping her."

"Richard's with her," Greenhouse said. "She's going to be OK."

"Not according to her," I said. "She thinks the chief is going to arrest her because of that earring."

"The earring proves nothing," Greenhouse said. We merged into the Hutchinson River Parkway. Along the sides pillows of still-clean snow glinted in the sunlight, reminding me of the camphor flakes my mother heaped in bowls at the bottom of our winter clothes closet each spring.

"Did you know she used to live here?" I asked.

"All I know about Kesho is that she appeared on the stoop next to mine twenty-two years ago. She was only twelve, without a mother or father that we could see, and clearly in need of a lot of loving. She lived with her aunt Rose who made great dresses. Rich East Side ladies would come by in cabs all the time."

"Your side's rich too, Dad." Willy lived with his mother on East End Avenue, right across from the mayor's residence, Gracie Mansion.

"It wasn't rich then," Greenhouse said, pulling at an

eyebrow. "My father was still alive when Kesho moved in next door. He took a shine to her and so did I. She used to take my NYU notebooks and fill them up with drawings which always got my mother mad. Kesho never talked much about herself, Rose always had pins in her mouth, and with them being black, my mother said it was rude to ask. I was twenty, in my second year at NYU. I didn't care where anyone came from. 'She's a nice, smart kid, that's clear as ink on the page,' my father would say. 'What else do you need to know?' "

I watched Greenhouse twist his eyebrow into a dreadlock. "He must have been a wonderful man," I said. A partner in a financial printing company, Greenhouse senior had been killed one night in a mugging in the elevator of his building. Greenhouse quit NYU and joined the force. "It's my way to help," he'd told me. He'd gotten a college degree years later by going to NYU's continuing education program.

"I'm sorry Kesho's lost that house," Greenhouse said. "It's the only material thing she's ever wanted. She's obsessed with it."

Willy sat up. "She wasn't going to get it even if the woman didn't die."

"What do you mean?" Greenhouse asked, slowing the car down as he looked at his son.

Willy let triumph rest on his face. "Elisabeth called Mr. Dobson last night sometime and told him she wouldn't sell."

"How do you know this?" I asked.

"Mr. Dobson said so this morning. He was standing with his wife, you know, by that big bush just outside the inn, watching the police rope off, you know, half the lake. She said something like, 'It doesn't matter. She's dead anyway.' " Willy twisted around under his seat belt so I could see his profile. "Mr. Dobson said, you know, in that geeky voice of his?" He paused for effect.

"What did he say?" I dutifully asked, ready to throw those "you knows" out the window.

"He said that he knew all along she didn't mean it, the house would always stay in the family. She was too emotional, and only wanted to hurt them, the Dobsons you know, because of something 'Walter' did, whoever he is. Then he—"

"Her husband," I interjected.

"*Thennn* he asked"—Willy graced me with a flash of annoyed cornflower blue eyes—"if they should have the ice-skating party anyway."

"You're getting to be a regular detective, aren't you?" Greenhouse said, trying hard, I thought, to sound pleased with his son's eavesdropping.

"Yeah. I'm going to be head of the FBI and you'll work for me, Dad."

"The police do *not* report to the FBI. What were you doing out there and what time was this anyway?"

"When you slipped out to visit Simona this morning."

"I did not slip out. I had to tell her about Grandma."

"What else did you hear, Willy?" I asked quickly.

"Mrs. Dobson wanted to cancel the party. She said they could always give the marshmallows, you know, to the church's poor program and the hot chocolate would keep till next year." Willy laughed. "I'm sure glad Grandma's not tight. I didn't hear anything else. I was cold and I had to pee, you know, so I left."

"Go to the bathroom," Greenhouse corrected.

"In the car?" Willy asked, with his father's poker face.

Greenhouse had a hard time holding back a smile. "Listen, son, there's no need to tell Kesho what you overheard, agreed? What happened at dinner was bad enough."

"Agreed." Willy grinned. Dad was off the hook.

That picked up my mood and made me rash. "Maybe

Willy and I *should* go back to Fieldston to be Kesho's cheering section." I liked Kesho and I did so want to please Willy. Besides, my unhealthy curiosity was acting up. "Why does the medical examiner think it's murder?"

"You promised to stay out of this," Greenhouse said, his eyes sliding to the rearview mirror and making contact with mine.

"I will, of course," I said, wanting to add, can't you see we're on neutral territory in Fieldston? There I have my one chance to get closer to Willy.

"Well, let me think about it as I drive." He gave me another glance with those warm eyes of his. I wanted to grab that mirror with his eyes still in there, and slip it into my pocket.

We drove on down the practically empty Hutch, by now exchanging inanities such as the sky being "such a bright blue"—that was me—"don't forget to put on suntan lotion"—me again. "The sun's so bright on that snow, *you* guys had better watch it"—Greenhouse. Willy said he hoped that while Dad was gone we'd have a "real bad snowstorm so the National Guard has to come and dig me out." I was obviously the one who would stay buried.

"So why does the medical examiner think it's murder?" I asked again. "Come on, it'll be in the papers tomorrow, so why not tell us now?"

Greenhouse huffed. He hates the media for its tattling tactics. Then he puffed.

"Why?" I prodded.

"All right. The back of the victim's neck had fresh bruises which could have been made by a hand holding her under."

"*Dio*, don't call her 'victim.' She was a woman with a name—Elisabeth Dobson—with a life history. A bad one, too, I bet."

"Simona, I was trying to answer."

"I know, I know." I raised both my hands in surrender. Was I witnessing the birth of a smile on Willy's lips? "You're a policeman. You need to depersonalize. But Elisabeth Dobson didn't have to be held under. She had at least twenty kilos of rocks around her waist. And bruises can't be enough. She wouldn't let herself be led to the slaughter without a fight. If someone was holding her under, she must have scratched and kicked."

"She'd also been hit on the head. Hard enough to knock her out."

"Oh." Why did I suddenly think of Chuck, in Jean's kitchen, snow clinging high on his pants? He'd been angry, kicking the door shut. At dinner he had blanched at the news of the house being sold. "That house is the reason she was killed. I'm willing to bet—"

"Sim," Greenhouse warned.

"Right." I sat back and focused on the baseball cap covering Willy's head, trying to wipe away the whole problem of Elisabeth's death. Greenhouse concentrated on his driving, his chin set in a way that made me suspect he wasn't telling me all. Willy, who had slipped a Walkman headset over his ears, bobbed his head, mouthing lyrics. Music bled through the earphones. The Grucci family fireworks is what it sounded like.

We crossed the East River under the towering, cathedral-like arches of the Whitestone Bridge. In the distance New York looked like a Lego construction Willy abandoned years ago. An unreachable city, I thought, with a pang of nostalgia for the bobbing skyline of Rome. I leaned back and closed my eyes, suddenly wanting to take a plane too—for the sight and sound of the *zampognari*, the Abruzzi shepherds who came down from the mountains to announce the Christmas season with their bagpipes; for the Pope's Mass in Piazza San Pietro under a white winter sun, while my father moved the forty or more figures of our Neapolitan *presepio* a little closer to the manger. It was a crèche of finger-high peasants—fishermen, vegetable and fruit vendors, cheese-makers, offering their animals and wares to *il bambin Gesù*. The bright hand-painted terracotta figurines—a legacy from my Neapolitan grandmother who died giving birth to her only son—had followed my father in all his diplomatic posts and were unwrapped and set up every eighth of December, on the Feast of the Immaculate Conception. After Mass, we'd sit down to the traditional *pranzo di Natale* of *capelletti*, little pasta hats in chicken broth; a garlicky, lemon-doused capon; roast potatoes with *pancetta* and a spinach flan. We always ended up with a glass of Asti Spumante, a slice of *panettone*—a mound of yellow cake with raisins— and oranges, tangerines, dried figs and nuts always served in a Venetian swirled glass bowl—a legacy from my mother's family.

Just as I was dreaming that I would wake up starved, Willy's whisper pierced through.

"Dad, I can't do this to Mom. She'd hate it if I stayed in your apartment with Simona."

"Willy, your mom doesn't love me that way anymore. She's got a boyfriend now, and I've got Simona. You have to understand that."

"She'd die," Willy whispered back, his pain so raw that when I pried open my eyes, I found tears in them.

On the curb at LaGuardia, Greenhouse announced that if Willy wanted to stay in Fieldston, it was OK by him but only if I stayed too. Willy shrugged. I was grateful Greenhouse was still trying to get us together.

"Give Kesho a hand if she needs it," he said. "She doesn't like to make it easy on herself. But please stay out of trouble." He looked torn, unhappy.

"The only trouble out there is maybe a patch of ice," I said, borrowing Jean's words, "and a sea of prejudice."

Greenhouse gave me a quick hug, whispering "love you," as if it were something to be ashamed of. I gave him a meek kiss on both cheeks. All Willy got from his dad was an awkward double pat on his back. We both wished grandma well.

"Willy, about last night," I started to say after going around the airport twice to find the exit. Willy jiggled his Guns 'n' Roses tape. The Walkman sat on his lap. "I'm terribly sorry that happened. It was embarrassing for all of us."

Willy slipped the tape into the deck on the dashboard and flicked the volume knob up with the smoothness and rapidity of an often-repeated gesture. I wondered how his mother handled rough spots.

I flicked the knob back down. "Can't we talk?"

"Not." He was adamant.

"How about using your Walkman then?"

"Are you going to solve the murder?"

"No, I think that's something the police should do."

"That's not what my dad tells me." I got a sullen look, his jaw sticking out, straight straw-colored hair falling over his eyes. There wasn't a freckle of friendliness showing.

"I promised." I turned to face him, one hand swooping in front of the windshield from nervousness. "Look, Willy, your father means a lot to me." I just couldn't say "love."

He reached over and turned the steering wheel a few degrees to the right. I whipped my eyes back on the road in time to see the Buick miss the metal divider by a couple of inches.

"Sorry about that," I said, gripping the steering wheel with both my hands this time.

Willy flicked the volume knob back up. I added American power steering and gargantuan cars to my hate list. We made it back in time for church services at eleven. As per Greenhouse's worried instructions, I dropped a very silent Willy in front of the white clapboard, towering Episcopal church on Main Street, just to one side of the village green. Well-dressed couples and children with red and navy gold-buttoned coats were already filing under the arched doorway festooned by a garland of pine branches.

"Are you going to be OK?" I had also dressed in my Sunday best, a black skirt and beige sweater that turned my olive complexion into extra-virgin-oil-green, but made me feel very puritan. My coat was vintage lower Broadway, very chic on a Downtown eighteen-year-old, but tawdry and cheap on a Downtown thirty-seven-year-old. Cheap is what had gotten me to buy it and if Myrna Dobson got a glimpse of it she might feature me as Miss-Cheapo-of-the-Month in her *Prudent Times*.

"Sure you don't want me to come in with you?" I tried again. Out of the corner of my eye I saw Richard's red Corvette barreling down Main Street. Willy and I turned in time to catch a fast glimpse of Kesho at the wheel. "She's going to get a speeding ticket." She had to be going at least seventy.

"No way." Willy was now eyeing the church door with longing. I had a firm grip on his shoulder, more for safety than to stop him from going in. My heels were guaranteed to send me skittering across the sidewalk at the least provocation, such as Willy exhaling too hard. Despite the radio's prediction of warmer weather the sidewalk was still one sleek shine ready to crack bones.

"I could sit through the service with you." Why didn't I just let him go instead of staring at the week's pastoral message.

Have You Forgotten God? it asked from the white clapboard wall.

"You're Catholic," Willy said, with a tone of finality.

"Catholic, that's right." I let him go. "I'll pick you up in forty-five minutes," I said, wiggling fingers as he loped off on his big sneakered feet.

Barricades were being found and set up to guard the fortress. I'm Catholic, he's Jewish, you're Episcopalian, I'm white, you're black, someone else is yellow. How comfortable we have been taught to feel in the safety of our own particular enclave.

CHAPTER

8

❄

Staring at the Have You Forgotten God? message, I remembered, not my religion—which as a Roman is hard to forget even if you want to—but that Greenhouse had mentioned that the chief of police wanted "to chat" with me again. Now I was sitting on a hard metal chair in a small, very warm room on the second floor of the Fieldston police headquarters complete with bow window, marble fireplace, and mantelpiece topped by an oval mirror framed in carved wooden roses. Frame, wainscotting, walls, and ceiling with intricate moldings still intact had all been painted a Halloween orange.

"Don't you feel as if you're in a pumpkin?" I asked to get the conversation going, shifting my coat from my lap to the floor. "Maybe it'll turn into a magnificent carriage and take us to a disco." I'd been sitting there almost three minutes—which in an overheated police station after a possible murder feels like hell's eternity—while Copper George tried to squeeze drops into his blinking eyes. He had dry-eye syndrome, Jean had told me.

"When was the last time you saw Elisabeth Dobson?" Copper George lowered his head to look at me. Drops trickled down his face. I didn't feel sorry for him.

"I told you, at dinner," I said, automatically tearing off a paper towel from the roll on his desk and offering it to him. That's the kind of gesture that really annoys Greenhouse. He calls it "possessive"; I call it "considerate."

The drops kept trickling, but Copper George didn't take the towel. Maybe he needed a good cry. His face didn't look quite as large or strong as it had at three o'clock that morning, but then I doubted that he'd gone to sleep. He was wearing the same shirt and red knit tie, except now the shirt was buttoned. I hoped he'd gotten a chance to brush his teeth, too. The rest of him was hidden behind a beat-up partner's desk that put him at a breath-proof distance.

"You saw her leave?" he asked. He moved his desk flag to get a better look at me.

"No, I left first." On my way up I had noticed the orange house was strewn with Fourth of July flags and Christmas lights, making the place a confusion of holidays. But then, putting a police chief's office in a lady's upstairs sitting room was a little schizo too. "In fact most of us—that is, the five guests of the inn—left in the middle of the main course." He asked about the dinner and I explained the pleasant events, my hand itching for a trash basket in which to dump the unwanted paper towel.

He followed my words with interest, keeping the blinking to a minimum, as if he were learning about the dinner for the first time. I forgot the towel and spoke freely, letting my anger at Myrna and Charles Dobson's racism show.

"Mr. and Mrs. Dobson are very respected in this town." He wiped the drops off his face with the back of his hand. "I'd watch what you say." I eyed a wooden crate piled high with discarded papers sitting inside a delicately carved marble fireplace. Two pizza boxes still oozed oil.

"I'm not making it up." I stuffed the paper towel in my skirt pocket. "Myrna and Charles Dobson definitely didn't want RockPerch sold to Kesho and Richard. Neither did Chuck."

"The way you heard it isn't necessarily the way it is." Copper George sat back in his swivel chair, flicking his tie on a tight stomach.

"Didn't the murderer leave footprints? There are twelve inches of snow out there."

"Seven to be exact." His eyes half-closed, he looked like a big ginger tom biding his time. "Ice was swept for the skating party. Her driveway plowed. Your prints wandering all over the place on Elisabeth's property, then coming down the hill in a hurry. Size eight Sporto boots. No other footprints."

"Maybe Elisabeth met her murderer on the ice."

"Maybe not. What were you in such a hurry for?" The tie stopped flicking.

"I told you. I saw the fawn drowning."

The tie started up again. "Elisabeth Dobson, you'd seen her once in the afternoon and then at dinner."

"Correct."

"Did you notice any marks on her neck either of those times?"

"Her hair was too long." I remembered the wilting movement of her head and neck as she told me her husband had made her suffer. A strand of wavy brown hair had fallen forward with her movement, giving her, for an instant, the wistful look of a young girl. "No, I can't say I ever saw much of her neck. But don't forget the fawn. She was right under him." I showed him the red cut in my palm. "He might have bumped her on the head."

"What bump?" The tie flicked faster.

"An educated guess." I didn't want to bring up Greenhouse. "With all those rocks around her waist, why didn't she sink to the bottom?"

His eyes opened. Deep brown eyes. If he got some sleep he'd be nice-looking, I realized.

"Detective Greenhouse warned me about you," he said.

"Warned?"

"You like to interfere in things, especially murders."

"Did he also tell you I'm good at it?" Which wasn't really true. With my emotions running a high fever all the time, I got confused a lot, but with my stubborn prying I did manage to stumble onto some truths. Greenhouse had no right to set this big blinker of a policeman against me. It was a good thing he wasn't with me. I'd have grabbed his precious "privates" and sliced them up as sushi, I was so angry. Not unlike cutting off your nose to spite your face.

"He was concerned, that's all," Copper George said in a gentler tone. "Perpetrators don't like interference." He edged closer and gave me the blink, blink, blink of his eyes. "Tell me how Kesho reacted at that dinner," he said. The man was trying to hypnotize me.

"With her temper," he added, "Kesho must have been ready to spit teeth."

I sat up and focused on that tiny American flag. "Kesho has a last name too, just like Mr. and Mrs. Dobson. It's Larson, but I expect you know that since you knew her when she was a 'black squirt of trouble.' " Behind the flag, his face hardened. "Miss Larson spit nothing. Not even the overcooked beef. If I'd been in her place, I'd have thrown that whole platter at them." I could have used a loaded platter right then and there.

Copper George leaned forward half an inch with only one blink. "Maybe she did more than that. Are you ready to swear that while you were cooling off from a fight with your boyfriend in fifteen degree weather"—what the hell else had Greenhouse told him?—"you didn't see your new friend Kesho running on that lake like the KKK was after her? Isn't that why you ran down the hill? You had to have seen her! If not on the lake, at the house. She was up there, I got witnesses to that. And she was good and mad. Called Lizzie Dobson a lying bitch, said she'd ruined her life and she was going to have to pay for it. Didn't you hear Kesho say that?"

"No!" Had she really said those things? "Who are these witnesses?" I was too frightened to doubt him. "Who told you Kesho was anywhere near Elisabeth after the dinner?"

"Did you see or hear anything?"

I'd heard a branch crack. I'd heard the soft *plop* of a snow clump falling. A repeated, hurried crunch that I'd thought might be a deer loping between trees. Then a rock tumbling down the slope. "No, nothing at all," I lied.

"Come on, you can save this *omertà* crap for the likes of John Gotti." He was leaning forward on his desk, his face large again, strong, mean. "Why are you protecting her? You said you just met her yesterday." Copper George looked at me as if I were gray and furry with a predilection for city sewers. "You must be one of those knee-jerk liberals who think all blacks are innocent."

And you must be a jerk, period. "I trust her," is what I said. "Can I go now?" I picked up my coat from the floor, remembering that trusting people had gotten me into trouble before. What the hell, maybe my knees were jerking. Maybe I was just being protective after that disastrous dinner. Maybe I was even patronizing. "Someone's waiting for me on—"

The phone interrupted me with a polite chirp. Copper George picked up, raising his hand to me. I half stood up, impatient to go. I stopped when those thick lips of his spread in a satisfied grin.

"She was doing what?" He let out a low whistle. "Fast little car."

My ass hit the chair.

"What's that?" The words came out as a bark. "Another lawyer, from Stamford?"

I squirmed.

"Jesus, how'd the news get out so fast? OK, put him on."

I tapped a foot on the floor.

"No, wait a minute." Copper George lowered the phone on his chest. "That'll be all, Miss Griffo."

"What happened to Kesho?" I stood up.

"Pretty perceptive, aren't you? She tried to outrun a police car and now she's on her way to the Danbury Hospital."

I ran out of the room.

"The Corvette's totaled," he shouted after me.

9

The last of the worshipers was shaking the minister's hand in front of the Gothic doorway of the church.

"They're going ahead with the ice-skating party. Postponed it from today to tomorrow," the woman was saying to the minister as she wrapped a purple mohair shawl around her head. "And Elisabeth not even buried yet. You should have stopped it."

The minister rubbed his bare, elegant hands together. "The children look forward to it so."

"Excuse me, have you seen a young boy?" I asked, skittering to a stop in front of them. "Blue down jacket, Mets baseball cap? He was supposed to wait for me here."

"Nobody stops Charles Dobson," the other man said, the words coming out in cartoon-like clouds of condensed air.

"Poppycock!"

"Blond, fourteen years old?"

"Merry Christmas," the minister said affably, giving my coat a barely perceptible once over. "Your son?"

"No, not my son," I almost yelled. "I'm sorry, I'm in a terrible hurry."

"He got a ride with the Dobsons," the woman said, jutting her head out from her shawl.

Good. Willy was taking care of himself. At this moment I didn't care about his rebuff. For all I knew Kesho could be dying. "How do I get to Danbury Hospital?"

"You're staying at Sleepy Hollow!" the woman declared, resting a purple mohair glove on my arm.

"Take 35 North, then 7, after a while you'll see the mall," the minister said, "get on 84. . ."

"You're the young lady who found Elisabeth?" The woman tightened her grip. "You must be."

"Edith, let's go," the man said, stomping his feet. He held out a cane for her.

"You poor thing!" Her neck stretched, the face came in close. Beak nose; parched, crisscrossed skin. "Don't feel sorry for her." The perfect turtle. "She killed poor Walter."

"Edith!"

"Well, she did. If she hadn't been a Dobson, she'd be in jail!"

The minister disentangled me from her clutch and was pushing me along the sidewalk. "Exit 5. There'll be signs."

I turned to have another look at the purple turtle. "Did she really kill her husband?"

"Of course not," the minister whispered.

"She has to be the one who found her," Edith overlapped. "Jean's only got two women staying with her and we know she's not Kesho Larson. Where's she running to? Who's in the hospital?"

The minister opened the car door for me and practically dropped me in. He hadn't stopped smiling for a second. "I hope whoever is in the hospital gets well soon."

"I hope so too."

"New Yorkers are so rude!" Edith exclaimed as I swung the car door shut.

⤙   ⤙   ⤙

Richard was sulking in the kitchen of the inn, eating caramel popcorn while Jean stuffed the turkey. I blurted out the news about Kesho, while those infernal bells jingled on the radio.

"Jesus!" Richard said, dropping popcorn on the floor. Jean turned off the radio, startling me with silence.

"Come on, I'll drive you to the hospital," I said, readjusting the volume of my voice. "Where's Willy?"

"He said he was going up to the Dobsons until dinnertime."

"Tell him where we are. I'll be back as soon as I can."

"No, you stay here!" Richard's face was the color of uncooked turkey skin. "Just lend me the car."

"Not even in your dreams," I said, pushing him out the door. In his state he couldn't drive a tricycle.

"I'll hold dinner," Jean yelled after us. "And let me know how she is!"

"My God, did you see what she was stuffing that bird with?" I said as I careened down the narrow, curving road, flying by a string of For Sale signs. "Caramel popcorn!"

On Route 7, just past the Indian Trading Post, the shock of a red stain of metal halfway up a tree made me brake to a halt. The Buick did a protest boogie, then settled down. I stared. Richard invoked Christ. The Corvette had charged an enormous copper beech and lost. The front half looked as if it had been discarded from a recycling-can machine. Only the unmarred trunk, shining red in the snow, told me this had once been a car. The license plate read BISTRO1.

"Keep going," Richard urged, pushing his foot against the floor of the car as if the accelerator were at his command. "To hell with the car. Get to the hospital!"

Anxiety got me lost, the minister's directions buried under Edith's murder accusation. Instead of driving past the mall, I turned off at the first sign that read Downtown Danbury. We slowed down through empty streets strung up with straggly holiday lights, looking for the blue hospital sign. A well-dressed woman got out of a Mercedes parked in front of an abandoned store. I saw her MD plates and stopped, confident she would know. She told me it was somewhere behind us, but she couldn't tell me how to get there. As her arm pointed to the hill in the distance, she underlined the blue-and-white For Rent sign screwed to the empty store's door. Dobson Realty it read.

I thanked her, got back in the car, and drove in the direction of that "somewhere" looking for someone else to ask.

"I didn't want to get married in Fieldston," Richard said, leaning forward, his nose practically against the windshield. "I told her the Plaza. Invite three hundred people. Tell the world how happy we are." The words came out like a pressure cooker's steamy spurts. "She insisted. It had to be in Fieldston, at Jean's inn. She'd lived here as a kid. Jean was a friend of her dad's. If she had the wedding at Jean's, he'd come." He slammed himself back in the seat. "Her dad's been dead twenty years."

"She meant in spirit," I said, scanning the street for some help. Lunchtime on Christmas Day didn't offer many candidates and there were no gas stations in sight.

"Keep going!" Richard barked. "It's bound to be up there, that big brick building, turn left, no, no, turn right, I meant right." My stomach churned.

I stopped the Buick next to a man dragging a sled full of empty cans across the street. Behind him a billboard told me Drugs Don't Work, Kids Do. I asked.

"You bet, I know where that's at. Got my arm cut up last year. Real bad too." He reeked of alcohol, but I received precise instructions.

It was on a hill, an anonymous structure of concrete and brick with multi-level parking lots that made me think of beehives. Across the street, a cemetery sloped down the hill. What a fun view for the patients, I thought, dropping Richard off at the emergency entrance and picking, from the four colors offered, the Green parking lot for luck.

When I found Richard in the emergency room, he told me Kesho was down in Radiology.

At least it wasn't the operating room.

"She's going to be OK," Richard told me, repeating what the doctor on duty in Emergency had said. "A few superficial lesions. But she twisted her knee on impact. It doesn't extend. They're going to keep her here overnight."

We were sent up to 12 Tower East—the Orthopedics unit.

As we got off the elevator, Richard looked so upset I gave him a hug, even though I couldn't help wonder if he'd been the reason Kesho had driven out of town at that speed.

"What if it's something permanent?" Richard repeated, pacing down the length of the blue carpet. "What's that mean, 'it doesn't extend'? She's strong, you know. Athletic. She runs and goes to the gym every day. Lifts weights. Muscles like iron." Richard flexed his biceps. "Great body. I don't mean in the sexist sense. She's strong, that's what I mean. God, what if—"

"She's going to be OK." I followed to keep him company, to let him know someone was listening. It stopped me from thinking how happy and beautiful she'd looked before dinner last night, leaning against Richard's shoulder, making fun of her white man.

We passed the nurses' station with its fake Christmas tree propped up next to stacks of sealed rubber gloves. I asked the nurse which room Kesho would be in, then went back to pacing the corridor with Richard.

"I love her, you know," he said. "We had a fight, but that doesn't mean anything. I love her. She loves me. We're getting married next Saturday." An old woman with a knee-brace hugged the wall and watched Richard pace with widening eyes.

"Watch it," I said, and Richard stopped to apologize, hovering over her, asking her if she needed help, wishing her a Merry Christmas in a loud voice, scaring the woman half to death. I took him by the elbow and propelled him into Kesho's designated room. Both beds were empty. We sat down on the Naugahyde-covered chairs and waited, with me taking peeks out the window, looking at a Christmas card scene thick with snow-covered trees, the requisite white houses and church steeples. I wondered how this Christmas had gone so wrong.

Then Patrolman Joe Pertini, his black tag pinned to his shirt pocket, walked in and after a perfunctory holiday greeting, hauled a chair to the hallway.

"You certainly get around," I said, watching him straddle the chair outside the door.

"What the hell are you doing here?" Richard asked, more directly.

"It's Christmas, we're short on men." He shook his wrist watch.

"Why the company?" I said.

"Waiting for Miss Kesho Larson, who's under arrest for murder. She's already been read her rights by Detective Sherman."

"What?"

"Where the hell is he?" Richard yelled, making an abrupt movement that loosened his dark, long hair. He looked like Samson about to bring down the temple.

"In Radiology, where else?"

Richard bolted out of the room, leaving me on the doorsill of 12T27, too surprised to move.

"How can you arrest her? Based on what? A stupid plastic earring? Some argument someone supposedly overheard? Come on! What's going on?"

"Don't look at me, I just have to sit here and make sure she doesn't go nowhere. Is it for real those two are getting married?"

"Next Saturday."

"Before you know it, we'll all be the color of cappuccino." He twisted his mouth, making a smacking sound. "I guess there's nothing wrong with that. The wave of the future, huh?" Leaning forward, his arms resting on the back of the chair, Joe Pertini didn't look at all sure. He had a friendly kid's face and sported a dark moustache he probably thought made him look older. I was willing to bet he'd worn a cross or a saint's medal around his neck since his christening, not that that was any guarantee of good behavior. A nice *figlio di mamma*.

"Come on, Joe." I dropped down on my haunches, using the door jamb as support. "May I call you that? You must know something. It's not a racist thing, is it?"

"No, the chief makes jokes and stuff, but he doesn't mean anything bad by it."

Of course not. What's an insult or two. "Then there's got to be some hard evidence."

He gave me a look, as if deciding something. "Will you go out with me tomorrow night?"

He surprised me. "I've got a man."

"I've got a woman."

"*Allora?*"

Joe smiled. "*Nonna* says that all the time. '*Allora*, Joey, you gonna be President of America?' '*Allora*, you gonna *mangia* or do I have to whip you with those noodles?' '*Allora*, when you gonna get married and give me great-grandchildren?' "

"*Allora*, why do you want me to go out with you if you've got a girlfriend?" I had to stand up. My shins were killing me.

"I've got a problem. You can help me solve it," Joe said.

"What's the hard evidence on Kesho?"

"She had the means, right? Anyone can push someone as thin as that lady underwater."

"That's right. *Anyone.*"

"She sure had opportunity."

"So did everyone. Come on, Joe, what else has come up?"

He looked doubtful again. "It's no secret, they're probably telling her and her lawyer, right?"

"Right."

"Chief's got the MOM now."

"The what?"

"Means, opportunity, motive."

"That's ridiculous. No one's going to kill someone for reneging on a house sale."

"That isn't it. Some lawyer from Stamford called and said Elisabeth Dobson came to his office a year ago last July to write a new will. She left that fancy big house on the rock, with practically everything in it, what's it worth? Two million, three million? She left it to your black friend, Kesho. How about that? Good enough motive for you?"

10

"I swear I didn't know Elisabeth was leaving me anything." Kesho was lying on her side on a gurney, wrapped in a wrinkled, pink flowered hospital gown. An attendant wheeled her down the corridor. After agreeing to meet Patrolman Joe at the Whipping Post Bar the following night at eight, I had joined Richard in the Radiology Department. The X-rays had shown no abnormalities, but Kesho still couldn't extend her left knee. They were now going to photograph her knee with the magnetic resonance imaging machine—MRI—"to get information about tissue, metabolic, and bio-chemical data," the doctor had explained. "Tissue" was the one word I understood, and that only because I was balling up a Kleenex in my pocket. I was nervously trying to figure out if there was any chance Kesho had killed Elisabeth.

"You'll be fine, honey," Richard said, his eyes small with worry. "My lawyer is tracking down the best criminal lawyer in Connecticut. It's your health that counts. You've got to stay strong." He had said nothing about the inheritance.

"Why would I kill her?" Kesho's words slurred from the painkiller they'd given her. Besides the bad knee, she also had a painful contusion where her left shoulder had hit the door on impact. Her face was untouched, but she looked tired, her eyes as blurry as her speech. "We were buying RockPerch. It was all set. Why would I kill her to inherit the house, if we practically already owned it? It's dumb, this whole thing is dumb."

Even if she didn't know that Elisabeth had changed her mind about the sale, saving three million dollars could be considered a motive for murder in a lot of circles. But she would have had to know about the inheritance first. And if she did, why buy the place? Nothing made sense and with Detective Sherman ambling behind us, pretending to examine the white walls, I didn't ask questions. Such as, "why the hell did Elisabeth leave you that house in the first place? What's your connection to her?" Besides, I'd made a promise. I was here only for moral support.

"*In bocca al lupo*," I said, blowing her a kiss as we were about to reach the swinging doors of the MRI room. I had to get back to the inn. I didn't want Willy to have Christmas dinner alone. "*In bocca al lupo* means 'in the mouth of the wolf.' "

Kesho grabbed my wrist. "You said it, girl!" Her fingers were colder than last night's ice.

"It's for good luck."

"Getting the house wasn't luck. After what that woman did to me and my family, I deserve every inch of that place."

"What are you talking about?" Richard asked.

"You, too, honey." Kesho let go of me and flicked her wrist at Richard. "That property should have been yours by birthright."

Richard grabbed the gurney out of the attendant's hands, shoving Kesho through the double doors.

"Hey!" the attendant shouted.

"Whheee!" Kesho laughed.

"Mister, you can't do that!" The attendant chased after them. I tried to follow but was firmly asked to leave by the Indian technician. I walked out, toward the exit, asking myself why Richard knew so little of Kesho's past. What exactly was his birthright? As I passed, Detective Sherman gave me a look as sterile as that hospital wall.

Jean was in her kitchen, wrapped in a lemon yellow housedress with Bill's Gas stitched over one breast. Bing Crosby was groaning "White Christmas" on the radio for the thousandth time and Premi, the cat, was curled up on the stove.

"Any more news on Kesho?" Jean asked, putting a lopsided frozen pie in the microwave.

"Her left knee's still locked." I'd called Jean from the hospital to let her know Kesho had survived the crash. "An MRI will tell them more."

Jean shook her head, her thick straw-colored curls held back by a spidery net. "God's hand was on her shoulder. She raced out of here this morning faster than a tornado. Pre-wedding jitters. Me and Bill had our biggest fight night before we got married. Now those two have been fighting since after that god-awful dinner. She stormed out of here last night and he let her go, didn't go looking for her like he should have. Something bad had to come of it."

"I think they've made up now." So Kesho had gone out last night.

"I smashed six plates of my good dinner set. Made Bill laugh so hard, I forgot what I was mad at."

I slid down into a cushioned kitchen chair by the table. "Where's Willy?" I'd looked for him everywhere, even in the bathrooms.

"Still with Chuck. Those two have taken to each other."

"The runaway kids," I said, disappointed Willy wasn't there for me to make friends with. "Did anyone call?" I pushed my chair closer to the oven. I needed food.

"The only call I got was from Edith Holmes who met you outside of church. She wanted to know if you'd been the one to discover the body. Edith had you down for a New Yorker. She was real surprised to hear you were Italian."

"That's because only New Yorkers are supposed to be rude. Italians, instead, charm you with their eyes and steal with their hands!"

Jean tilted her head at me. "What's the matter, dear?" *Ping!* went the microwave. For a nanosecond I thought it was the phone.

"I don't know." I was surprised by my own bitterness. "I guess I've been thinking about stereotyping, how easy it is to fall into it." I had also been hoping for a call from Greenhouse in Florida. And then there was Kesho's bad news.

On the radio, a male voice was urging me to run out to Radio Shack and buy that forgotten present. "Kesho's been arrested for Elisabeth's murder," I said.

"That's terrible!" Jean grabbed an open bag of pretzels, her face a soft mound of surprise. "Why would Copper George do something so silly? He doesn't even think Elisabeth was murdered!"

"He does now. It seems Kesho inherited RockPerch and that's a good enough motive for your chief of police. Never mind that a few other people probably thought they'd get the house and might be willing to murder for it." Petite Myrna Dobson swilling eggnog, the disdain on her face as thick as a mud pack. She might consider RockPerch a family heirloom, like her pearl choker. Barrel-chested Charles Dobson of the ear-choking voice probably thought he should own the whole town. Then there was

Chuck, the forlorn runaway son who'd only gotten as far as Jean's inn. He hadn't liked losing the house at all.

"Elisabeth left Kesho RockPerch?" Jean cracked into her last pretzel.

"Apparently she did." I eyed the salt and crumbs left in the pretzel bag and stood up. It was time to get Willy. "We'll be eating soon, right?"

Jean opened the oven door, and Premi wavered on the brink of the stove, probably debating whether he could still manage a pounce at the venerable cat age of seventeen.

The absence of enticing smells made me sidestep Jean and take a peek inside the oven. All three of us stared at an anemic turkey, still all gray-pink goose bumps. "Poor Chuck," Jean muttered, and for a moment I thought she was talking about the bird.

"I guess we've got a few more hours," I said, my stomach now howling its empty fate. Willy had to be hungry too. Maybe I could fix him something. I looked out the window. All I could see, between the hanging Christmas cactuses, was Jean's iced-over pond the size of an Olympic swimming pool. Behind it were tall birches blending with the snowy knoll which led to Goose Lake. Willy was out there behind those trees, probably skating. I could make an appetizer of the rigatoni he had given me for Christmas, tossed in butter. He'd like that.

"The lake feeds that pond in the summer, keeps it clean and pretty," Jean said, carrying Premi over to the window. "You should come back in the summer, that's my best season. A lot of honeymooners in June and folks who prefer ponds to the chlorine of swimming pools." Premi jumped out of her arms, his hind legs buckling as he landed on the counter. He looked mortified. I gave him an encouraging pat.

"I've got a nice green thumb," Jean said, "and the place

is full of roses, dahlias, impatiens, you name the flower I've got it. I put out wicker chairs and serve white wine with crackers and cheese. Some grapes. You know, real elegant."

Jean started plucking dead pink flowers from her cacti, stuffing them in the pocket of her dress. "That pond's my big seller. It's what makes me different from the other inns around here."

"I think Willy should come in," I said. "It's beginning to get dark. I'll go look for him."

"Oh, I'm sorry. I thought you understood." Her lips had turned into a perfect cherry Life Saver. "You see, the electricity went off for more than two hours and so the turkey didn't cook, and the boy kept saying how hungry he was." Jean wrapped Premi around her neck and opened a cabinet. "He asked Chuck if he could go with him to his parents' for dinner. They both looked so pleased about it all, I didn't know whether I should stop him or not. Chuck has such a hard time being alone with Charles and Myrna. The boy said you wouldn't mind."

"He did?" Mamma! And Merry Christmas to you too!

"I'm sorry. It's always hard with stepmothers." Jean offered me a half-empty bag of Cheez Doodles.

"I'm barely a step-girlfriend!" I snatched the Doodles and dropped down in my chair again. "Greenhouse and I have made no commitments." Myrna and Charles weren't the only hard ones to be with, apparently.

"The boy's scared." Jean and Premi joined me at the table.

"So am I." What was I going to do with Willy? Or rather what was Willy doing to me? I felt blotted out, my existence eliminated. With everything else that was going on, that was ridiculous. I was giving him too much power.

"Think how Kesho must feel," Jean said, her face flushed and wet from the oven's heat. "I've cleaned up plenty of Kesho's battle scars, but I don't know what to do about this one."

I shook out more Doodles. "How long have you known her?"

"Since she was knee-high. Bill and I used to own the only gas station in town before he got it into his head to go 'genteel' and buy this inn." She pointed to the Bill's Gas stitching on her yellow breast. "This was his idea, and sweet and loving as he was, he never made it to 'genteel.'"

"Jean, do you know what Elisabeth did to Kesho and her family?" I was breaking my promise not to interfere, but I was too hurt and angry with both Greenhouses to care.

Jean dug in the Doodles bag, coming up with orange fingers. "Well, I don't know it all." She crunched louder than I did as a grim expression settled on her face. "I think Kesho better be the one to tell her own story."

"Copper George is going to find out, if he doesn't know already," I countered. "And when he does know, he'll use it to incriminate her even more. It'll probably show up in the *Fieldston Ledger*."

"Oh, Lord, I hope not. There was enough written and said about it at the time."

I leaned over. "Jean, I want to help Kesho. I like her, she's a good friend of Greenhouse and Willy's. Copper George is racist, he seems daunted by the Dobsons, and he's gone after Kesho before. She doesn't stand a chance unless we help." I realized as I spoke that I meant every word. The real reason I was breaking my promise was Kesho Larson. Knee-jerk liberal, maybe. Too emotional at times to see straight, also, but I just didn't think Kesho was a killer.

"I don't know," Jean said. "I'll have to check with her. I just can't believe Copper George arrested her!" She was ironing the cellophane bag, now empty, with the palm of her hand. "He's a good man. He can't hold onto a wife, but he's a good man."

"Maybe he's just doing his job. Who hires the chief of police?"

Jean looked up, wisps of hair escaping her net and sagging over her eyes. "A five-member elected Police Commission."

"Is Charles Dobson on the commission?" I wondered how much pressure Charles could bring to bear on the investigation.

"Sure." She blew her hair away. "There's always been a Dobson either on the Police Commission or on the Board of Selectmen. It was the town's thank-you. Whenever the town was in financial trouble, the Dobsons bailed them out without a word. That was true of Charles's father and the Dobsons before him. Charles counts the dollar bills he gives out, then expects the town to make a big fuss over him." Her hand angrily punched air. "The way he treats his son, awful!"

"How *does* Charles treat him?"

Jean got busy unwrapping the cat from her neck. "Lord, Premi, you make my neck sweat!" She dropped him on the table. The kitchen was now bulging with oven heat and the luscious smell of roasting turkey. Premi and I sniffed the air.

Jean's face glistened. "Charles Dobson claims he's giving the ice-skating party tomorrow, with his sister-in-law not even buried yet, because he doesn't want to disappoint the children of the town. But he sure doesn't mind buying out their homes at bottom dollar when their parents lose their jobs."

I unbuttoned my sweater. "Do you mind if I open the back door for a few minutes?"

"Sure, Premi could use a stretch."

I hurried over to the back door, sure I would melt before I got there.

"He loves to roll in fresh snow. Thinks he's a dog. But it's got to be fresh." She rubbed her nose against the cat's, then lowered him to the floor. "Snobby little thing, aren't you, hon?"

I opened the door, slipping into an envelope of cold air. A tall silver pine divided the driveway in half. Behind it, fifty feet beyond the garage, half hidden by a tall stack of firewood, was a red shed where Chuck built his Shaker tables. Jean had proudly shown it to us after we arrived yesterday. A perfectly swept, neat shed with no trace of sawdust or wood curls. All the tools hung clean on the wall in order of size. The electric saw was covered in blue plastic. The long work table looked more pristine than the Danbury Hospital. Planks of different woods, resting against the far wall, were divided by size and thickness. A large sawed-off wooden barrel offered an assortment of table legs.

"Chuck says Shaker furniture is elemental, the way our lives should be."

"He means simple," she added after we made no comment. We were too cold to speak and the place was stifling in its austerity. "He's happy here," she said simply, closing the doors and hitting the padlock shut. We had gladly tramped back to the inn for tea and warmth.

I took a few steps now into the plowed driveway, gulping cold air. Premi whipped past me, speed a newfound resource.

"Oh, don't let him run away," Jean called out.

I followed the cat, then stopped.

"Jean, you'd better come look at this!"

CHAPTER

11

The sky had turned to charcoal, and the driveway lights were already on. I now faced the shed, its doors wide open. Inside, the place was a mess of dark shadows.

Jean ran out of the back door as fast as she could, slowing down as she hit the unplowed snow beyond the driveway, her slippers sinking deep. Premi meowed mournfully from somewhere ahead of us. We made our way past the garage, the residue of kitchen warmth replaced by straitjacket cold, and stopped short on the threshold of the shed.

"Oh, Lord, Bill, help me!" Jean cried, clasping a hand over her mouth.

The walls of the shed were stripped of tools that now lay scattered on the floor. Sawdust, piled like anthills, surrounded the electric saw. The blue plastic covering was torn to shreds underneath a mound of broken, splintered, sawed wood that was screaming for a match. The barrel had been crushed, the table legs thrown across the shed.

"Oh, poor Chuck!" Jean said, breathing hard, tears streaming down her cheeks. "Who did this to you?"

"I'm sorry." I flung an arm around her shoulder. She stiffened and stepped back, swinging the doors closed so fast she almost left me inside. To the right of the shed, I could see part of the dam that fed the pond from Goose Lake.

She smacked the padlock shut with the butt of her hand. "I gotta call him. I gotta call him."

A familiar sky blue down jacket glided through the dusk above the dam.

"Willy!" I shouted. Willy hesitated a moment, then doubled his skating speed. He was coming in. A dark figure skated past the same spot.

"Is that Chuck?" I asked.

"Yes, yes, it is." She half ran to the driveway, body heaving like a ship in bad seas. I went after Willy.

"He did it himself," Willy said as he hung up his skates in Jean's entrance closet. As usual his Mets cap was planted on his head, the visor hooding the back of his neck.

"Chuck trashed his shed! Why?"

"Did Dad call?"

"No."

"You sure?"

"Yes, I'm sure." I was trying to keep up with him in the corridor. "I'm not going to lie to you. Willy, I'm really hurt you left today."

He whipped around, the weak light of the wall sconce giving him a yellow, unfriendly cast. "And I'm pissed you went off to the hospital without me."

"I apologize. I was nervous. Richard was going crazy worrying and you weren't there." Why was he always putting me on the defensive? "She's going to be fine."

"I know that." He walked into his room, leaving the door open. I took that as a friendly cue and followed. "Mr. Dobson let me call the hospital from his house," he said. "The MRI showed she's got a bucket handle tear with a locked knee." He sounded like Kesho's doctor. "She's having arthroscopic surgery tomorrow. She'll probably go to jail on crutches."

"They'll set bail, Willy. Richard has plenty of money to meet her bail." The prospect wasn't pleasant, but I wanted to make light of it for Willy's sake.

Willy threw his jacket and cap on the bed. "Shit, I wish Dad was here." He combed fingers through his hair, giving me his worst sullen look. "Listen, are you going to get into this thing or not?"

"You made me promise to stay out of it."

He narrowed his eyes. "You're just a sissy. You think I'll rat on you to Dad to try to break you up."

"No!" I sat down, stunned. "It never even crossed my mind."

"Sure it did. You just think I stink, don't you? I'm in the way. You don't want some ex-wife's kid around. You want kids of your own."

"Your dad and I haven't even mentioned marriage!"

"You will after Kesho gets married! Then you'll take Dad to Italy and I'll never see him again!"

"No, Willy. No! I'd never separate you two." Who was feeding him this crap? "You've got to believe me!"

He was bouncing on the bed, an unhappy, little boy. "I don't trust you. You're different."

"How am I different?" I sat at the tip of the bed, my hands spread out to steady the mattress, as if that would calm him, too. Had his mother been trickling poison in his ear? She'd bared barracuda teeth over this shared vacation, only giving in because she had her own romantic vacation planned.

"You have an accent," Willy said. "You dress funny."

"I don't wear jeans, is that what you mean? They make me look like a jug; I'm too hippy. If you want you can call me vain. And I can't help my accent. I try hard, but my tongue gets twisted. It's a teeny teeny accent. Not that bad, is it?" I was smiling, trying to break his resistance. "Come on! Half of New York City has an accent!"

The bouncing continued. I dropped my elbows to my knees and got serious. "Look, Kesho's different, but you love her."

He stopped. "She's not screwing my Dad."

"I do *not* screw your dad," I yelled, slamming my hand against the bedpost and killing my fingers. "I *make love* to your dad. And I told you I'm sorry about the other night, but I'm not ashamed of it.

"Willy, I love him and I want to love you, if only you'd let me. Even if I wanted to lure your dad only as far as New Jersey, which I don't, but even if I did, Stanley Greenhouse wouldn't move anywhere without you." I sucked on my aching fingers.

"He left Mom."

"That's it. He left Mom. Not you." I got closer and dropped a hand on his shoulder. "Or maybe they left each other, huh?" Actually Irene had left Stan, saying she was bored with being a wife. A few months ago, in that moment of vulnerability that can come after too much lovemaking, Greenhouse confessed he'd discovered Irene had had a lover at the time, who dumped her the minute she became marriageable.

"He'd never leave you."

Willy actually leaned into me, and I held my breath so as not to squeeze him in my arms. *"Piano, Griffo, piano,"* I whispered inside my head. Go slow.

"Now why don't you tell me about Chuck?" I asked. "Then we'll talk to your dad and see what we can do about helping Kesho."

"He's totally mad at Kesho for getting that house," Willy said, leaving me, alas, and crossing his legs on the bed. I followed suit, facing him. Maybe, just maybe, we had found peace.

"Who told him?"

"The police chief." Copper George had called while Mr. Dobson was carving the ham. No one had eaten anything after the call except Willy, who said the food was "the best," cooked by Myrna who had gotten "zonked" on wine. Chuck had tugged on his hair, chewed the inside of his cheek, looked like "you know, a bump on a log." Dobson had thundered about betrayal.

Willy socked a fist into the palm of his other hand, getting as excited as if a fly ball were coming his way. "It's like there was this pact, you know? The land is supposed to stay with the Dobsons. You're not supposed to leave it to anyone else. They've been doing this since the settlers. Usually it's written right in the will, you know, when a male Dobson dies and leaves it to his wife, it's supposed to say she can only leave it to her children."

"What about female Dobsons?"

"Same thing. If he or she doesn't have any children, the land goes to the Dobson side of the family. Except Walter died—no, they declared him dead because he disappeared, and he didn't leave a will, what's that called?"

"Intestate. So Chuck thought he was going to inherit?"

"No, his father did. 'Goddamn Lizzie!' That's what his father said. 'That house was mine!' "

"When did Chuck trash his shed?"

"I don't know." Willy shrugged. "Wait till you see their house. It's like my friend David's floor-through on Park Avenue, except bigger." Willy went to Dalton, a private school on the East Side whose tuition couldn't be paid for on a detective's salary. And he wasn't on a scholarship. Either Mom had money or Greenhouse had inherited enough from his father. Money was another subject we never discussed.

"They're humongo rich. If Chuck doesn't get Rock-Perch, you know, he'll get the other house. So no big deal. Anyway, Jean says that RockPerch brings bad luck."

"I hope not to Kesho and Richard." Although the way things were going . . .

"You know that fancy thing Myrna wore last night?" Willy clutched his neck.

"The pearl and emerald choker?"

"She showed me three pictures of ancestor ladies wearing it. I think that's neat. Stuff, you know, staying with the family like that."

"I like that too,"—the physical threads of family weaving through generations—"but it doesn't have to be fancy stuff, does it?"

Willy rolled eyes. "Why not?" The phone rang down the hall. "Hey, I bet that's Dad." He jumped off the bed and ran to the door. There were no phones in the rooms.

"Willy, your dad." Jean called out. He took off.

Finalmente! There were a few things—such as the exact meaning of 'interfering' and 'promise'—that I wanted to discuss with that gentleman. I followed slowly though, wanting Willy to have the luxury of some privacy. The phone was in a corner of the entrance hall.

Jean came down the corridor toward me, the floor boards groaning. She had changed into a red sweater encrusted with pearls and a green wool skirt. "My Christmas uniform," she explained. Her hair, free of constricting nets, curled messily around her head. "Turkey's done. I'll bring it out in the dining room." She sounded tired, but it was hard to gauge her expression in that weak light.

"I'll help. Chuck joining us?"

She shook her head. Behind her I heard Willy ask, "Dad, do I have any rich ancestors?"

If only I could squeeze him. "Jean, didn't you hear any noise coming from the shed? Those planks were shredded with a saw."

She leaned under the mirrored sconce. "He loved Elisabeth, you know." Her eyes had conveniently disappeared into the shadows of fake candlelight. "Her death's got him crazy."

"He must have trashed the shed while I was gone."

She leaned away from the gold paisley wallpaper and opened a closet. "Shortly after the three of you left for the airport." She reached for a large turkey platter from one of its shelves. "The shed door was shut but I could hear the racket anyway. I thought he was making another table for me to find a place for."

This morning. When he knew that Elisabeth was dead and the sale would not go through. When Copper George had not yet announced the news of the inheritance.

"Come on, Simona!" Willy called, flagging me over. "It's your turn to talk to Dad." That wonderful acceptance swept the Dobsons away.

12

"Kesho's mother and father worked for Walter and Elisabeth as cook and gardener," Jean said as we sat clustered at one end of the dining room table—which seated twelve—in a play for "cozy." Last night's expensive silver appointments were gone. I had set the table with Jean's mismatched flatware and faded plates, feeling right at home.

"It had to be real tough for them," Jean added, having agreed to discuss Kesho's past only after calling the hospital and getting her permission. "They were the only black family in Fieldston." Willy held out a hand for some pie.

Jean winked, topping a wide slab of her lopsided apple pie with vanilla ice cream. Her mood had picked up after Chuck showed up at the last minute to carve the turkey. Now the dry bird rested at the other end of the table, looking as if set upon by hyenas.

From a chair, Premi contemplated the turkey and another suicide leap. Chuck looked like he might stop breathing any minute himself.

"Kesho and I are only four months apart," he said, tugging at his glasses. "Her mother, Shirley, would set us both up by the barbecue pit in the back of RockPerch where the pool is now. She'd give us paper and mostly broken crayons. I would tear the paper in small pieces. Kesho would draw for hours." His voice was as limp as the shock of straight hair that fell over his narrow forehead.

"At two, she had mastered the cartoon. She drew an emaciated, bespectacled mouse that is a dead ringer for me. I still have the drawing."

"You're supposed to freeze mice," Willy said, his lips white with ice cream. "You know, if your cat catches too many in one night or you've already fed him."

I swallowed hard. "What?"

"That's what I read in that paper Chuck's mom puts out. You save on cat food that way. Is that what you do, Jean?"

"Whaddya think is in this pie?" She kept on cutting.

"You're kidding?"

Chuck shook his head to Jean's offering of pie. "What I remember," he said, "is being goddamned incensed at Kesho's talent—she wasn't paying any attention to me. I have a knack for remembering the lousy parts." No ironic smile appeared.

Jean sat down. "Kesho's parents rented a small house behind the cemetery, which her mom hated." She stopped to watch Willy bend over his plate and peer under the pie crust.

"I bought that pie at Grand Union, young man," Jean said, laughing. "It's just fine. No mice." She took a huge bite. "Well, seems Kesho's mom wanted to go back to Africa. That's all she ever wanted. I got all this from Kesho's father, mind you, after Shirley died. Hewley'd come by the gas station, looking for Kesho, knowing he'd probably find her sitting in my kitchen, making her drawings. Later I'll show you the autographed copy of the first *It's Ruff* book she sent me. 'To Jean and her kitchen table, where it all started.'" She nodded at Willy, obviously pleased he was taking his first bite of pie.

"No." Chuck thrust his elbows on the table. "She started drawing by the barbecue pit, inspired by the squirrels. And Dad. The landlord squirrel, the one who kicks Ruff out of his tree for non-payment of walnuts?" He was looking at Jean. "Dead ringer for the pater. And now she's got the whole damn place to draw in!" The tableware jingled.

Jean gave him a worried glance. "Why would Elisabeth give her the property? That's what I don't understand."

"Revenge," Chuck answered. "She hated Walter, she hated my father. They were both gaga for her and she despised them." He narrowed his eyes, as if savoring that negative sentiment. "She used to like Mother until Walter took off. Then they ended up hating each other, too."

"Elisabeth always loved you." Jean's voice was reassuring. "You know that." Their eyes locked, their minds probably running on the same track of memory. They'd forgotten we were there.

"You're the child she never had," Jean said.

"Well, this child didn't inherit."

"Did you expect to?" I asked, breaking the moment. Premi jumped on the table and stood perfectly still, as if shocked he'd made it. I thought of a glass figurine poised too close to the edge of a shelf, which is about where I stood with my prying.

Chuck set his eyes on me. "I thought the focus was on Kesho." Jean scooped the cat up.

I met his gaze. "The focus is on anything and anyone that can bring some light."

"Don't look to me for that." Chuck shoved his clean plate away. "Yes, I did expect to inherit. Elisabeth always told me I would. She said she approved of the things I did. Encouraged me when I started painting even though I was terrible at it. Encouraged me again when I took up carpentry. Gave me the money for the tools and the wood, even though I have no talent there either. She even gave me money to stay here at Jean's when I couldn't stomach my father anymore. That's about to run out, Jeanie."

Jean smiled. "You're hired as handyman then."

"My record on holding down jobs is about three months, but I thank you."

Willy punched his discarded baseball cap. "You expected to inherit because of the Dobson clause in the will."

"I have no expectations from Dobson customs," Chuck said. "I just believed the line she fed me. Christ! You'd think I'd know better by now!" He shoved hands through his hair.

"What was her line?" I asked gently.

" 'This place is yours,' she'd say, with that wistful look of hers. 'I'm safe here. You'll be safe here.' "

Safe from what?

Chuck released his head and looked back at me. "Yes, I expected to inherit. Now Elisabeth has the last laugh, and you've got less light than before."

Agreed, the story was murkier, but I did have another solid suspect.

Jean helped herself to more pie. "I expect your father will take that will to court."

Willy leaned over his plate. "Yeah, he thought he was going to get the place, too." His tongue flicked down to his chin to catch a runaway ooze of melted sugar.

Chuck's face went slack. "Maybe she told him the same thing."

"How does Kesho fit into all this?" I asked. "Was she close to Elisabeth?"

"Heavens no!" Jean said. "Well, she used to play up at RockPerch but that was before her mother left for Ghana."

"She left Kesho?"

Jean lifted penciled-in eyebrows, furrowing her narrow forehead. "Hewley didn't want Shirley to go, wouldn't let her take the baby. So off she went by herself. Then she got on some rinky-dink toy plane and crashed. So at four years old, Kesho found herself with no mom."

"She meant to come back, right?" Willy asked. "Kesho's mom was going to come back?"

Was this another terror he would bring into his sleep? I wondered, wishing him away from this story.

"Sure, honey, Shirley meant to come back," Jean said, with the same reassuring tone she had used on Chuck. "Hewley kept telling Kesho. Shirley was going to come back to her little girl."

"Not in Fieldston," Chuck said.

I sat up. "Why not?"

"She'd have been arrested."

"You see, Shirley didn't have the money to go to Africa," Jean said. "Hewley wouldn't give it to her. What they earned, he put away for Kesho's college. So Shirley went into Walter's study one day, when he was on some business trip, took two thousand dollars from his desk drawer and made off to Ghana."

"That's what Mother meant by 'thieving servant,' last night at dinner." Chuck leaned back on his chair and, with a finger, pressed his glasses against his nose. "You probably considered her looped." Was he smirking behind that hand?

"The whole dinner was looped," I answered.

Willy squirmed in his seat. "Two thousand isn't that big a deal."

"We're talking twenty-eight years ago," Jean pointed out.

"Who says she took it?"

"That's right," I joined in. "It doesn't sound like the action of a very proud woman. Did someone see her?"

"I can't say. I didn't know her," Jean said. "But Hewley had no doubts." She waved a hand. "The two thousand was missing and how else would she get the money to go to Africa?"

"Uncle Walter called the police." Chuck was now circling the table, hands deep into his pockets, his tall, thin frame looking permanently curved. "But he didn't fire Hewley even though my father insisted." He gave a close-mouthed grin. "Uncle Walter wasn't all that bad."

Jean shook her hair. "Nothing wrong with Walter that a loving wife couldn't cure."

Chuck stopped. "What would it take to cure Dad?"

"Oh, Chuck! Your father means well." Jean stood up and began to pile dishes. "Like Hewley meant well by Kesho, except he just didn't know how to go about it."

"My father never means well."

I got up to help, my feelings about Chuck confused. He was really like a forlorn, gawky goose who had missed the signal to migrate to better climes. And yet, he was a suspect, with a very good MOM. Whoever had killed Elisabeth had to be someone she trusted enough to go walking with at night across a frozen lake. Chuck had come back into the kitchen with snow up to his thighs even though the snow on the ground was only seven inches deep. And now he'd just confessed to an excellent motive. Kill Elisabeth before the sale of RockPerch and, as far as he knew, the place would be his.

CHAPTER

13

The news of the theft spread across town like mayflies,"
Jean said. "Even made the *Ledger*. Edith Holmes has
her share of the responsibility. She's going to keep those
teeth clacking even after the grave digger's shoveled dirt
down her throat." Flatware clattered into the empty
creamed onion bowl.

Edith Holmes, who gathered broccoli, as we say back
home, broccoli standing in for gossip. A woman who
claimed that I was rude and that Elisabeth killed her husband. I shouldn't forget her.

"Kesho became a handful after her mother left," Jean
said. "She'd kick and bite anyone who mentioned Shirley.
'My daddy gave birth to me,' is what she told me that last
Christmas when I took her to see the nativity scene over at
my church. That's how ashamed she was."

That's why Richard knew so little of her past.

"She was twelve that Christmas. A month later Hewley's heart gave out and a sister showed up to take her off
to the big city."

"I remember when she left," Chuck said, looking out
the window at a starless night. "My mother breathed a
sigh of relief. She said they never belonged in this town.

Kesho and I were both twelve and I wanted to leave, too. Go off to New York and be an artist. She never came to say good-bye." His face relaxed into sadness.

"How could she?" Jean asked, her arms full, pushing her back against the swinging door to the kitchen before I could get to it. "She wasn't about to set foot on Dobson property."

"Willy, could you please help clear?" I asked, loaded down with dishes and feeling very daring. He gave me a sharp look, then to my surprise, got up and started removing glasses. As I followed Jean into the kitchen, I wondered what punishment Willy would exact later.

"Tomorrow night the meal's on me, Jean," I called out loud enough for Willy to hear. "Comfort Pasta. We could all use some of that."

"Between you and I, Chuck," Willy's voice came through the door, "if a friend of mine was leaving, I'd make sure *I* said good-bye."

To hell with his grammar. I was so proud of him, I picked up the empty ice cream dish and finger-licked it clean.

"Well, what did Dad say about breaking the promise?" Willy asked me, from his bed. *Julius Caesar* lay skewed underneath a leg, next to his baseball cap.

While I helped Jean clean up in the kitchen, the events of the past twenty-four hours had finally hit me in the knees. Barely standing, I had come to wish Willy good night.

"Did Dad say it's OK?"

"He thinks Richard and the lawyer will take good care of Kesho." I hadn't mentioned my sleuthing. Greenhouse had been too worried about his mother. The doctors had discovered a heart condition and were afraid to operate on her. He didn't even know when he'd be able to come back.

That stopped me from bringing up his "interfering" label or my threat to make sushi out of his genitals.

"Did you make up that story about the frozen mice?" I asked.

"No, totally real. Myrna gave me her paper to read while we waited for dinner. You thaw them out in the micro."

I made a face.

"She also says to walk, you know, not drive. It saves health and gas. Another one is, use toilet paper to blow your nose instead of Kleenex. That one freaks me out."

"Myrna could probably learn a few tricks from my father." During World War II, in lieu of toilet paper his family used newspapers cut into squares. He still insists he's got Mussolini's words printed on his ass. "Which is where they belong," he invariably adds.

"We're going to help Kesho, right?" Willy's earnest, young head looked lost in a thicket of ruffled pillows and shams. Behind him, vines of morning glories crowded the wallpaper. "Aren't we?" He didn't know about his grandmother's heart condition.

"If we can." If I could get some sleep first. I did like that "we," though.

"I was thinking about the weather," Willy said. "You know how yesterday the radio said it was going to drop below zero today?"

"Yes, Jean said something about that."

"I think the killer, you know, was counting on that." Eagerness buffed Willy's face to a shine. "He stuffed her down there with a lot of rocks, then everything was going to freeze, and when they found out she was nowhere around, you know, no one was going to think of the lake. It's all frozen over, see? She wouldn't have been found for months, years."

"Good for you, Willy. That's clever!" It made sense, too. "What made you think of it?"

His lips disappeared into a mouth-splitting grin. "Chuck said if it got any warmer, we couldn't go ice-skating."

"That sure wouldn't have triggered any thoughts in my fuzz brain. Except relief maybe. I like my weather hot and sunny."

"I'm good at logic." Willy edged forward on the bed. "Next year, I'm going to take deductive reasoning as an elective. That's a class seniors take."

"Good for you. Then tell me how it works, OK?"

We didn't connect. He was following his own thoughts. "Chuck's got a good motive." Willy reached the end of the bed now, those enormous dirty sneakers stretching his legs down over the edge. "But if he killed that lady, he wouldn't tell us all that, right?"

"Right." I didn't want to explain about deceitful ploys.

He caught my hesitation. "Dad won't mind if you break the promise. Really. I know Dad."

I smiled, wanting to kiss him, to steal a quick hug. "Who better than you." I didn't move. I was still afraid of a rebuff.

"Mom says she knows him best."

"Yeah. I guess. Well, good night." I stepped back to the door. "The ice-skating party's tomorrow. That should be fun." I started to close the door.

"I got a paper due the first week of school on *Julius Caesar*." He waved the thin blue booklet.

I stepped back into the room. "That doesn't seem very fair."

"It sucks. 'Discuss Shakespeare's handling of loyalty and betrayal.' Yuuck!"

"Heavy duty subject." Yes, let him learn about deceit and murder in Shakespeare. "*Ciao*, Willy. See you in the morning." He waved and I closed the door.

This time he was the one to open the door again, just as I was stepping into my room.

"Hey, Simona. I bet you know my dad pretty well, too."

"I'm getting there." I flashed him a truly happy smile, but he had already slipped back into his room.

I was too tired to sleep. I was hungry. I was thirsty. I wanted Greenhouse in bed with me. The room was a furnace; I would never get used to American heat, to American air-conditioning. I didn't know Dad "pretty well." I didn't know him at all! Why didn't I just go back to Rome? I paced the room. I couldn't lift the stupid bay windows overlooking the pond. Why didn't America have easy windows that opened out? I cursed. I went to the bathroom, leaving the light off to avoid extra heat.

How the hell was I going to help Kesho? I turned on the sink faucet and sank my face into cold water. I couldn't flash a badge on Charles Dobson and demand, "Tell me everything you know about the evening of the twenty-fourth of December."

"Not a creature was stirring," was the kind of answer I'd deserve. With water dripping down my face, I tugged at the smaller bathroom window. Frozen mice! Mamma!

If I didn't come up with something to help Kesho, all the pasta dishes in Italy wouldn't save me with Willy. To my surprise the window slid up. My nose hit a storm pane. I gave up, kneeling on the sticky plastic of the stuffed toilet seat, my knees grateful for the foam. I leaned my forehead against the cold pane. The moon, just above the silver pine, had lost a thin slice of yesterday's half, but still managed to give off a muffled lantern glow. The bathroom faced the end of the driveway on the other side of the house. The garage was only a few feet away, a giant dark shadow.

Deceit was the amateur sleuth's tool. Eavesdropping, fawning, snooping, snitching. Blunt questions that caught people off balance. Downright lying at times. Not something I enjoyed, having suffered my share of lies from my ex-husband and my ex-best girlfriend. The means was not honorable, but the end was good. Good for the innocent. My mother always accused me of having a *faccia tosta*, a hard face, the meaning of her words a negative concept of chutzpah. I would just have to put on that hard face.

I heard the rustle of a whisper. Someone was out there. I pressed my ear against the storm window.

"Simona?"

I let out a feeble cry, hitting my temple against the window sash as I turned to look.

"Are you peeing?" It was Willy whispering, hidden behind the bathroom door I'd left ajar. Why had I thought the voice came from outside?

"No, just getting some fresh air." I rubbed my head, checking my pajama top for open buttons, and walked out. He stepped back, my table lamp picking up his red, excited face, the down jacket askew over his pajamas, his untied high-top sneakers. As always, his Mets cap was backwards—worn the "cool" way. Without thinking I hugged him.

"Love that cap," I said, letting him go. "What's up?" My hand tugged at his jacket. "Been sleepwalking?"

"Shhh! They're out at the shed. Jean and Chuck. They're cleaning up the place. Destroying the evidence." His freckles stood out darkly on his face. His eyes stretched with excitement. "I can see them from my window."

"What evidence?" I whispered back to his chin. Willy was an inch taller.

"I don't know, but why else clean up in the middle of the night?"

"Maybe they couldn't sleep?"

He made a boy-you're-dumb face. "Come on, let's go listen."

"No."

"Shhh!"

"Why are we whispering? They can't hear us. I'm a pretty permissive woman, but eavesdropping is not something I'm going to promote. Before you know it, your Dad's going to say I'm leading you down the path to perdition."

"What's perdition?"

"If you read Shakespeare you should know. If you don't, never mind. And it's 'between you and me,'—between takes the objective case—but the thought was wonderful."

He spread his mouth in a grimace. "You're weird. And stop worrying about eavesdropping. Kids of divorced parents get real good at that. I mean, they should make it an Olympic sport for the parent-impaired. Come on! We'll miss all the good stuff."

How could I say no? I had visions of a six-year-old Willy curled against a locked bedroom door, listening to his parents argue their marriage to death. I'm good at heart-wrenching scenes. "OK, let me get my coat and shoes." A move was of the essence. My eyes were beginning to feel prickly.

We didn't get very far down the corridor. Light seeped under the kitchen door. They had moved back inside. Jean uttered the cliché of the season. "Want a turkey sandwich, hon?"

Willy tugged at my arm and pointed to the living room. I followed. For some miraculous reason, the floor boards didn't creak. Maybe that was another talent of the parent-impaired.

Under the mistletoe of the living room door, I dared whisper. "Where are we going?" Not that I could see the mistletoe. The only light, coming from the bay window, had to fight its way through the Christmas tree. I just remembered the mistletoe being there, trussed up in red velvet, the berries looking as appetizing as cocktail onions. I quickly flashed to Greenhouse being slobbered by one very horny, slightly overweight *Italiana di Roma*.

Willy led me by the hand into the dining room. Clever young man. The swinging door let us hear perfectly. I would have snuck around the outside of the inn, ending up with an ear pressed underneath the kitchen window. And a bad case of pneumonia.

"Well, I'm glad that's over," Jean was saying as we crunched against the wall, choosing the hinge side of the door for some sense of safety. She sounded a little winded. "Hand me that mayonnaise jar, will you?"

This was ridiculous. I was going back to bed.

A chair scraped. "Are you going to tell Copper George what you saw?"

"I'm not going to tell that idiot anything." A few seconds of silence turned into light years. They were eating. I could almost smell it. A chair scraped again, along with something in my stomach. I patted Willy on the shoulder. I would never make it into the FBI.

"*Buona sera.*" I gave the door a shove. The kitchen brightness hit me like killer headlights. I blinked. "I'm so hungry I can't sleep." Behind me Willy groaned.

14

I can't believe you butted in like that!" Willy said. "They weren't saying anything important." I turned onto Exit 5 on 84. This time I'd listened carefully to Jean's directions. We were off for a quick visit to Kesho with a set of clean clothing for Richard who had spent the night at the hospital. On the way I'd pointed out the incriminating copper beech to Willy. The Corvette had been towed. "And we found out what we wanted to know, right?" All the more reason to pay this visit.

I'd asked Chuck point blank, after Jean had shoved the turkey platter my way.

"What did you see that you aren't telling Copper George?"

Chuck had given me a snowman's charcoal smirk. Jean's mouth turned into a maraschino cherry. Premi lifted his head from the top of the refrigerator and gave me one of his prolonged croaks. I raised palms to the heavens.

"I know, I know. None of my business. But I am trying to help Kesho. I don't know how you felt about her in the past, Chuck, but I do know that Jean used to fix her cuts and bruises. If either of you still care, and if what you aren't telling the police chief has something to do with Elisabeth's murder, then tell us. It might help."

"Us?" Chuck asked.

"*Cavolo!*" My golden mouth. "Willy, you might as well come in. We were both hungry."

"You were eavesdropping," Jean corrected. "It's a good thing you're paying guests and I need the money. Come on in, boy, no one's going to eat you."

Willy did a slow roll into the kitchen, a boy facing never-ending ice, *senza* skates. Even his freckles had blanched.

"We weren't eavesdropping. We overheard, there's a difference." I didn't like lying to Jean, but I wasn't ready to trust Chuck. I still didn't know why he'd trashed his shed hours before anyone knew of Kesho's inheritance.

"What's *cavolo* mean?" Jean asked, curiosity winning over hostility.

"Cabbage. A euphemism for *cazzo*, penis. Italians like using genitals to swear with. And to ward off the evil eye. Help yourself, Willy." I waved at the turkey carcass spilling popcorn from its gut. "Pretend you're at the movies."

Willy had gulped, but played along.

"Sorry about that stuffing I made you eat," I said now. The Buick lifted its nose up Hospital Avenue. On my left, the cemetery reached away and down, a white sheet broken by the dark pattern of crosses and tombstones.

"I think Jean did it," Willy said.

"What reason could she possibly have to kill Elisabeth?"

"She's a lousy cook."

"That makes her a murderer?"

"Well, it's a tragic flaw, you know." He bit into a chocolate-covered Dunkin' Donut, his breakfast of choice. "Mr. Jensen my English teacher talks about tragic flaws all the time. Julius Caesar's was pride. Flaws can ruin your destiny."

"I don't think bad cooking comes under that heading."

Willy's face turned serious. "With that food she doesn't have a whole lot of guests, and if she doesn't have guests, she'll have to declare Chapter Eleven, and that's pretty tragic."

"You've got a point," I said, wondering what the Reagan-Bush legacy did to a teenager's view of his own future. I gave him a reassuring smile. "Thanks for your support last night. I owe you."

"It's OK. You bought me these." He hit the doughnut box, his voice guarded. Last night's friendliness had waned a bit. The sky didn't look very friendly either. Gray foam dropping down to engulf us. "A snow sky," Jean had called it. But the temperature had shot up above the freezing mark and was expected to reach forty degrees. Tomorrow most of the snow would be gone, taking Christmas with it.

"Your father will kill me for feeding you junk." He was a banana and cereal man at breakfast.

"Dad won't know."

The Green parking lot was full. Willy chose Orange for the Mets. "Lying is out with your dad. In fact, it's out period. Last night I was cornered."

"Loosen up." He offered the last doughnut after I parked the car. "The FBI lie all the time." He'd eaten the other five. A boy after my own stomach. "So do the politicians. It's the only way we're going to find out stuff, you know."

"I don't like it. From now on, I'm going to be honest."

Willy sank down on the seat, his cap slipping over his face. "I don't believe this!"

In the hospital gift shop Willy picked out a brown teddy bear the size of his hand, then didn't have the money. I had to convince him to let me pay.

"Dad'll pay you back."

No, the trust wasn't completely there yet. I hid my disappointment by peering past the ATM machine at the gaudy blue-and-gold list of Patrons and Friends of the Hospital, a display of the regional who's who which the rich of my country would shun for fear of the tax collector. MR. AND MRS. CHARLES DOBSON were third on the alphabetically arranged patron's list. They'd been generous since 1986 when the Strook Tower had been built, but the absence of a gold button indicated that this year they hadn't given. Elisabeth's name wasn't on either list.

"What are you going to do about Richard?" Willy asked. We were now in a yellow-walled elevator that had just informed us, in a serious mellifluous male voice, "You are going up." I took it as a good omen.

"I'll do with Richard what I did with Chuck." Who had finally answered my question, thanks to Jean's prodding.

"Ask him a direct question." I raised my arm, pretending to beam light in Willy's face, and lowered my voice. "Richard Mentani, what were you doing up at RockPerch at 11:17 last night?"

Instead I asked Kesho, "What's arthroscopic surgery?"

Willy grunted.

I had changed my mind in the corridor when the smell of antiseptics and the sight of an empty gurney reminded me of injury. I didn't want Willy as witness to important or personal revelations. If there was any danger in my probings, I didn't want him anywhere near it. A little game of Clue was all right, but no more.

Kesho made a face. "All I know is tomorrow they're giving me a local to drill three holes in my knee. After that I don't want to know. Forty-five minutes work for thirty-five hundred dollars that doctor's getting. That's the advance I got on my first *It's Ruff* which took me two years to write and illustrate." She tugged at her blanket, yellow to match the flooring. "But I guess it's fair. He saves bodies. I'm only trying to get to kids' hearts."

Richard kissed the top of her head. "Now you get a couple of more zeros to that sum." He looked besotted, tired. Innocent of anything more serious than love. "And that's only the advance. My baby's going places."

To court, if no other suspects popped up.

"Simona and me are going to get the real killer." Willy thrust Kesho's teddy bear against her chest.

"Baby, thanks," Kesho said, giving him a one-arm hug. The other arm was curled into Richard's. "You're as wonderful as your dad. Stan the Man, your grandfather called him, after Stan Musial."

"I know," Willy said. "Outfielder for the St. Louis Cardinals. Great batter. Dad's not that good."

"He's great!" Kesho protested. "When he married your mom and moved out of the neighborhood I was heartbroken. He was my first real love and now his boy wants to help me out of this mess. I think that's neat."

Willy did a sneaker shuffle that sent pained noises from the linoleum. "Well, Simona'll help. She's done this before."

"I'm all for it." Kesho offered a low five which Willy met.

"So we gotta ask questions." He shot me a low-lidded look.

"You're kidding," Richard said. He gave me an easy, politician's smile that put me on my guard.

I leaned against the window. The gray foam seemed to hold just above the twelfth floor. "We thought we'd keep receptive eyes and ears, hoping to discover something that might help Kesho."

"You're on!" Kesho pushed herself up on one elbow, wincing as her bad leg jerked.

"How did you two meet?" I asked. Willy went bug-eyed. Why didn't he go for a soda and give me five minutes of privacy with these two?

Kesho laughed. "That question's easy. In a Fieldston real estate office." She grinned at Richard, her cheeks pushing up against those dark wide eyes of hers. Without a trace of makeup and covered in that regulation gown of flowered wrinkles, she still managed to look good. "Richard took one look at me and was smitten."

"Smitten by her guts," Richard said. Willy, disbelief plastered over his face in neon colors, pressed the power button on the channel selector. Bugs Bunny chomped on a carrot in silence.

"Here she was," Richard went on, "the color of hot chocolate on a cold, rainy day, asking this glue-white Martha Stewart clone at Dobson Realty if RockPerch was for sale. I had to fall in love."

"Why live here when you got New York?" Willy sounded like Woody Allen.

"Kesho means 'tomorrow' in Swahili." Her face was grave. "I remember my mom telling me it was a special name. She'd hold me up on her hip, a skinny hip that hurt, and carry me round and round the vegetable garden, by the rose patch.

" 'Tomorrow,' she'd say. 'Tomorrow it will be yours.' I guess she was talking about the future, about taking me to Africa. But I always thought of that house. So one day after I signed a neat four-book hard/soft deal, I rented a car and came to ask. That broker tightened up as if she'd been goosed.

" 'That belongs to the original Dobson estate.' " Kesho mimicked the broker's lockjawed speech. " 'I assure you it will never be for sale!' Then she tried to show me some property here in Danbury which 'you might find more suitable to your needs.' Meaning I'd find other blacks." Kesho leaned back against the pillow.

"I never thought it was going to be available." She spoke up to the TV, into Elmer Fudd's shotgun barrel. "I just wanted to show them I'd made something of myself, that they weren't the only ones with money. But that broker thought I was nuts so she never told the Dobsons. I should have gone straight to Edith Holmes." Kesho broke out into a smile. "She's got all the news that's unfit to print flying off her tongue like spit."

"You never told us anything about your mom." Willy flopped down in a chair just as the shotgun exploded in silence. "I remember when you got real mad because I asked you to show me a picture of her. I'm sorry she's gone."

"So am I, Willy, but thanks. I remember telling you off, too. You'd showed me about fifteen pictures of your dad. That was right after the divorce, wasn't it? I was a real bitch to you."

Willy shrugged, embarrassed.

"I'm sorry, sweetie, I had my reasons. Anyway, when you guys walked in, Richard had just finished telling me that I can't possibly remember my mom telling me those things. He thinks my storytelling fantasy is taking over."

"You were only four at the time," Richard said.

"I remember."

"So how did you two almost buy RockPerch?" I asked.

"Richard had already contacted Elisabeth directly before I met him, and she'd refused. When we decided to get married, we tried again together. This time she said yes."

"How did you know about that house?" I asked Richard. Greenhouse had told me there was only one reference to it, in *Architectural Forum*.

"I used to rent a place near here."

That's right, he'd mentioned it at dinner. Great sleuth I made. "Since Kesho dropped the word *birthright* yesterday, I thought you had a special connection to Rock-Perch."

Richard slowly shook his head. He was still wearing yesterday's clothes, gray flannels that had lost their sharp crease and a stretched-out sweater with the unmistakable

Missoni mix of colors. His hair, falling to his shoulders, made him look older and a bit silly. Someone trying hard to look cool.

"Come on, Rich!" Kesho hugged his waist with her good arm. "What's the harm in telling?"

Willy looked away from Bugs Bunny stuffing Elmer Fudd into a foxhole. "Did you tell the cops you left the inn after dinner?" he asked, his blue eyes set on Richard. "I saw you from my window." Was he making it up? The bum hadn't said a word to me. "I mean, telling them might help Kesho. Confuse that police chief."

"Like hell it will!" Kesho jerked up to a sitting position and pain twisted her face. "Dammit, I hate this leg!" She slammed her fist on the bed. "Listen, if you guys want to help me with this asinine murder charge, let me tell you straight off, Copper George is full of it. I was never anywhere near RockPerch that night."

"If he arrested you," I said, "he must have a witness to prove you were there."

"I don't care how many witnesses he calls in!" Kesho cried out. "I've got my own witnesses." Richard's hand slid up her arm and pressed. What were they hiding?

"Me, for one," he said. On the TV screen, Bugs Bunny gave way to Popeye. "We took a walk. We needed fresh air."

"How did the earring get on the island?" I asked. "Did you drop it somewhere and Elisabeth picked it up? When I last saw you in the kitchen after dinner, you still had it on."

Kesho started twisting her short hair into tiny, tight dreadlocks. "Someone's trying to frame me with it," she finally said.

Richard let go of Kesho. "Thanks a lot, both of you. We appreciate the effort, but it's all taken care of. I've got the best criminal lawyer in Connecticut on the case. Look out there." He waved at the open door. "Got rid of the cop in less than two minutes." Neither Joe nor Detective Sher-man were anywhere in sight. "And he's already found a hole in Copper George's case that's bigger than Goose Lake."

"Which is?" His swagger was putting me off.

"They've got to prove Kesho knew about this new will. Or else why kill Elisabeth?"

"Hey, that's great." Willy clapped a hand on the channel selector, blasting us with Olive Oyl's screaming.

Then the thought hit him at the same time it hit me. Above him the TV winked off.

"Maybe *you* knew," Willy said.

Richard hit a foot against the wall. "What are you talking about?"

I jumped in, forgetting my keep-Willy-out resolution. "What Willy means is that Chuck claims he saw you up at Elisabeth's last night after dinner. He went up to talk to her about the sale of the house, but when he looked through the glass of the entrance, he saw you. You looked 'mad as hell.' His words."

"So that tells you I didn't know about the will. If I knew, why be angry?" Richard's tasseled foot settled back on the floor. "I'd have to wait a few years maybe, but I'd save three million bucks."

"One and a half," Kesho said. "I was going to pay my share."

"She'd changed her mind about selling." Willy's voice cracked. "That's what Mr. Dobson said. She called him and told him she wasn't selling. She must have told you, too."

"Are you accusing me of killing her?"

"Rich!" Kesho called out in warning. For a moment, Willy was in a Spielberg frame, hanging on by one finger, facing a pit of giant roaches.

"Of course he's not accusing you," I said, rushing in to save the boy. "He's trying to figure out the truth. Everyone's spinning tales around here."

"I'm investigating, that's all." Willy swung his cap around. The giant roaches had turned back into speckles in the linoleum. "Just going over the possibilities." He fiddled with his visor, ready to pitch a curve ball. "So did she tell you?"

"Get out of here, kid!" Richard jerked his chin at the door.

"Richard!" Kesho reached out one arm helplessly. She was pinned down by her bad leg. "Willy, he doesn't mean it. Come here!"

Willy was already out the door, his shoulders and back a perfect T-square.

"I do mean it," Richard said. "I don't need this." His voice would have frozen mercury.

"God, Rich," Kesho said, "what's the matter with you? I'm the one arrested for murder."

"He was only trying to help Kesho," I said, feeling as put down as Willy. "You don't have to be a bully. His father's a detective, for Christ's sake! What's the boy going to play at? Owning bistros?"

"You can get out, too." He was by the window now, looking down at the church spires breaking through the cover of trees.

"Did you see anything while you were up there? Notice anyone on the property, walking around the lake. Anything that can help Kesho?"

He didn't answer me.

"Willy meant no harm. Neither of us do." I leaned down to kiss Kesho. Through the half open door, I could now see Willy waiting for me by the nurses' station. "I'll come back tomorrow before your surgery."

Behind Willy, a blur of orange. A narrow face looked at me, then moved quickly out of sight again. Not fast enough. I'd seen him before. A thin, weaselly man, wearing that same orange sweater. A color that had matched the pumpkin walls of the police station exactly. Richard's powerful Connecticut lawyer was full of it. The police were still watching Kesho.

"Get some rest, Kesho." No need to tell her.

She held me back, her hand tight on my wrist. "We're both scared, Simona. Tell Willy that. And for God's sake, ask questions across the lake. Those Dobsons are full of locked closets, and Copper George is too much of a coward to even get close."

CHAPTER

15

Well, we were standing in the middle of the lake, my balance precarious, Willy sure-footed on his beloved skates. The ice-skating party was in full swing. The townsfolk had turned up despite the murder, their bundled children whirling in bright colors to the sounds of *The Nutcracker*'s "Sugar Plum Fairy Waltz." While some watched, others were gathered in talkative clusters, nodding woolly heads toward "the island of death"— that's what the *Hartford Courant* had called it. Yellow tape, held up by orange cones, cordoned off the northern end of the lake. Two patrolmen stood on guard, neither of whom were tonight's date, Joe Pertini. In daylight, the policemen looked like movie extras who'd wandered into the wrong lot. The horseshoe of Dobson land—with its cover of pines, oaks, birches, and maples—was just too postcard-pretty, the skating party with its fairy-tale music too colorful and gay a scene. Elisabeth had died somewhere else. In some other time. This place belonged to Bambi. I wondered where he was now, my scraggly half-drowned fawn.

"He's hiding something," Willy said, skating in small circles around me, each circle a little wider, as if he were picking up courage to fly the nest. I was happy to be considered a nest, even if only for those five minutes. Willy, to my surprise, had not been visibly shaken by Richard's anger. On the drive back to Fieldston, I'd tried to find out how he felt and his only comment had been a neutral, "He's got a right to his feelings." Which made him much fairer than I was.

"I'm really sorry Richard treated you that way," I told him now.

"You said that."

"I'm saying it again." I unwrapped the red plaid scarf I'd tied around my head. It was just past noon. The clouds had lifted and the sun was turned on high. The snow would soon melt, leaving dark stains on that white hill, maybe bringing back some reality. "I'm sorry we ever got into this." I could smell the marshmallows roasting on a grill stretched under a huge willow fifty feet back on land. The red brick house where Charles and Myrna lived was barely visible behind a row of pines. "Sherlock and Watson are on vacation from now on."

"Right, that's our cover."

"No, that's for real. Someone's been killed and asking questions can be very dangerous. We almost lost a friend for one."

By the time we got back to the inn after a quick stop at the supermarket for vegetables and beef chuck for tonight's Comfort Pasta, Richard had already phoned. When I returned the call, he apologized, adding casually that he'd gone up to RockPerch for reassurance about the sale, which he said Elisabeth had given him. Which didn't explain being "mad as hell." But then why believe Chuck over Richard?

"Did you really see Richard leave the inn?" I asked as Willy did a triple turn on one skate.

"No," he said with a smile, pleased either by the lie or the perfect turns.

"Let's leave this death to the police. Is that a deal, Willy?"

He skidded to a stop, his skates ending up in a perfect T. "You don't mean that!"

I explained. In the white sunshine of a beautiful Christmas scene, I talked about danger, death, lying; how at fourteen he should involve himself with the bright side of things like skating, enjoying the good weather, good food, joining the other teenagers who were playing ice hockey in a curve of the lake.

"I'll stop if you'll stop," he said, head turned to the hockey players, his expression bored, unhappy, sullen? Who could tell with a teenager, a boy I barely knew.

"Deal." We didn't shake hands. I knew I was lying. Once that curiosity grips me, I can't stop myself from burrowing. Maybe he was lying too. Maybe Willy had my same need, a need to grasp people, to scan them for mysteries, for sudden shifts, in a vain hope of being prepared for any more betrayals. Divorce can do that to a spouse or a child for a while; leave them floating, untethered, in some nebulous loveless space. I had the added condition of being a diplomat's brat. Every four years we'd pick up and leave a country. Places, people would suddenly be miles too far for friendship or a child's memory. I learned to hook my eyes hard onto my surroundings, coming away with a strong picture to glue into my mind's scrapbook.

That's what I was doing now, staring at the island. Behind it, two hundred feet up the hill, the thick rock ledge commanded attention. Layered, intricately folded, baked in intense heat thousands of years ago, it was a powerful reminder of nature's dominance. We would all disappear along with Walter and Elisabeth; the Wright house would crumble, but that ledge would still be there.

Above the ledge, a swath of sunlight shimmered, reflected from the band of windows where Elisabeth and I had stood together. Every day, looking out those windows, she had a perfect view of her future deathbed. It wasn't visible from this side of the lake. I had been trespassing on her property when I sighted the fawn. The murderer must have felt safe, thinking no one would wander on private property late on Christmas Eve. Actually the killer had been lucky. Chuck had gone to Elisabeth's house; so had Richard; so had, according to some mysterious witness, Kesho. Very lucky.

Through a thicket of trees a narrow stone path plowed of snow snaked its dark way down, stopping at the edge of the lake, between a hedge of evergreen mountain laurels—the state flower, Jean had informed me. On each side of the path, behind the junipers, I could barely make out what looked like two stone troughs, similar to the ones the shopkeepers of Main Street would fill with flowers in the summer. I stared at that path, imagining the murderer leading Elisabeth down to the lake, careful not to leave footprints. I was the only one clumping through snow with my size eight Sporto boots. Everyone else had walked on plowed paths. Even in the panic of Elisabeth's sudden death, the Dobsons had been careful not to tread snow. That thought was chilling.

"Want some hot chocolate, Willy?" On a wide beach of snow-patched lawn, underneath another giant willow, Myrna was silently handing out hot chocolate from two giant thermoses. Twenty feet from her, Charles, heavy chest this time cresting a black-and-white hunter's jacket, had taken over the barbecue pit, rubbing gloved hands. His voice was loud.

"You should have seen my camel spins and butterflies. Olympic quality. My waltz jump was almost always a ten." His audience was two young boys who looked at the roasting marshmallows with longing. Charles shifted weight every few seconds as if it were still bitterly cold, his voice sounding like the constant rush of cars on a highway. "It takes hard work, a great deal of discipline to be good.

Remember that, boys. The puritan ethic. Hard work, and then more hard work." The marshmallows burned.

"I'm going for something to drink," I said, spotting Edith Holmes, wrapped in blankets, being wheeled to Myrna's table. Her head was wrapped in a tight beehive of purple mohair, and all I could see of her face was a purple lipsticked mouth working nonstop, probably giving Myrna hell for having the party. "Want anything, Willy?"

He shook his head, looking at two girls skating by, holding hands. They were both pretty, his age at the most, wearing white leggings under short fluffy skirts. Willy took off ahead of them, suddenly looping in the air and landing on one skate, the other leg straight behind him.

"Bravo!" I yelled. The girls giggled. Finally a healthy pursuit.

"Sorry I was rude outside church yesterday," I said, walking up to Edith, "but I did have an emergency on my hands."

"Kesho Larson should never have come back here," she said, unwrapping her scarf to peer at me. Her husband stood behind her like an ever-faithful butler. "She's stirring up a lot of past trouble." She narrowed eyes paled by age. "Since you're snooping around, young lady, you should ask yourself about that innkeeper of yours."

"I'm not snooping."

"Of course you are. You've got that look about you. I always recognize a snoop."

"By looking in the mirror!" Myrna snorted.

Edith grinned, dentures sparkling. "I gave up mirrors in my teens. Comes with being ugly." Her nose outdid mine in length, a straight pointed weapon. If I kept up with my prying, maybe I too would become the village gossip when I was her age. I could see myself at eighty, setting up shop on a bench in Washington Square Park, exchanging the latest malicious scoop with the drug dealers or giving bad advice to lovelorn NYU students.

"I don't know what Jean's been blabbering about me," Edith went on, "but she was no friend of Elisabeth's. By next summer that place of hers was going to go bankrupt 'cause Elisabeth was cutting off her water. Shut the dam right up so there'd be no pretty pond for her guests to swim in, that's what sweet Lizzie was going to do. That pond's the only thing that brings 'em in the first place. And it would have served Jean right, too."

Edith's husband looked away.

"Shut up, Edith," Myrna said. "What has Jean done to you?"

Edith's eyes glinted like a hawk's spotting meat. "Nothing to me, but she should have kept her hands off Walter. Elisabeth didn't like that. There she sat, coiled in that reptile house of rock and glass all by herself, while Walter was down at the gas station or over at the inn, listening to Jean's dumb mouth, eating her foul food. She even killed Jean's stupid cat, ran right over her in Jean's driveway. Said it was an accident, but you know damn well, Myrna Henderson Dobson, that Elisabeth was just hissin' pissin' with jealousy."

An affair between Jean and Walter? Was that what she was implying?

"Elisabeth didn't give a damn where Walter was!" Myrna snapped. "She didn't love him for one minute."

"But you did, didn't you?"

Myrna laughed, a short, scratchy sound. Edith took my hand. Hers trembled with age or Parkinson's. Her head had that Hepburn shake, too, but none of the poise. "Now Myrna and Walter and Charles, that's another story you should get into."

"Edith, please," her husband said, standing behind her. Myrna opened a flask.

"Are you here for some Italian magazine?" Edith asked me almost kindly. She looked behind me, as if expecting a photographer to pop up.

"No, sorry. I'm here on vacation."

"No one's going to believe that." Edith wrapped her shawl around her head again, her nose pointing over my left shoulder. I turned and saw Copper George talking to Jean on the narrow strip of land that led to the dam.

"Henry, take me over there. I got a few things to add to whatever that woman's telling him." She spoke to the air in front of her. "And I'm sick and tired of this moronic music." The "Sugar Plum Fairy Waltz" in fact had been spinning like her tireless tongue.

Henry grasped the handles of the wheelchair and tugged. As he turned her around, she held out her cane, which for a moment pointed straight at Myrna.

"Jean's done the same thing to your son, except you're too soused to see it. Hypnotized him so that he's never going to come home. Just like Walter. I think that woman's a Circe. She's even managed to turn herself into a pig." Her husband pushed her wheelchair hard out of earshot. Edith waved her cane in parting. "Next year, let's have some Elvis!" she shouted.

Myrna raked fingers down her short gray-streaked hair. "That woman thrives on parties. She can kill thirty birds with one mouth!"

"I'm surprised so many people came to this one," I said.

"You expected signs of grief and respect?" Myrna handed me a steaming paper cup half full of chocolate. She looked older in daylight, clearly in her late fifties. The dark brown parka she was wearing made her look dowdy and sallow.

"Well, yes."

"Emotions aren't given their due in this part of the country. We've been bred to pretend nothing has happened." The sun struck her weary eyes, ran down the grooves of her cheeks, stopping at the wrinkles, thin as paper cuts, hemming her tight lips.

"Elisabeth wouldn't have minded." Myrna looked like she minded very much.

"Where is Edith's hate coming from?" I asked.

"That is none of your business, actually."

"We wallow in hate around here," Chuck said, appearing from behind the willow tree. Sunlight favored him, flushing his face with some color, bringing out the green of his hazel eyes. Jean's Christmas present—a dark green and blue Sutherland plaid—cocooned his neck, as protective as an Ace bandage. "Centuries of money metamorphosed into hate." He smiled at me, as if we had become friends overnight. "Edith's captain of the nasty ship. Her family came over on the *Mayflower*. She used to reserve most of her bile for FDR and the Democrats in general," he said, "then when Jean, a lowly gas station attendant, got the inn, Edith's focus changed." Even his whine was gone. "You see, Edith wanted the place for herself. It's not as big as what she's got now, but she'd be able to indulge in her favorite pastime."

"Which is?" I asked, putting down my cup after one sip. The brew was twenty parts water to one part chocolate powder. No wonder there was no one lining up for the stuff. "What is her favorite pastime?"

Chuck watched as his mother poured clear liquid from a flask. "Keeping a close eye on the circus act of the Dreadful Dobsons. She lives on the other side of the hill, behind RockPerch. Can't see a thing except the property line."

Myrna gave her son a crooked smile. "Disagreeable, direful, delirious, dreadful Dobsons."

And dipsomaniac, I might have added. "Edith said Elisabeth killed Walter. What did happen to her husband?"

"God!" Myrna groaned, her nose disappearing into her cup.

"I'm sorry." Maybe I was getting to be worse than Edith.

"Walter was the delirious one," Chuck said. "He died by his own hand."

A woman on the edge of the lake was waving her arms. "Jennie, careful. Watch the red flag!" A tiny thing in a sequined pink skating outfit swerved around the obstacle. Her mother dropped her arms.

"What are those flags for?" I asked. On this side of the lake, several red flags stuck out of the ice like wild poinsettias.

"Ice holes, damn it!" Chuck stared angrily at his mother.

"Blame that on your father." Myrna turned her back on the lake, as if she wanted no part of it.

I searched the lake for Willy, found him still showing off for the two girls, well away from the flags. "Just how big are the holes?"

"Come on, Mother, you're the one who charges the locals for the great privilege of fishing on the property. Didn't want to break a crisp twenty for another gin bottle?"

"I'm sick of your attitude, Chuck. There wasn't supposed to be a party! Not with Elisabeth dead. But your father can't stop playing lord of the manor."

"How big are those holes?" I almost shouted. Beyond Chuck's shoulder Willy was racing straight for a flag, the girls fast behind him.

Chuck turned to follow my gaze. "Big enough to sprain an ankle."

"Willy!" I screamed. He jumped over it, knees high, and landed perfectly. The girls glided on each side of the hole, applauding him.

"Your kid's smart." Chuck smiled.

"Thank God." I felt a little silly. Maybe I'd overreacted. "He's not mine."

"Willy knows what he's doing. Just like me, right, Mother?" Chuck laughed.

Myrna downed her drink. "Do shut up, Chuck. You have nothing to be happy about."

"But I do. No more expectations of wealth. Father's disowned me, Elisabeth picked Kesho for her little Wright plum, and you haven't a cent to your name except that pearl choker which, in true family tradition, you'll hand to me when I show up with a wife."

"You know perfectly well your father will contest the will." Emotion flickered across Myrna's red-rimmed hazel eyes.

"Of course he will. But I'm still disowned." They had the same eyes. Small, deep set and hard to decipher.

Myrna crushed her Styrofoam cup. "You'd pawn that choker the minute you got hold of it. You hate our traditions." Leftover chocolate and gin dripped down her small, liver-spotted hand. "You hate everything about us!"

"So do you, Mother. The only difference between us is that I'm free now. I won't have to pawn anything. I've been offered a job I'm going to keep for once. Jean's handyman and carpenter extraordinaire. No more stranglehold." He took off his glasses and looked at me, his eyes shrinking, suddenly vulnerable. "All Dobsons are born with their umbilical cords wrapped tightly around their necks. Ask over at the hospital. 'The Dobson choke' they call it."

"Don't believe a word of this." Myrna still held her crushed cup in her hand. Behind her, the willow tree dripped melting snow.

"Real or imagined, it's there," Chuck said, raising his cup. "How about a toast to my growing up?"

I tipped Styrofoam against Styrofoam. "To your new job."

"To Simona and Willy finding another suspect," Chuck said, "who is not I."

We both turned to Myrna. She was looking across the lake, to the house poised on the rock ledge, its eaves spread out for flight. She lifted her crushed cup, not to our cups, but to that house. "To Elisabeth," Myrna said as her eyes filled.

I was surprised, instantly moved.

Then her knuckle met our cups. On her face, a tear had caught in a groove above her cheek. Her breeding had betrayed her.

"And to dear Edith," Myrna added. "May word poisoning kill her quick."

Chuck laughed. "That's more like it, Mother."

CHAPTER

16

S o what'll you have?" The waitress of the Whipping Post
cocked a round hip practically in my cheek, all the
time giving Joe Pertini the full benefit of her anger.

On the wall next to him, a carefully stitched sampler
exhorted us to Make Whoopee At The Whipping Post. In a
Greenwich Village bar that might offer an off-beat array of
possibilities. Here I suspected the sampler was just asking
us to order one more beer.

"You know what I like," Joe Pertini said, his sweet face
now sullen.

"I'm not a walking encyclopedia of your wishes," the
waitress said. "And I don't have all night."

They fumed at each other. No one bothered to find out
what I wanted to drink. I had served my purpose, which
clearly was to get this attractive woman jealous. Under a
cupola of black curly hair, her frosted pink-shadowed eyes
had fulminated me with a quick glance, a mine sweeper
catching and detonating in the same instant.

"We've got a murder on our hands," was my peace
offering. "We also have the wrong person accused. I'm just
sitting here with Joe, hoping to get some help."

The hip retreated. A dark, thick eyebrow cocked.

"Honest," I said.

"You fink," she told Joe, whose moustache squirmed.

Those pink eyes shifted to me. "Copper George fucks up easy," she said. "Joey's been due a promotion three years now." She flattened her hand over a slice of air. "Three years and he gets *nient*. And the jerk"—her long-nailed thumb pointed—"instead of facing that other jerk"—her hands were flying now, her Italian origins taking over—"the jerk, he picks a fight with me, sayin' I flirt with all my customers. Me? You know, you should go fuck an egg, Joey."

I lowered my face not to show the smile creeping in. *Va fa' l'uovo* was my father's favorite road insult when my mother was in the car. Without her, the "egg" became an "ass."

"What part of Italy are your parents from?" I asked her after I tucked the smile away. "I'm *Romana*."

"My grandparents were Italian. On my dad's side, Nonna from Ancona. She missed the Adriatic, but she had two cousins here. Grandpa was from Calabria, the bottom of the boot. He liked it here 'cause it was all rock like back home. He could really relate to rock. He put up a stone fence around our house that's the envy of our street. My mom's great-grandparents were both from Catania, Sicily. What'll you have?" She lifted her dimpled chin. I'd been accepted.

"Sambuca with flies, if you've got them." Our booth, at the very end of the bar/coffee shop, had become a corner of Italy, even though the narrow room was dark-wood, red-Naugahyde, Tiffany-plastic anywhere-U.S.A., with last year's tinsel sagging in waves across the bar mirror. Christmas lights blinked.

"Joe, I need your help," I said.

"I'm a cop. I can't spy for you."

"I'm not asking you to do that. I just have some questions I want you to think about. My doubts, your insider knowledge, we might come up with the real killer. Maybe it'll help with your promotion."

A halo of black curls blocked the light. "*Maronna*, that jerk'll never promote Joey. He doesn't like Italians."

Joe was handed a rum and Coke. I got my Sambuca with three coffee beans, the odd number—the trinity—a must to bring good luck. Italians look hard for good luck, finding it even when a pigeon drops on us or our shoe squashes into dog litter. Enacting a pooper-scooper law would bring great bad luck, my father insists, mostly to the dogs, who'd find themselves homeless.

"Roxanne Santinelli." Joe's girlfriend offered me a hand, wet and cold from holding beer glasses. "Known as Rox in honor of my grandfather."

"Simona Griffo."

"Now if you two catch the killer, then Copper George gets egg all over his face, and my father's cousin, Sandy Santinelli, gets the chief's job. Mama would finally get a smile back on her face. Joey gets promoted and Rox, instead of being a waitress with a B.A., gets to be a wife with a B.A." Her red lips spread into a grin. "Works the same, but the benefits are better. Help her, Joey."

"I can't."

"Sure you can. Mama would love you forever." A hand called to her from a booth by the entrance. "Be right there." She bent over me. Estée Lauder's Beautiful prickled my nose worse than cinnamon.

"Watch it," she told me, lethal nail pointed at my eyes, her sneakers already poised for takeoff. "He's mine." The air moved as she strode away. Joe's eyes were rheumy with love.

A pang of longing for Greenhouse hit me in the lower abdomen. We had spoken briefly before dinner, just as Willy's Christmas rigatoni were seeping up the stew sauce. Greenhouse's mother's heart was better and they expected to operate on Tuesday. He wouldn't be home before

Wednesday night at the earliest. Willy was crushed at the news. After only three bites of my Comfort Pasta, he'd walked off to the den to watch TV. I tried talking to him, but got sullen silence in return.

"Joe, you don't have to report back to me," I said. "Just look into several things and decide for yourself. Copper George is so convinced Kesho is guilty that he's not looking for anyone else. It's a closed case." A sip of Sambuca coated my mouth with a sugary licorice taste that made me instantly feel better.

"The chief's a good guy," Joe said. "Maybe she is guilty."

Why was I so convinced she wasn't? Just because Kesho was Greenhouse's friend? TV was always showing neighbors and relatives saying, "He was a real nice man." "She was such a caring neighbor." "I've known him all my life." Was I trying too hard not to be racist?

I wasn't sure. Gut feeling and a few unanswered questions were all I had to go on. "I think Copper George is making a mistake." I lowered my voice, leaning closer to him. "Charles Dobson says he got a call the night Elisabeth was killed. She supposedly told him she wasn't selling the house after all, which makes it very nice for him because it leaves him without a motive to kill her."

"What's he need that house for? He's got a gorgeous colonial I would give my nails for." Roxanne was peering from the booth behind Joe, a sponge in her hand.

Joe looked annoyed. "Rox, this is business."

"Freddy Flintstone here. Listen, I asked a good question."

"Rox's right," Joe conceded, his eyes wallowing in the sight of her. "Dobson doesn't need that money."

"Not that you'd know it by their clothes," Roxanne said, her lip curling. "The homeless dress fancier."

"Have you seen the For Sale signs around here?" I pushed the Sambuca glass out of the way. "They practically outnumber the mailboxes. Everyone's selling and no one's buying. Not ideal for a real estate firm. In fact his office in Danbury is up for rent, and he isn't one of the hospital patrons this year. So the Dobson money situation is something for you to look into."

"My brother works over at Connecticut Seal where the Dobsons have an account. He might be able to tell you."

"Rox, I'll handle this."

"Sure honey. I'll keep the booth behind you empty for privacy. Not much doing tonight, anyway. People spent all their money on Christmas."

"Thanks, baby." Joe smiled, a boy who'd found a treasure trove.

She smacked her lips in a kiss. I was getting sick.

"Also check if that phone call from RockPerch exists," I said.

Joe looked into his glass, an annoyed look creeping across his face.

"These are only suggestions."

"Yeah, I know. It's just that I don't like it, you know, being told what to do. I'm doing my best."

"He's sweet. That's what his problem is." This time Roxanne brought potato chips. She winked at him and left.

"Who ever heard of a sweet cop, huh?" He was blushing.

"Greenhouse is sweet. Maybe even sweeter than you."

"Sure he is. You don't become a New York City detective by being sweet."

"Maybe he knows when to turn it off." Which was something I didn't like to think of. Nor did I like to think of Greenhouse as a policeman period. Not in New York City.

Joe took a long slurp of his rum and Coke, as if that might toughen him up. "What else should I be looking into?"

"Find out who told Copper George that Kesho was up at the house that night." I'd already asked Chuck, who said he'd only seen Richard.

Joe looked unconvinced. "All this information is going to go to the defense lawyers anyway."

"I'm hoping it doesn't get as far as a trial. If someone swore Kesho was having a fight with Elisabeth, that someone has to explain what he or she was doing out in the freezing cold, eavesdropping on Elisabeth. For all I know the whole Dobson family paraded up there. What alibis do they have? Were Myrna and Charles together?"

"Even if I look, I can't tell you anything."

"But maybe you'll find something that should be followed up. Maybe you can convince Copper George. If not him, Sandy Santinelli."

"I don't know."

"Just look into it, then decide. And another thing. With all those rocks around her waist, why didn't she sink to the bottom? Can you find out?"

"I can tell you right now. There's a ledge in that spot. About four feet under. Guess it got there when they dredged the lake about eight years ago. I didn't know about that ledge. I guess the killer didn't either. She got stuck, then that deer of yours must have kicked her hand up, and that's how you saw her. Otherwise she'd have been down there all winter."

"Weighted down by those rocks."

"She didn't need rocks to stay under. Not in that freezing water. I mean, in summer, she'd have filled with gas in a couple of days and floated. In this weather, she'd stay under for months."

Pleasant thought. "By then the bruises and the bump on the head wouldn't show, maybe." I told him about Willy's theory. "The space the killer slipped her into is barely wide enough. If the temperature had dropped, the next morning the entire lake, space and all, would have been frozen solid. Who'd think to look for her there?"

Joe sipped cautiously this time. "Could be he's got a point." I got the feeling Joe didn't like to take a stand, just in case he was wrong.

"Did the autopsy find anything unusual?"

"She had a lot of aspirin in her. Which doesn't mean a hell of a lot. The chief thinks that's why she was bruised. You can bruise real easy when you take a lot of aspirin, he says."

"Elisabeth suffered from arthritis." Roxanne popped up behind Joe. "Martha over at the drugstore told me. She runs at the mouth almost as much as Edith Holmes does. Joey has to go over to Ridgefield to get his condoms so the whole town won't know how many times he has sex with yours truly."

"Rox, have you been listening this whole time?"

"No, I've been cleaning. The people who sat here left a mess."

I couldn't help but laugh.

"Hey, wait a minute, Joey!" Roxanne clattered a cleaned ashtray on the Formica-topped table. "You aren't getting those condoms in Ridgefield because you don't want *me* to know how quickly you use them up, are you? That's a bad question, right, Joey?" She was looking at me now, the pink eye shadow narrowed to two thin strips of distrust. "Tell me I got this wrong."

"If you're thinking of me," I said, crunching into a potato chip, "you've got it very wrong."

"Very wrong," Joe repeated.

Her eyes didn't budge so I ignored her. "What's at stake for Copper George with this murder? Why did he arrest Kesho?"

Joe's leather jacket rode up as he lifted his shoulders. "What's he gonna do? The town's all scared. The ME is screaming murder, saying she was alive when she got that knock on her head. I mean, we're not in New York City here. This is a quiet town. The most you're gonna get in the *Ledger*'s police log is reports on sick raccoons we end up shooting in case of rabies, or loud music on Maple Street. Chief's gotta move or Santinelli gets his job for sure." He stopped, as if waiting for Roxanne to cheer for her cousin. She was still frozen in her unpleasant thought.

I crunched my last coffee bean. "Elisabeth being a Dobson might have something to do with it, I suppose."

"Yeah, God and the police are supposed to protect their kind, and their kind is more than half the town." Joe shrugged. "The rest of us are service personnel."

"My family thinks he's in the pay of the Dobsons," Roxanne said, her expression sad now. "When Elisabeth's husband disappeared, Papa swore Charles Dobson paid Copper George to keep it hush hush."

Joe widened his eyes. "Rox, what are you sayin'? The FBI got called in! They looked all over for the man. He killed himself. Went up to Toronto and drowned in the lake."

"They never found his body though." Roxanne turned her face to me, a pretty white oval tucked in a nest of curls. "Chuck killed Walter Dobson because Walter wouldn't cover a check he'd forged, that's what Papa said. Maybe Chuck drowned him in Toronto. Elisabeth drowned, too. Maybe Chuck killed both of them."

"I'd like to talk to your father," I said.

"You can't. He died four years ago of a stroke. But you can talk to Mama. She'd love to meet a real *Romana*. Come for lunch. She makes a baba ghannoush that'll curl your hair from good."

"What, no lasagne?"

"Naw, we're all citizens of the world now."

I wasn't. Not of Fieldston, at least. Someone had made that clear. At nine-thirty at night, with a coffee bean crumb stuck in my tooth, with my tongue still sweet from Sambuca, I was standing in the half-filled parking lot behind the Whipping Post. The temperature was thirty-two according to the Connecticut Seal Bank, a block down the side road. Zero in Celsius, which is exactly how I was feeling. Next door, on Main Street, an old-fashioned marquee announced the only movie in town: *Under Siege*. I had my own announcement, scratched neatly on the hood of Greenhouse's Buick.

Go Home!

All four tires were slashed.

I wanted to sink down into the snow and bury myself alive, but, in the white light of the street lamp, I saw widening puddles of ugly brown slush. I went and got Joe instead. Roxanne followed.

"Jee-sus!" she said at the sight of the car.

I brushed the scratches with my hand, as if they were dust prints. They were blood-letting sharp, the nail had dug deep. "Not my idea of making whoopee."

"Kids," Joe pronounced, giving me a consolatory pat.

"Some quiet town." What was I going to tell Greenhouse?

Joe shook his head. "I don't think it's our kids. More likely from the bigger towns like Danbury, Greenwich, Stamford. Kids bored with being poor."

"I'll give 'em bored." Roxanne stepped between us. "Right up their you-know-what." She shook her head. "Naw, this ain't kids," she decided, now that she had Joe's hand in her own. "You got New York license plates. There's people here don't like you guys. They say you pay so much for houses we can't afford to live here any more. You dress loud, talk loud, you want service lickety-split."

"Fieldston's not like that. It's kids."

Roxanne shrugged. "Like I said, he's sweet."

"What are the chances this was done by someone who doesn't want me to pry?"

"Who knows you're prying?" Roxanne said.

"The people I've questioned." Chuck, Jean, Kesho, Richard, Myrna. I'd even asked Copper George questions. "Besides, Edith Holmes declared me a snoop."

"Then all of Fairfield County knows."

"This is kids," Joe insisted. "I don't mean to put you down, Simone, but you're not the police or anything. You're just curious, right?"

"Simona. With an *a*." I don't like my name mispronounced. It makes me feel foreign.

"The killer wouldn't worry about you."

"What do you mean, he wouldn't worry?" Roxanne's hands flew skyward. "What, just because she isn't in uniform? You think that blue shirt gives you so much authority, makes us all quake and shake. Oh, boy, have you got a surprise coming to you, baby!" She gave me a long-lashed wink.

"I didn't mean it as an insult!"

My feet sloshed a puddle. "Listen, could one of you give me a ride to the inn?"

"Take her, Joey. I trust you." Roxanne waved a hand in my face. "I'm not really jealous, you know. It's a part I get into. You know what I mean? We're supposed to shake our hips a little, knock 'em in the eye with a boob, make a big fuss over them. If you've got Sicilian blood in you, then you threaten to pick their eyes out if they stray. It's sexy, harmless. But it doesn't mean we're dumb or anything, right?"

"Right." The Italian sex game. It made for some fun, horny moments and some pretty bad ones, too. Like the time a film director I was working for squeezed one breast as if to gauge its ripeness. I squeezed his balls right back. Hard, so that he couldn't use them for a couple of weeks. I didn't feel dumb at all.

We walked to Joe's old Chevy, Roxanne still trailing.

"Take her away, baby," she said, shooting her forefinger at Joey as she watched us get in the car. "If you're not back in ten minutes, you're dead."

Behind her, an advertising sign warned: Don't Compromise. Chain Saws On Sale.

CHAPTER 17

"Hi, Jean," I said, walking into the welcome, oven-hot air of that immaculate kitchen. Wearing her red bathrobe, her hair in neat rows of curlers, Jean was sitting at the round table, Premi curled on her lap, a newspaper in her hand. She smiled, last night's eavesdropping apparently forgotten. "You look like you got caught in a bulldozer sweep."

I laughed. "That's exactly how I feel. It's been a long day." I shrugged off my coat, not wanting to tell her about the car. I realized I was ashamed, as if I somehow deserved that Go Home. Jean tapped her pencil against the crossword page.

"What's the champagne town of Italy?" she asked. "Four letters."

"Asti." A vague whiff of Comfort Pasta still hung in the air, a reminder of failure. Willy had stopped eating my cooking after three forkfuls, which in turn blocked my appetite. Only Jean had enjoyed the comfort. "Is Willy still watching TV?"

"No. Joan and Jill, those sisters he met at the ice-skating party? They called him up and invited him to go see a movie."

"Here in town?"

"Danbury, I think. Don't worry, the girls' mother took them. I made sure of that."

"Thanks Jean. Was he feeling better?" I sat down next to her and rubbed Premi's ear.

"He asked to call his dad. I put him in my bedroom for privacy. Talked twenty minutes, but it didn't put a smile on his face. Then the girls phoned. He liked that. He even combed his hair."

"Did you see Kesho go to RockPerch Friday night?"

Jean dropped her smile. "Why do you want to know exactly?"

"Now, don't get upset again, please. Copper George has a witness who saw her up there, and I'm trying to find out who that is. Kesho swears she was never near the place that night."

"So you think I'm the lying witness?"

"Nooo. I don't think you're a liar, but I had to ask." Why was this getting to be so hard? I could hear Greenhouse's voice swirling in my head. "Think suspect, not man, woman. Suspect. Feelings cloud judgment."

"You're a great innkeeper, Jean." I smiled, meaning it, and just flunked out of P. I. school.

"That's not what Edith told you."

"I didn't listen to what she was saying." Premi stood up on Jean's lap, bumping his head under the table. I stole him from her and draped him over my shoulder. "Did Elisabeth really kill your cat?"

Jean looked up, eyebrows raised. "I thought you weren't listening?"

"I couldn't help but hear that."

"Well, I told myself Reg's death was an accident, though I didn't convince my husband. Now if Bill were alive, you could try to pin Elisabeth's death on him."

"Why did he dislike her so much?" Premi was filling my ear with a Rolls-Royce purr.

"I don't like to speak ill of the dead, but for all her ladling out soup for the poor down in the church basement every Friday, which she did, mind you, only after Walter walked out on her, Elisabeth Dobson was not a very nice lady. In fact she was no lady at all, and that's what started the whole trouble to begin with."

"Which trouble? Her death? Her husband's death?" Walter's disappearance was beginning to intrigue me. Was he a suicide or a murder victim?

"Maybe the two deaths are linked," I said.

"There's no real proof he's dead. And you can stop twitching your nose for more. You look like Premi in front of a mouse hole. If you want gossip, go talk to Edith. You'll end up with hot air balloons for ears."

"I'm trying to help." Being emotional, I wasn't the best of detectives, but I could stir things up, maybe scare the killer into making the wrong move.

"Let me tell you one thing," Jean said. "I understand you wanting justice and asking around to see what you can learn. But don't forget there's other people."

"The only other person I'm interested in is the killer."

"Well, that's jim-dandy, Bill used to say, but there's such a thing as privacy. And it's not as if anyone's given you the right to poke around."

"I don't want to stop." Was I being self-righteous? Kesho had a good defense lawyer; he would take care of her. But what if he didn't move fast enough and she went to trial? What if she was found guilty because the lawyer was too cocky, or because he didn't want to give a black woman his best?

"Maybe I can make a difference," I said.

"That's what we women always like to think, but sometimes we can't."

"Yes, we can," I said, standing up. I was learning that in this country. "Sure."

I was going to make a big difference to Greenhouse

when I told him about the car. Well over five hundred dollars worth of difference. I'd tell him tomorrow. After his mom had come out of the operating room. Maybe even the next day. Give him a chance to relax. I looked out the window. The frozen pond caught the glitter of the waning moon. Leaning forward I could barely make out one dark corner of the shed.

"Jean, I'm going to ask one more question, but I don't want you to get angry."

"What's that?" She peered at the ACROSS column, indifferent to my question.

"Why did Chuck trash his shed? Elisabeth was dead, the sale was off. He hadn't heard about the inheritance yet. So what got him angry enough to be so destructive?"

Her eyes never left the crossword puzzle. "Ask him."

"I did." After Myrna's morbid toast. He'd walked away, laughing at his mother, and I followed. "He told me it was none of my business." Which had been his mother's words exactly.

"Well, maybe it isn't." Jean bent over the paper. "First name in mysteries. That's easy. Agatha."

Go home, Griffo. "Good night, Jean."

She looked up in surprise. "Only four letters." Fingers started counting. "Not Dorothy. Not P.D.. Not Sue. Sara!" She started to write, then stopped. "No, it's got to be an E at the end."

"How about Erle."

"Oh, him!" She tried out the letters. "E-R-L-E. Thanks, that's who it is. He's not half bad."

18

"Did you and your date have a great time at the Whipping Post?" Willy asked the next morning, his face about to drop in his Grape-Nuts. The tone was not friendly. Premi, eyes half-closed, wavered from his perch on the stove, fighting sleep.

"How did you know I was at the Whipping Post?" I'd only told him I had to meet someone, not wanting to let on I was sleuthing without him.

I got a shrug in response, which I probably deserved.

"It wasn't a date, by the way. His girlfriend was there. But it's nice of you to be so protective of your dad."

He looked at me dumbfounded. "I just asked a question."

We were having breakfast in Jean's kitchen, despite her protests that paying guests should eat in the formal dining room. "Only family uses the kitchen," she'd said.

Willy's forlorn, "yeah," made her relent. His mood hadn't improved. So far communication on his part had been limited to a "Hi" and cereal-crunching silence. Outside the window, a steady rain tried to make inroads into the thick mist. What ground I could see had turned from white to mud brown. The thermometer on the window pane read thirty-five degrees. Which is what the kitchen felt like this morning, with Willy's shoulders hunched in rejection.

"Where's the car?" he asked, the last teaspoon of cereal down his throat.

"Your father's car . . . " I bit into a slice of coffee cake. How to tell him that while out on that "date" he so obviously resented, someone had taken a very sharp key to his dad's wonderful car.

"It's not his car."

"What do you mean?"

"It's rented. Mom's got Dad's Toyota."

"A Toyota? And Mom's got it?" Why did I not know the car was rented? Or that this man drove a Toyota? "Why did Mom get Dad's car? If I may ask?"

"That's between Mom and Dad." Was he smiling? If he was smiling I was going to punch him.

"Yes, I guess it is," I said, ramming the rest of the slice in my mouth. He'd managed to put me right in my place. Exactly nowhere. Nor could I retaliate because he was fourteen and I was thirty-seven, and his confusion was probably much greater than mine. But it did make me think, as we continued to eat in silence, about my lazy tendency to assume. I'd known Greenhouse owned a car, but since we only saw each other in the city, where the use of a car brings instant psychosis, I'd never actually seen the thing. When I arrived on his sidewalk and saw him loading the trunk of a maroon Buick, I had assumed. Just as I had assumed that since he had once told me he was picking up his son after church, that meant he was a Christian. I didn't care what he was or what car he drove, but I should have known. Now I felt excluded. And damn jealous. Why did Mom have to keep popping up? Why couldn't she have rented her own car?

The phone in the hallway rang. I perked an ear, wondering if it was Greenhouse. Only last year Willy's mom had made moves to get Greenhouse back. He'd turned her down, but Willy was the one string that held them together. Even without children, my ex-husband was part of my life just the way those six years of marriage were part of me. Not only a memory, but a stepping stone, a part of my education, my makeup. Except I had the benefit of distance. My ex was back in Rome along with those six years. In Fieldston, Connecticut, with a hostile Willy sitting across from me, I felt very much alone.

I could hear Jean chatting into the hallway phone. The call was not for me.

"Willy, why are you angry with me? I thought we'd become friends. Is it because we're not sleuthing together?"

He looked up, focusing on the door beyond my shoulder, his mouth open, lower lip twisted. "Who's angry?"

"How was the movie in Danbury last night?" I was giving it one last try. "Should I see it?"

Willy scraped his chair back and picked up his bowl. "We went right here in town and you wouldn't like it at all." He got up and clanked the bowl in the cracked porcelain sink. "This whole vacation's a drag." He walked out, slamming the door, leaving me with the ugly thought of an angry boy scratching Go Home on the hood of a rented car.

Half an hour later Mrs. Condlin and her daughters picked up Willy for "mall fun"—their words—over in Danbury. In my opinion malls are purgatory with only hell in the wings, so it was a good thing no one asked me along. Besides, I had work to do which was going to stop me from thinking Willy had anything to do with slashing tires and scratching cars. And stop me from feeling sorry for myself. I called Kesho.

"Can you believe it?" she yelled in my ear. "I almost got arraigned this morning! They don't even have a grand jury in this state. Just one man judging yours truly and you know how that's going to work out."

"You said 'almost.' "

"The lawyer got it postponed until Friday because of extenuating circumstances."

"Thank God for your knee. It'll give us more time."

"I can't believe this is happening to me!"

"Let me come over and cheer you up before the surgery." With what? I had no car and not much cheer to offer either.

"Too late. They've pushed it up an hour and right now some itty bitty woman is threatening me with a syringe the size of the Empire State Building. Anyway, I'm brewing one of my tropical storms and you don't want to get caught in that."

"Did your lawyer find out who supposedly saw you up at Elisabeth's?"

"No, they're giving him some kind of runaround. At least my bail's paid and I'll be back at the inn by tonight. We'll catch up then. Keep digging. I do appreciate it. So does Richard."

"Then tell me the truth, Kesho."

She hung up. Bad timing on my part. Before an operation isn't the moment to confront people. I do that often, butt in, blurt, bluntly ask, instead of waiting for that sensitive moment when the truth is on the edge of a lip. *Dare tempo al tempo*—that's the wisdom I used to stare at from my toilet seat back home as a child. Give time to time.

Here in the States I'd been learning that every minute counts. Taking the best of both worlds, I decided to leave the rented Buick where it was until I phoned Greenhouse to check on his mother. I'd tell him the news this afternoon. That left me a free morning for some library work on the disappearance of Walter Dobson.

Neatly dressed in nursery pink sweats and her new red slippers, Jean shut off her vacuum cleaner to offer me a ride in her truck. She even offered the keys if I promised to come back in an hour. I had no idea how long my research would take, but I knew I could use a brisk walk to get rid of the bad mood and half a box of Entenmann's coffee cake.

"Thanks, I'll brave the weather. When did Walter disappear? Do you remember the exact date?"

"You got so many question marks stuck in your throat, it's a miracle you don't choke."

She made me smile. "I can't breathe. That's why I ask. Do you remember?"

"April first of '85. Nice April Fools' for all of us."

"He was a real good friend of yours, wasn't he?"

She waved me away with an exasperated look. The vacuum cleaner whirred back on.

I borrowed Jean's umbrella, donned my Downtown coat and Sporto boots, ready to march out of the house and down Bishop's Lane in pursuit of health, fresh air, and the murky past of Fieldston's premier family. By the time I hit the cemetery, half a mile from the inn, I was sure I had pneumonia. Fresh air was really an army of frozen termites gnawing my face, and the murky past had become a muddy presence that was going to send me sprawling against a tombstone if I didn't walk at snail's speed. I lifted Jean's baby blue umbrella a few inches in case I was about to bump into a tree. To one side, drenched, ribboned wreaths of pine and holly leaned against granite crosses and marble tombstones. Christmas for the dead. What about the living, is what I wanted to know, as a gust of wind rolled a wave of icy rain in my face. What the *cazzo* had happened to the joyous, jolly, jingling holiday season?

I jumped as a shining black and chrome dinosaur whizzed by, spraying me with slush. I caught a glimpse of Myrna with something black sitting on her head. I called to her, hoping for a ride out of the cold and an illuminating chat, a first step to those locked closets Kesho had talked about. Doing at least fifty-five in a thirty-five-mile-an-hour zone, Mrs. Charles Dobson didn't see me. Or pretended not to.

"You're not setting a good example!" I yelled, waving my umbrella. The editor of the *Prudent Times* might have been saving health by driving in that rain, but in that relic of imprudent times, she sure wasn't saving gas. And she was going much too fast. If she didn't watch it in that rain she was going to end up being Kesho's neighbor after all. At the Danbury Hospital.

CONNECTICUT ENTREPRENEUR DISAPPEARS, was the *New York Times* headline in the "Metro" section's Connecticut page. The *Hartford Courant* headlined LEADING FIELDSTON CITIZEN MISSING over three columns of their front page. The *Fieldston Ledger*'s front page spread the news over five columns. Underneath a blue stripe telling me the paper had been established in 1872, I read: WALTER DOBSON GONE. POLICE FEAR FOUL PLAY.

Charles Dobson reported Walter's disappearance to the Fieldston police on Saturday, April sixth. "We thought he'd gone on one of his business forays," he was quoted as saying in the *Courant*, to explain why he had waited five days to tell the police. When asked why Walter would not have told his wife he was going, Charles admitted that his brother's marriage was faltering.

I could almost hear Edith Holmes clacking her teeth over the news. It must have kept her busy for years. She and her husband Henry had sworn they had seen Walter the Sunday before he disappeared, wrapped in his signature cape, walking at the edge of their property, which bordered the woods at the back of the RockPerch estate. Charles had confirmed seeing his brother that afternoon as had Elisabeth. Walter had driven off Monday morning, April 1.

The *Fieldston Ledger* dedicated a short human-interest column to the love story gone "bad." Walter had fallen in love the first year Elisabeth and her mother had moved up from New Hope, Pennsylvania. She had joined the tenth grade of the Fieldston High School. At the time he was in eighth grade in the same school, "a school that, as we all remember, owes its new gym to the generosity of Walter Dobson's father, Charles Dobson Sr., a man who never believed in fancy boarding schools for the rich." Elisabeth had refused to be interviewed.

"According to resident Jean Shaw, who was in Walter's high school class and is a neighbor of the Dobsons', 'It took Walt the better part of four years to convince Elisabeth. With all that courting, you'd think he'd flunk, but no, straight A's all the way through. He was our class valedictorian. That's Walter for you. A winner. Don't you worry. He'll be back.' "

On the *Ledger*'s front page Jean was quoted as saying that on Wednesday, March 27, Walter told her he was thinking of going away for a while. When she hadn't seen him the following week, she assumed he'd left although she was "a little disappointed he didn't drop in to say good-bye." She repeated, "Don't you worry. He'll be back."

But Walter didn't come back. Just hours after Charles's declaration to the police, Walter's car, a metal gray Jaguar XJS Cabriolet, was found parked in the long-term parking lot at LaGuardia Airport. A fingerprint check found many smudges and only Walter's prints. Elisabeth declared she had never driven that car nor had Walter let anyone else drive it. The airlines, checking back to when Jean Shaw had spoken to him last, found no Walter Dobson on their passenger lists. The FBI joined the search. Two days later, the Toronto police called to say that a Walter Dobson had registered in the small elegant Windsor Arms on the night of April first, had handed over his gold credit card and asked for a suite for one week, adding that he would be using it as a base while traveling around on business. The concierge thought nothing of it.

A zealous rookie reporter on the *Ledger* had flown up to Toronto and scooped both the *Times* and the *Courant* with details of what the FBI had found in the Windsor Arms suite. Walter had opened his Bottega Veneta suitcase on the luggage rack, laid out his toiletries on the marble bathroom counter, slept in the king-size bed, dropped a pair of striped boxer shorts on the floor along with a one-way American Airlines New York-Toronto ticket issued to a William DiRusso, and removed an eight-by-ten wedding picture of Elisabeth from its silver frame. The maid had found the picture torn to shreds on the thick, dark blue carpet.

"Well-versed in the erratic ways of the rich and famous, Mary Chambers, the appropriately named maid, discreetly gathered the myriad pieces that had composed Elisabeth Dobson's face and dropped them in a crystal ashtray the size of a soup bowl." When the FBI pieced together the photograph, the inscription read, "To my husband, forever." Walter was not found.

"Lake Ontario," the reporter concluded, "is 193 miles long, 53 miles wide and 802 feet deep. Is it also Walter Dobson's final resting place?"

A week later, a blurb in the "People" section of the *Ledger* wished that reporter good luck on his new job at *New York* magazine.

In the following weeks, the furor over Reagan's visit to Bitburg took over. So did Coke's announcement of a new formula. A five-week-long fire was steaming the giant turtles in the Galápagos Island of Isabela, and John McEnroe announced that men could beat women at any sport. In Fieldston, senior citizens were feted at the annual luncheon in their honor, and the police union worried about the delay in the budget referendum. Walter Dobson's story disappeared as he had.

I dropped the microfiche back on the library counter, startling a long-faced toothy woman dressed in a long hand-woven beige skirt with matching beige Shetland sweater.

"Sorry and thanks for your patience." It had taken her twenty minutes to find the fiche for me.

"Fascinating case, isn't it?" she whispered, towering over the counter. "Is this for a Rome magazine? Something like Deaths of the American Rich?"

Edith's fast-moving tongue was giving me a good cover. Journalists poke with impunity when they're not in a war zone.

"I don't know yet," I whispered back, liking my vagueness. It didn't make me a liar. "Now I need last year's *Ledger,* but I don't have a date."

"You'll want the presumption of death announcement." Her ponytail bobbed, flaxen and thick.

"Uh huh."

"June twelfth." Her mouth spread. Nostrils twitched. I thought of a palomino.

"It's my birthday," she said. "That'll be over here."

I pattered after her elegant, silent stride across the glass-walled library. I'd read that Connecticut's horse density was tops in the country.

She riffled through a neat stack of papers on a wooden rack. "Here it is, June eighteenth. The *Ledger* only comes out on Thursdays. The other papers didn't carry it."

Walter Dobson Presumed Dead

On June 12, the Danbury Supreme Court ruled that Walter Dobson is presumed dead after a continuous seven year absence. Charles Dobson's lawyer was able to show that there was no explanation for the disappearance and that a diligent search had been made. Walter Dobson left his beautiful home of Rock-Perch, didn't use his bank account, and left behind a loving wife and personal property worth a considerable amount of money. The court ruled that there was no satisfactory explanation for his absence other than death. A memorial service will be held this Saturday at 10:00 A.M. at the Congregational Church on Main Street.

A small picture showed the same strong face I had seen over his studio's fireplace.

"I was in Elisabeth's high school class," the librarian said, keeping her voice low. She had stood over me while I read, her ponytail dropping over my shoulder. "She was going to leave him. That's why he did himself in. She had a lover."

T hat's what I heard, too," Mrs. Santinelli said, taking a
sip of coffee that left a half-moon of blood red lipstick
on the rim of her cup. After a delicious, healthy lunch of
baba ghannoush, roasted red peppers, and salad, she had
made espresso that we were drinking in a small peach-col-
ored living room. Mirrored shelves, covering one wall,
creaked with a lifetime's collection of dancing figurines. A
skinny Christmas tree was jammed against the other wall,
between the gold velvet sofa and the matching armchair I
was sitting in. On the windows, glass snowflakes hung
from silver ribbons.

"Papa said it, right?" Roxanne sat next to her mom,
looking like a sister, barely younger. "Didn't he overhear
something?" The halos of curly hair were identical, so
were the overly made-up saucer eyes with long lashes, the
wide red lips, the perfectly oval faces. Roxanne was
vibrantly pretty and thin. Her mother's good looks were a
shade quieter, her body a few inches thicker. Their voices
were the same. They both boomed.

"What do you remember, Roxanne, huh?" Mrs. Santinelli's fingers met and shook in doubt under her daugh-

ter's nose. "You was a kid at the time. Too young to know about such things."

"Mama, I was fourteen!"

Mrs. Santinelli leaned back against the gold sofa, her black skirt hiking up her knee. A wine red sweater, hand knit in a complicated open pattern, hugged her tightly. Roxanne wore the same sweater in Christmas red over jeans. Under the TV set, a basket brimmed with knitting needles and wool skeins.

"I heard Walter was the one with the lover," I said. At least that's what Edith Holmes had been implying.

Mrs. Santinelli smacked her shiny mouth. "He was devoted to his wife, the whole town knows that. That's why he left her." She pulled at her skirt. "Emilio, my husband, he was a building contractor. He also did patios and pools. He was working for the Dobsons, Walter and Elisabeth, at the time."

"Yeah, and he heard them fight," Roxanne broke in. "He called her a slut of the worse kind. That's devotion for you."

"Who's telling this story? Who did your father say this to? You or me?"

Roxanne grinned widely, clearly used to this. "You, Mama. It's your story. You tell it like it is."

I sipped strong black coffee. *Dare tempo al tempo*. Give time to time.

Mama waved a hand. "This girl of mine has no respect. Always hiding behind things, listening to everyone. Not like her brother, who works in the bank instead of a bar."

"Johnny's an *angelo*," Roxanne said, grabbing red candy from a dish on the mirrored coffee table. "The boy's always the best." She winked at me.

"Your father never would have said anything if he knew you was squeezin' those Dumbo ears of yours against the door."

"When did Walter call Elisabeth a slut?" I put my coffee cup down. "The day he disappeared?"

"No. Three or four days before, I think it was. You remember, Roxanne?"

"Yeah, I guess a few days before. Papa went and reported it to Copper George after Walter disappeared. He was sure the man was killed and that Chuck did it."

"Why Chuck?"

"You see, at that same time, there was some kind of scandal about Chuck making out a bad check using Walter's name. The thing was pretty hush-hush. I got it from a friend who overheard teachers talking in the john at school. Papa told me to stay away from Chuck because he was bad."

Mrs. Santinelli poured more coffee. "Papa didn't think Chuck was the killer because of the check. Uncle Walter was his meal ticket, always giving him money, presents, treating him like he was his own kid. No, Emilio was sure Chuck killed Walter because Walter found out he was the lover."

Roxanne's mouth gaped. A red dot of translucent candy rested in the center of her tongue. "Mama, I never heard that!"

"That's about the only thing you didn't hear."

"Eight years ago he was, what, twenty-four?" I said. "And Elisabeth was in her mid, late forties. That's quite an age gap for loving."

"No, it isn't," Roxanne said, snapping her fingers. "You see it in the movies all the time." She popped another candy in her mouth. "So Chuck was making it with the princess."

"Why did Chuck have to kill him?" I asked, not believing any of this. "It should be the other way around. Walter killing Chuck."

"Maybe it was self-defense. I don't know." Mrs. Santinelli rocked on the sofa. "My Emilio was sure. He even knew where he buried the body."

"In the lake?"

"The police dredged that," Roxanne said.

"In the pool," Mrs. Santinelli said. "Walter was getting a pool put in back of the house. A few days before Walter disappeared my husband and his workers had poured the Gunite."

"Mama, you have a grid of steel rods before you pour Gunite. You can't get a body through unless you hack it into little pieces, and they didn't find any blood."

"No, no, it's the deck around the pool. Emilio laid in the pre-fab slabs that Friday. There's fill underneath. On Saturday he went over to check things out. 'The slabs don't look right,' that's what he told me. And that's what he told Copper George who did absolutely nothing about it. My husband never got another job in this town." She rocked herself, tears filling those dark saucer-eyes. "It broke his heart."

"Filled it with bile," Roxanne said, her eyes filling up too.

"I'm sorry." Mrs. Santinelli's story had cracks all over it. Just because Walter had called Elisabeth a slut didn't mean she was having an affair with anyone. Women have been called sluts since Eve did her defiance bit, for any number of reasons. Once at a party my ex called me *troia*—sow—for jumping into a dance circle and rolling my hips to Michael Jackson's "Beat It." I should have taken Michael's tip then and there.

"You're saying your husband noticed the deck wasn't right on Saturday," I said. "But several people saw Walter that Sunday."

Roxanne's chin shot up, fingers brushing off tears. "His brother, big deal. He's been after Elisabeth for years himself. Isn't that right, Mama?"

"I don't know." Mrs. Santinelli was dabbing her eyes with a handkerchief. "I don't know."

"Edith Holmes and her husband also saw him," I said, lowering my voice, thinking the hurt of my words would be less.

"Roxanne said you was going to help." Mrs. Santinelli tucked the handkerchief up her sleeve. "Some people said Emilio was off his head and you don't want that said about your husband. Emilio was solid, strong. Put a brick on top of another brick, dig the pool of your dreams, get sand and gravel all over this house, those things he was good at. Making up stories, no."

Roxanne patted her mom's hand. "Eight years is a long time, Mama. And the Dobsons, they're big in this town. A hell of a lot bigger than the Santinellis."

"What about your father's cousin?" I asked her. "The one who wants the chief's job? Hasn't he been able to help clear your father's name?"

"Sandy? He don't dare," Mrs. Santinelli said. She reached behind the base of a cut glass lamp. "He's gotta think of his career." Her hand came back with a small blue box of Baci Perugina.

"Joey's stuck too," Roxanne said. "Not that he's in a position to do much, thanks to the jerk."

Mrs. Santinelli offered me a silver-covered mound of chocolate and nuts. "Copper George hates Italians, you know why? His first wife, Verna. Real pretty, blond from the bottle, but still nice. Now she's got a shop up at the Danbury Mall. Calls it DiRusso T's. Tease is right. She made out with every man in town behind his back and now all Italians are bastards. Joey doesn't have a chance. I told Roxanne already. He should quit and go over to Ridgefield. An Italian's chief over there, a stable man with only one wife."

"That jerk's had two wives since Verna," Roxanne said. "None of them any good. None of them Italian either."

Mrs. Santinelli looked at me, a chocolate raised to her mouth. "You help the black girl, and maybe you'll help my husband, too. That possible?"

"Sure." I smiled. "Did you know Kesho or her family? She didn't live too far from here." Only two streets back, according to Jean, who had given me directions to get here.

Mrs. Santinelli's face tightened. "Far enough. Don't get me wrong. I've got nothing against blacks. It's just that, well, they got their ways, we got ours."

I stood up, disappointed, even angry. "What about being citizens of the world?"

"That's me, I'm the citizen," Roxanne said. "You got to let the older folk be, right, Mama? You make great baba ghannoush, but you're stubborn just like Papa. Even the pope's not gonna budge you."

I thanked Mrs. Santinelli, who had the grace to look ashamed. We said good-bye and Roxanne walked me to the dry-stone wall her grandfather had built. It had stopped raining, but it was still cold and damp.

She walked her nails along the wall. "Twenty-five thousand miles of stone wall in this state. We're part of history." Behind her stood her blue frame house with yellow shutters and eaves. Christmas lights blinked around the doorway. A diminishing snowman, pelted by yesterday's sun and this morning's rain, watched from under a pine tree.

"Mama says dumb things sometimes, but she's all right."

"She was very nice to feed me so well and give me all that information."

"Which you don't believe for one minute. Listen, I know some of it doesn't make sense. Maybe it wasn't Chuck, maybe it wasn't even Elisabeth, but Papa laid the slabs himself, troweled the grouting to a smooth finish. He just knew somebody had fooled around with his deck."

"That's not enough to go by. Your father's dead and can't tell us more."

"He'd cry if he saw the pool now. It's got more cracks than Edith Holmes' face."

"I'm sure the FBI looked into things thoroughly."

Roxanne shivered. She wasn't wearing a coat. "They couldn't dredge Lake Ontario, could they?"

I shook my head.

"Maybe that's the way Walter went," Roxanne said. "He cut quite a figure in town, you know. He looked like an actor. Not the movies. More theater. A WASP Raul Julia, if you can believe that. Sexy."

"Any news from Joey?"

"Oh, good thing you didn't try him at the station. Blip, blip, blip, that's what you get when you call. Drives me nuts! They record everything. Here's four things for you." She lifted four fingers, showing off those perfect long real nails. "Elisabeth was looped. Not completely blotto, but high enough not to know what hit her." She marked off the item with thumb against finger. "What hit her was smooth and round, and RockPerch called Charles's house Friday night."

"Elisabeth called? Is Joey sure?"

"Never mind who's sure. Two calls came out of that phone, one at 4:33 P.M. when she called the liquor store for a bottle of Amaretto, barf—"

"What about a maid? Does she have help living with her? They could have made the calls?"

"Naw, Pat down the street does for her once a week. Place never gets real dirty. That huge house and Elisabeth only lives in the studio, even sleeps there. Mama thinks it's out of guilt. There's a portrait of her husband in there."

"What time did she call Charles?"

"Ten forty-seven. Can you imagine getting drunk on Amaretto?"

More than an hour after the dinner had broken off.

Time enough to get drunk and change her mind about selling.

"Maybe she was barfin' so bad she fell in," Roxanne suggested. "Copper George would love that. He'd buy anything not to have to move his ass."

"What's the fourth item?"

"A good one. Dobson Realty's going to declare chapter eleven after the holidays."

"*Grazie*, Roxanne." Whether Charles knew Elisabeth wasn't going to sell didn't matter now. With Dobson Realty going bankrupt, Charles still had a strong motive for killing her. He expected to inherit.

Roxanne was thinking the same thing. "Yeah," she said, those long-lashed eyes widening. "Money'll beat it over racism any time. Greed's the big one."

CHAPTER

20

My butt got the first throw. I jumped. "Hey!" As I turned something moved soundlessly behind a deep hedge of junipers thirty feet up the hill. "What the hell are you doing?" Something blue. Or was that the sky? *"Basta!"*

My left shoulder twisted back with the next pitch. I dropped behind the stone trough for protection, bunching my legs up to my chest. The trough was only about three feet long, but it was better than hiding behind a laurel. Whatever my friend up there was hurling, it was bruisingly hard. My left butt cheek burned with pain. I shifted my weight and sank into slush and mud.

I tried to listen for my assailant and got the silence of winter—creaks and groans from trees, the drip of snow still melting on shaded branches. A quick rustle of a bird or a squirrel. Too light to come from a person. Unless . . . I stopped myself from thinking.

Behind me was the lake, shimmering with a coat of rain and melting ice. Above me was the hill with its many saplings and trees, and a thick hedge of junipers. Even higher was the metamorphic ledge from which RockPerch surveyed the lake. I lifted my head. Another bomb skimmed the top of my hair and crashed through the mountain laurel behind me.

I splashed back into the slush and twisted my neck to observe the gleaming white ball, resting on the edge of the lake. A cannonball made of ice. Hitting the frozen lake had barely dented it. Better an ice ball than a bullet, I guess. I slid forward in skin-firming mud and peeked, this time around the trough. The view was of stubborn patches of old, dirty snow pocked by the rain, and two curves of the stone path that led to the house, with clusters of birches in between.

I whipped up, my hands over my head. Hit me, but let me see you at least. I stood there waiting, my eyes doing a 180 degree scan. Nothing, no sighting, no ice bomb. Just that eerie winter silence again. I almost felt the woods hemming in, trying to claim back the land. First cedars and junipers. In about a hundred years, RockPerch would disappear within a dense forest of oak, maple, and hickory. In a hundred years this story, this event wouldn't matter.

I sat on the edge of the trough, a muddy mess. The raid was over as abruptly as it had begun. Kids?

Or was it Elisabeth's killer warning me off gently? Maybe he or she didn't want me here, staring at this trough, more than two feet deep, piled high with rocks of all shapes and sizes. Rocks Roxanne's grandfather would have fingered lovingly, nostalgic for home. I picked one up, heavy and round. Smooth.

"What hit her was something round and smooth," Roxanne had said. I dropped the rock back in the trough, repulsed. A rock the killer might have used to knock Elisabeth down, more rocks to girdle her and plunge her into ice water. Not that it made any difference in the end whether he had hit her here or up at the house. Except that one discovered detail leads to another. If nothing else it makes the killer nervous. That's when mistakes get made.

Feeling newly charged with the authority to detect after my lunch with the Santinellis, I had come to walk across Elisabeth's property, looking for I don't know what exactly. A sense of atmosphere, a clue to her rich unhappy life, for brilliant ideas to ricochet off the trees.

Standing up, I could see the red flags of the ice holes, brighter under this afternoon's pewter sky, markers for the killer as he hauled his drunk, unconscious load to the island just a hundred feet ahead. Had he used skates for speed?

While the rest of the town clinked eggnog cups and sang carols, had he led Elisabeth down the meandering stone path for a view of the beauty of Goose Lake shimmering under a half-moon, at midnight? A friend, not raising her suspicions, maybe consoling her for her drunken unhappiness, an arm over her shoulder in case she stumbled, then a quick, iron-hard grasp around her neck, a tap on her head . . .

I caught movement from the corner of my eye. I cried out and lifted my arms to my face. Nothing came at me. Slowly I lowered my hands to see a squirrel frozen on a bare branch. He was as scared as I.

I turned around and kicked the ball of ice, watching it skitter across the lake. The spot had been too silent for kids. No guffaws, no crunch of feet running away. The killer, I told myself. It's bound to be him. I want it to be him. Better him than Willy.

"You're trespassing!" Charles trudged down between trees. The squirrel leaped across branches.

"This is Kesho's now," I yelled back.

"We'll see about that." He stopped ten feet from me, barrel chest safe in his black-and-white hunter's jacket, baggy brown pants clasped at the bottom by hiking boots. His jowly face was firm, set in smoldering anger.

"What do you want?"

"I could ask you the same thing, Mr. Dobson. I was here first."

He lifted the flaps of his red hunter's cap, freeing his ears. For a second I thought it would help the communication problem, but I was wrong. He just stood there like a moose, trying to stare me down, his lips twitching.

"Actually, I do want something, Mr. Dobson, now that you ask."

"Charles. I thought we'd established Charles." He lifted a gloved hand in sudden peacemaking. I was obviously no threat.

I walked a few steps up the hill, to meet him halfway. "I'm Italian, Mr. Dobson. I've been taught to reserve first names for friends. Did you throw ice balls at me five minutes ago?"

He widened his watery blue eyes. "What are you saying?"

"Just that someone was taking potshots at me with some ice balls."

He looked around, up and down the trees, jowls trembling. He wasn't the one.

"I think you're safe, Mr. Dobson."

"Of course I am." He didn't seem so sure. I walked up closer, to see his face better. There was one more question I wanted to ask him. "Are you the witness Copper George keeps talking about, the one person who saw Kesho arguing with Elisabeth?"

"You are trespassing now, Miss Griffo." He gave me a closed-mouth smile of satisfaction, his large strong face relaxing. He looked like a man who'd just given that final handshake on a multi-million dollar deal. My heart sank in the mud.

"Your account of that night will never hold in court, Mr. Dobson. You're a biased witness."

"Do you think your friend is any less biased? She

stands to lose that inheritance and her freedom. The jury will have to decide which one of us to believe." His smile cracked open and I held back an urge to pummel his teeth with my fists.

"I wouldn't be so smug if I were you. The political climate is changing for people like you."

He ignored what was only a hope of mine and gestured towards his house across the lake. "I'd invite you in for tea; you look like you might welcome it, but Myrna's out. Some other time, perhaps. And may I give you some fatherly advice? Take better care in selecting your friends."

"That's exactly what I'm doing."

He walked past me, taking the lake route home. He made his way slowly across the ice, the raised flaps of his cap making him look like an overfed, floppy-eared old animal. His unpleasant voice continued to buzz in my ear.

"It's rented," Greenhouse said over the phone. "Hertz will take care of it." He didn't sound worried. That's because I hadn't told him about the slashed tires or the Go Home scratches, just that the car was kaput. He would have had Willy and me on the first train to New York. "If they can't get it started, they'll get you another car."

"I thought it was your car." There was silence on the other end. I was fully aware of sounding petulant, but being pelted with ice balls, possibly by Willy, wasn't my idea of holiday merriment. My lying didn't sit well either.

"What's the matter?"

"I just thought it was your car."

"You said that. Look, is this about my not telling you I'm Jewish?"

"Maybe. We'll have to sit down one day and input our backgrounds, tastes, habits in one of those police data banks with a guaranteed monthly update." I was calling from Jean's room, an immaculately neat, ruffled, and

laced shrine to her past. Photographs were everywhere as
was a pink, peachy-smelling potpourri. A young Bill and
Jean, embracing a gas pump, stared at me from the
dresser. They had both been large even thirty years ago.
And happy, judging from those grins. "We'll just press buttons instead of speaking to each other."

"What's going on? You sound worse than my mother."

"I think Willy's miserable here." I inhaled, liking the
smell of peaches.

"Let me talk to him."

"He's over at the Condlins." He'd been watching televi-
sion when I came back. His sky-blue parka dripped on the
coat rack in the hallway. He'd mumbled a "Hi," and
answered my "How was the mall?" with "I'm really into
this movie. Can we talk later?" I was grateful to get away. I
didn't have the courage to ask him outright—"Are you
throwing things at me?"

Now I explained to Greenhouse about the skating sisters, about his having dinner tonight at their house.

"Sounds like he's having fun and you're not," Greenhouse said. My eyes surveyed the pictures of Jean's life,
cluttered over the dresser, the night table, framed by silver-
tone flowers, ribbons, and lacy hearts. All happy pictures.
Throughout the years, her son grinned, Bill grinned, she
grinned. Even the cats curled on top of their respective gas
pumps, Regular and Premium, looked into the camera
with eyes lengthened into satisfied smiles.

"I miss you." And Willy, which I didn't say. Next to my
elbow, Walter was grinning at me from a paisley cloth
frame, towering behind Bill and Jean. Then I told Greenhouse that I suspected Kesho and Richard weren't telling
the truth; I talked about the newspaper stories on Walter's
disappearance, about Edith Holmes claiming Elisabeth
had murdered him, implying Jean and Walter were lovers;
I told him about Elisabeth having a lover; how I was sure
Charles was the witness.

"That's bad."

"He's biased."

"He's a respected citizen of the community."

"He's horrid."

"I thought you weren't sleuthing this time!" Green-house did a perfect imitation of my previous petulant tone.

"*Ehi*, you're as good as Billy Crystal."

"I *am* Billy Crystal."

"*Magari.*"

"What's that mean?" His voice was suddenly gruff, sexy.

"I wish. Listen, the Santinellis think Chuck's the lover, but I'll bet it's Copper George." The thought had just come to me, looking at yet another of Jean's pictures, this one of a much younger and trimmer Copper George in swimming trunks by Jean's pond.

"He's the right age, actually good-looking if he smiles, can't keep a wife—he's on his third, I think—a ladies' man according to Jean, and he's tall and powerful-looking. Elisabeth told me she liked that. And Copper George said all men had a weakness for Lizzie."

A sigh came from the other end. "Sim, wouldn't it be safer watching the soaps?"

"Maybe, but boring. I like real-life drama. If you're worried about Willy getting involved in this mess, he isn't. We made a deal to break up the team and stop sleuthing. It's an unsavory occupation for a kid."

"A deal you're not keeping."

"I'm trying to help Kesho."

"Well, don't expect him to appreciate it."

"That lawyer Richard hired is a *pallone gonfiato*—a blown-up balloon." I told him how he'd conned Richard into thinking he'd gotten rid of Kesho's police guard. As I spoke I could hear my voice rising, getting defensive.

"Willy doesn't know what I'm doing. He's never around me." But he probably did know, like he knew I'd been at the Whipping Post with Joey. Another children-of-divorce talent. Not unlike the talents of a cheated wife, I realized.

"I'll admit I don't know what I'm doing," I said, "except that as things stand now, Charles is a good candidate for murderer. He thought he was going to get that house and he's going bankrupt. With his pompous pride, that's a fate worthy of death."

"Listen, honey, don't jump to conclusions and start accusing someone of being a killer. You can make big enemies that way."

I tried to move my shoulder and winced. "*Grazie tante* for the vote of confidence, Greenhouse." One side of my ass didn't feel much better.

He chuckled. "Well, you're not the most analytical, cool-headed person I've met, but I do love you. Be careful. I'm on the noon flight on Wednesday. Tell Willy to call me tonight."

"Sure. Hope your mother's operation goes as well as Kesho's. In fact, she should be here by now." I'd called her from the Santinellis' house after lunch. "Richard's going to bring her to the inn in a white Mercedes he's gone over to Stamford to rent. It's their wedding car."

"That's the car he should buy. Corvettes aren't made for three."

"Three? Are you saying what I think you're saying?"

"You didn't hear that."

"OK," I said, instantly annoyed. "I'll add it to the list of things I don't know. *Ciao*." I started to hang up.

"Hey, Sim!"

"What?"

"You knew I was Jewish."

"How could I? Picking up Willy after church was the only time we even came close to mentioning God."

"Oh, he got invoked a few times that I can remember."

"Sure, when I made you drink a voodoo love potion or I splattered you with spaghetti sauce."

"Or when we make love."

"That's another god entirely."

"You're always telling me how you think my circumcised penis is 'bellissimo.'"

"My handsome Jewish hunk, all American men are circumcised." Could I stay annoyed? The memory of him, Adam naked, was too mouth-watering.

"How would you know?"

"I read it in the *New York Times*, that's how. It's more hygienic or something." Actually I'd lost my virginity to a Columbia med student—a Southern Baptist from Louisville—my junior year at Barnard. After we made bad love, he'd told me his family wouldn't take kindly to a foreign girlfriend, a Catholic to boot.

"I love you," I said, blowing Greenhouse a kiss. "We'll talk tons when you get back." I might even tell him about senior year and my second lover, who was Jewish and a gentleman. He told me *before* we made love that with shiksas he only had one-night stands. I'd been too horny to care.

❄

Jean leaned against the back door as I walked into the kitchen. She was trying to kick her boots off.

"Hi, Jean. Welcome back."

She stomped the floor with one foot. "Gosh darn boots, I can never get them off."

I dragged a kitchen chair from under the table. "Here, sit down, I'll help."

She heaved herself over to the chair, out of breath, cross, huge in an old blue down coat that skirted her ankles.

"Do you have a bus schedule?" I asked. After hanging up with Greenhouse I'd called Hertz. "I've got to pick up another car in Danbury."

"Maybe Chuck can give you a ride when he gets back. I just came from there and I'm not about to go back. I went over to pay Kesho a visit."

"I'm sorry. I should have phoned you to tell you she was checking out. She's supposed to be on her way over here by now." The kitchen clock said five o'clock. I turned my back to Jean and gripped her calf with my knees. I grabbed the heel of her boot and started pulling.

"I didn't miss her. Careful! They're a Dobson fit, meaning—"

"I know. Tight." I clenched what few muscles I had and pushed harder. My shoulder groaned. The left side of my butt did a death rattle. "Mamma, how about a bigger size!"

"They're keeping Kesho overnight to do some more tests in the morning. Her blood count's dropping. She could have a ruptured spleen."

The boot slipped off and I practically fell in Jean's lap.

"Hallelujah," Jean said in reference to her boot.

"Oh, *Dio*," I said in reference to that "three" Greenhouse had spilled. What if Kesho had lost the baby? I leaned against the table and peered down at Jean.

"Is anything else wrong with Kesho?" Did she know?

Jean was busy pushing the other boot off with her redsocked foot. If she knew, she wasn't telling. "Thanks for freeing my foot. I gotta get me some thinner socks. It's cheaper than buying new boots." The second boot clunked to the floor. Jean leaned back in her chair, wiggling her toes. Premi rubbed against her calves, letting out his characteristic croak.

"I'm going to call her." I marched off to the hallway and dialed the hospital on an old black rotary phone. Richard answered. Kesho was downstairs having some more blood syringed out of her.

"Jean told me. What's the latest?"

"The doctor's not worried. I don't know why, but he's not worried." Richard was mumbling, the words mushy. He sounded as if he'd gnashed his teeth down to the gums.

"Is there anything I can do? Want me to come over, bring anything. A funny video maybe. Books? Comics? I'll make you both some pasta." Pasta is the cure-all in my family.

"No, Simona, thanks. Just keep your fingers crossed. There's a lot riding on this."

I stopped myself from saying, "I know."

"Kesho's going to be all right," I said to Jean back in the kitchen. Another thing I'd learned in this country. Think positively. Easier to do with others, I'd found.

"Lord, I hope so." Jean was still in her chair, holding Premi against her white angora sweater. Her coat had disappeared, probably already hanging in its designated closet. "I'm beginning to think this wedding was not meant to be."

"Don't say that." I rapped knuckles on wood, incurably superstitious.

"Well, it sure isn't going too good so far." She pointed down to the floor by the door. "That bag's for you."

A stapled Hay Day shopping bag rested on the orange-and-white hooked rug. "How Nell can shop in that place is beyond me. With those prices you'd think they were feeding the Pentagon."

I picked up the bag. It wasn't very heavy.

"Nell's convinced you're some hotshot journalist. That's the power of Edith's tongue." She bobbed her head. Not a blond hair moved. "You aren't, are you?"

"I won't deny it if someone else asks. Who's Nell?"

"The librarian. Trotting Nell, we used to call her in school. I was Rockin' Rollin. Bill was SteamRoll. You could break into reporting with an article on the lore of nicknames. Too bad they've gone out of fashion now."

"Politically incorrect. What was Walter's?" Maybe Nell had sent over more articles on Walter's disappearance.

"Stupid is what he was, for loving that woman so much." She bent over and picked up Premi. "He was always Walter. Nothing else would fit."

"Handsome man. I saw his picture in your bedroom and a portrait up at RockPerch. Elisabeth sounded lost without him."

"Of course she did. He left her with no money. He liked to spend it as fast as it came in. Charles had to end up helping her out. 'It's the dignified thing,' he tells anyone who cares to listen. He's a big one for letting everybody know how generous he is."

Having to give Elisabeth money could have been one more good reason to get rid of her.

"Walter was made of another cloth. Charming, grand, the most popular guy in school. Then he ended up hanging around at the gas station instead of going home."

"You must miss him."

"I miss Bill most of all. Then my son up in Maine. Walter. Kesho. Heck, I even miss Chuck if he's gone more than a couple of hours."

"Sounds like you're good at running a shelter. You should hang up a shingle: Home to the Emotionally Disenfranchised."

Jean's angora shoulders hunched. "I was looking to have ten kids. Instead I got one so I supplemented my diet with friends. Elisabeth wasn't one of them, though. She never did love him, and she shouldn't have married him."

"The Dobson life can be tempting from the outside." I sat down next to her. "Was Elisabeth really going to cut off the water for your pond?"

Jean nodded, frowning. "You know, curiosity only works with cats."

"Meow?"

She grinned with those very red lips of hers. "I'm well padded. If you want to make me into a suspect, I can take it. This past year Elisabeth threatened to dry out my pond, make the place worthless so I'd have to sell cheap. I'm barely holding on as it is."

"Was she that jealous of you?"

"She didn't like Chuck being around me. None of them do."

"I meant Walter."

Jean tucked in her chin. "Well, she didn't like that either. Not that she loved him. She just wanted him to be as miserable as she was." She gave a grunt of a laugh.

"Don't you go believing Edith's nonsense. Walter liked coming here to warm himself up a bit, that's all." That "nonsense" seemed to please her.

"I'd love to know why Elisabeth left RockPerch to Kesho."

"Don't ask me. Though Elisabeth always did have a special feeling for outcasts. With what happened to Kesho's mother, she must have felt sorry for the girl."

"That's not a good enough reason."

"Well, as I said before, I don't know another. Like Kesho, Elisabeth never did belong here. The town made sure of that. They don't like outsiders marrying their most eligible bachelors. Besides, if you haven't lived here for at least three generations, you're considered a newcomer. No, it wasn't easy for her. No one really liked her."

"I heard a rumor she had a lover, and that's why Walter committed suicide."

Jean straightened her back, clutching Premi to her chest. She reminded me of a big bird ruffling her feathers at some threat. "Walter never said anything. He was too much of a gentleman."

A man who calls his wife a slut wasn't my idea of a gentleman, but then my idea of something wasn't necessarily someone else's. There are always so many versions and this story seemed to have more than most. At least I knew that there had been a lover. Jean's reaction told me as much.

I stretched an arm to rub Premi's chin. "Could Chuck have been that lover?"

Jean sat back again, feathers unruffling. "Is that Edith talking again?" She snorted. "Chuck Dobson falls only for very young, bosomy, dark girls."

"African-Americans?"

"Probably any color that would get his father's goat."

"Fun family," I said. "Would Copper George fit the possible lover bill then?"

"Nah. He was newly married to wife number two when Walter took off. Lola, a skinny thing with stuffed breasts who wanted more and more money and made his eyes spin like a roulette ball. Made George build a big fancy white colonial with black trim, like all the rich people around here. Over by Route 35, just before you get to Ridgefield." Her hand slammed the table. "Two years later she divorces him and keeps the house." Premi lifted a sleepy head from her chest. His white whiskers trailed angora. "As Walter used to say, you gotta be crazy to get married in Connecticut. He was a lawyer, so he knew." She stopped and looked at me crossly, her lips pursed. "Anyway, who said she had a lover?"

"Do you think Walter killed himself?"

Jean nodded slowly. "He was a passionate man married to a limp ice-water fish. He was unhappy. He was broke. He had a flair for the dramatic. That's why he went for RockPerch. 'A house of genius,' he said it was. Charles dubbed it 'The Aberration.' " She clucked her tongue and lifted Premi eye-to-eye. "Beware of Italians bearing questions. Walter was a private man, he wouldn't want me talking about him like this."

"It's for the greater good."

"I hope so. Anyway no one did find his body, so you never know. Sometimes I fool myself into thinking he's going to walk through that door with Bill behind him, both of them yellin', 'Jeanie, big mama, give us a hug.' " She turned her face away from that memory and gave me one of her photogenic grins. "Well, at least you look happier after your phone call."

If Kesho didn't lose the baby, if the real murderer would please stand up, if Willy would give me a hug, if Greenhouse would walk into that kitchen right now, I'd be a lot happier. "Thanks for letting me use the phone in the bedroom."

"Sure. Even with no one around to eavesdrop, my hallway's about as intimate as Grand Central Station. What did you think of my pictures? Kodak's got my whole life up until Bill died. He was the snapper."

"You looked happy in all of them." A car braked in the driveway.

"Still am, most times. You can't be too fat or too glad, is my motto. To hell with what other people think. You know, you should start smiling a bit more too. Stop worrying about your weight for one thing. I thought Italians knew better."

"American ways travel well," I said, getting up. Footsteps were crunching on the driveway gravel. Chuck was back. "Exercise salons and liquid diets are the rage now. My mother's joined a place called Figurella."

"What a shame." Jean fished in the pocket of her red checked skirt. "Here, have some holiday goodies." Her fist held a half-eaten bag of red and green peanut M&M's.

"Thanks," I said, taking two.

"Have more."

I shook my head, M&M's already in my mouth, and headed out the door with Nell's bag, wishing I would one day rediscover Jean's kind of assurance.

"Give me fifteen, twenty minutes," Chuck said, readjusting his glasses to survey his newly tidied shed with a cigar-sharing grin. "Then I'll drive you over to Hertz." He dropped a bag from Nails and Pails Hardware on the work table. It clunked against the wood and split apart, spilling rolls of sandpaper, boxes of nails, a shiny new sander. "My next tables are going to glow with perfection."

"What made you do it?"

"What? Fuck up the tables so that no one in their right mind would buy them?" He looked at me through one lens, the other filled with the fluorescent white of the ceiling bulb. He had dropped his self-congratulatory grin.

"No, turn the place into a kindling wood storehouse. With Elisabeth dead, as far as you knew, RockPerch was yours."

Chuck panned the shed again, slowly raising a hand to finger his hair off his forehead. His hair was the exact color of sawdust in that cold light.

"Or maybe after Richard left Elisabeth, she told you RockPerch belonged to Kesho."

"No, I thought that place was mine." Chuck reached up for a hammer hanging from the wall. "Always did think that." He picked up a six-by-six-inch square of plywood and a fistful of nails. "I must have fucked up again."

With fast concentrated blows he hammered the nails into the soft wood. I watched mesmerized by his intensity, the rapidity of the hammer. The silvery flat nail heads formed a square edging the wood. He hammered another square within the square. I stepped closer and he looked up startled, both lenses picking up the ceiling light this time. He'd forgotten about me.

"As I said, give me fifteen, twenty minutes." Then he went back to his pattern of squares, back to his own deep pocket of thought.

CHAPTER

22

I cuddled into the lilac-and-pink puffed chintz by the bay window in my room, squinting next to an old glass globe of a lamp. The sound of Chuck's electric saw buzzed right through the double windows.

Nell's letter was written in a large, nonetheless extremely precise hand. She'd used green ink.

I thought this copy of a *Ledger* editorial might be of interest for your article, especially since the family involved was Italian. As you will see, RockPerch has not brought any of its inhabitants good fortune. I always did think, as did my mother, that Mr. Frank Lloyd Wright should never have built that house where he did.

I don't know how it is in Italy, but here all small towns have their legends and their ghosts. Our legend relates to the supposed great heroism of the townsmen fighting the British, when the truth is that most of the town was Loyalist. I have much more affection for our resident ghost, the widow Bishop. In 1777, the British burned her house down, and being poor and friendless, she came to live in a cave that now is part of Charles Dobson's property.

One winter, at Christmastime, they found Sarah Bishop dead of the cold, huddled on the ledge where RockPerch now stands. She had fallen and broken her leg, according to the doctor's log that is housed here in our library. The pain must have been too great for her to move, and if she called out, no one heard her.

I cannot help but think that all the misfortune visited on RockPerch might be Sarah's revenge against a town that ignored her plight. Do warn Miss Larson to be careful if she does indeed wish to live in the place.

Should you want any more assistance, please let me know. The library would appreciate a copy of your article, even if it is in Italian. There are still a few residents who remember their language of birth.

Sincerely,
Nell Bishop

She'd added a postscript.

PS My mother's name was Sarah and she always felt a special affinity for our unfortunate ancestor.

I dropped the letter on my lap and looked out the window. It had gotten darker outside, and the reflection of the orange globe of the lamp looked like a small, incongruous sun. Chuck's saw had stopped.

Nell was a nice woman, who didn't deserve being led on. I owed her an apology.

On the second page the handwriting was less careful.

PPS Did you know that Wright's lover, Mamah Borthwick Cheney, was killed by a crazed butler at Taliesin along with her two visiting children and four guests? The butler then set fire to the buildings. There was a second fire in 1925. Wright had his own share of bad luck! His fellow architects referred to him as Frank Lloyd Wrong. And wrong he was to desecrate that ledge. It broke my mother's heart!

Nell's outrage was sad, somehow sweet and naive. And she was so eager to help. A wonderful American trait.

Italians are in general more suspicious of humankind, although the tourist might never suspect it.

I picked up the *Ledger* editorial Nell had included, quickly skimming its contents. Any minute now Chuck was going to knock and say he was ready to go. Halfway through I caught "Three-year-old son, Richard." "Her husband, Frank Mentani."

Richard Mentani. Mamma, this was about Richard! Wonderful Nell, thank you. Curling my legs under a warm, worn quilt, I started over.

The editorial, headlined AN AMERICAN INJUSTICE, appeared on September 8, 1955. The first paragraphs gave background information.

In 1934, Charles's father Charles Dobson, Sr., who suffered in the Depression, sold the forty acres on the other side of Goose Lake to a Riccardo Di Marco who had just arrived from Genoa with his wife and five-year-old daughter. Di Marco, owner of a prosperous pharmaceutical company back in Italy, who came to this country to find the freedom Fascism did not offer his young family, contracted Wright to build RockPerch. The imposing structure was completed in 1935, with a great deal of criticism from architects in the area and local residents.

"Unfortunately the Di Marco family did not prosper in this country, and by the time Mrs. Di Marco died in 1953—her husband Riccardo had died five years earlier—all that was left of their wealth was what many locals dubbed 'Wright's Folly.'"

"Livia Di Marco, by then married and with a three-year-old son, Richard, inherited the house. Her husband, Frank Mentani, died a year later, in Suwon, Korea, fighting for our country."

I moved closer to the light. The copy was very dark and blurry. So far I had to admit Nell was right. The house was definitely not a lucky charm. Down the corridor, the phone rang.

"Now the Connecticut Seal Bank, whose motto matches our state motto—*Qui Transtulit Sustinet*—he who transplanted still sustains—has not sustained a war widow, has not sustained the birthright of her son to his home. Despite a fund-raising effort by the Italian community, the price of the unpaid mortgage has not been met. Tomorrow the bank forecloses. It is rumored a buyer has already been found. Tomorrow we will be ashamed. The Bank Board of Directors should be ashamed. So should that buyer."

Nell had added in her bright green ink, "The buyer was none other than Walter Dobson, who bought the house for his new bride. And you know what happened to them!"

So that was Richard's birthright! Elisabeth had planned to sell the house back to Richard—maybe to correct this old injustice. No, that didn't make sense. She'd willed the house to Kesho last year. Had refused Richard's first offer. It was only when Kesho had come on the scene that she'd relented and asked three million dollars.

Then Christmas Eve she changed her mind. Why? Pressure from the Dobsons not to sell to an African-American? I didn't believe it. Anyway, she'd had the last laugh on that one. Had she told Richard she wasn't selling? It would explain the "mad as hell expression" Chuck had seen. If she had, did Richard kill for that house?

There was a knock at the door. I slipped the papers back in the Hay Day bag as if they were something secret.

"Come in."

Chuck opened the door. "If you still want to go to Danbury, I can take you now." Sawdust fell from his shoulders like dandruff.

"Yes, thanks." I looked at my watch. Thirty-five minutes had gone by. "Now I want to go more than ever."

He flicked his hair back with a toss of his head. More sawdust sprinkled down. "Edith Holmes just called. After you've picked up your car, she wants you to stop by her house. Forty-five Elm Street. She said to tell you she goes to bed by nine o'clock sharp."

And if I didn't show up, she'd haunt my dreams for the rest of my life.

"My father's the one you should look into closely," Chuck said. We were on Route 7. "He's perfectly capable of murder." There was a laughing edge to his voice. I couldn't tell if he was putting me on. In the darkness of the road, only the brief sweeping flash of headlights brought his face into view, showing me a sharp, white profile.

"What about motive?"

I heard a chuckle. "I have a basketful of motives for you. Prestige. That's always the first concern with my father. Selling RockPerch to a black servant's girl is out of the question."

"Elisabeth changed her mind about that."

"We have only his word that she did."

"The telephone company can prove Elisabeth called your father's house that night."

"They can't prove what she said."

"If racism were the motive, or prestige as you call it, Kesho would be the dead one."

"Money's another one. He's about to declare bankruptcy."

"One thing I don't understand is why *both* of you expected to inherit. Did Elisabeth make promises to your father, too?"

"My admirable father, full of love for his only son, had a piece of paper tucked away safely that could get my ass ripped in jail. I inherit the house, I hand over the house." A passing car caught a broad smile on his face. "The immense relief of not getting that house has finally seeped in. Can you understand that? I have nothing, he can ask for nothing."

"I did notice an extra spring to your walk." Roxanne had said something about Chuck forging Walter's signature on a check. Was that the paper he was talking about?

We were on the overpass now. On Chuck's side, I could see the small airport. Beyond it loomed the mall, like a huge bomb shelter, stuffed with anything anyone might ever want, except light and fresh air. "Who's got that piece of paper now?"

"Christmas morning Dad handed over an envelope. It had his business card inside, name crossed off, with two sentences scrawled underneath. 'It's in the shed. Up to you to find it.' He didn't bother signing it or wishing me Merry Christmas."

"That's when you trashed the shed."

"It took me a while, but I found it. He'd folded it up tight and tucked it under the baseboard. Then I went crazy and tore the place apart. I don't know if I was ecstatic or furious." Chuck turned right for downtown Danbury.

"May I ask what hold your father had on you?"

"I did something dumb to cover up something even dumber."

"How dumb?"

He said nothing as he drove through Danbury. At least here he knew where he was going.

"You forged a check," I prompted.

Chuck stopped the car in the Hertz parking lot and started pulling his cheek out with thumb and forefinger, as if it were made of dough. He was generating enough power with the tremor of his knee to light up my Village studio.

"To pay someone off?"

More cheek pulling, knee jiggling.

"I met an incredible girl at the Whipping Post. Stella Himenez." His voice was barely audible. "Eight years ago, about a month before Walter disappeared. She was up from New York for the weekend. She was funny, sexy, beautiful." Chuck released his cheek, revealing a dark red patch. "She liked me. Unfortunately she was one month shy of the statutory rape cutoff. Her mother caught us in this car in fact. Haven't been able to afford a new one since." He tried for a laugh and didn't make it. "Her mother demanded I marry Stella. Stella would have liked that too. She said she was in love with me. Instead I did what I'd always seen my dad do. I tried buying my way out with a check. Except mine was forged with Walter's signature. I was sure I could talk my way out of it with Uncle Walter."

"Did they cash the check?"

"No. Stella sent it back, but instead of mailing it to me, she sent it to my father. 'You should be ashamed to have such a son!' That's what she wrote. Well, he always has been." His eyebrows rose above the wire rim of his glasses. "I was hoping to be some kind of artist and he hates that. I wanted to be like Kesho, be able to pick up a pencil and come up with Art."

"Why are you telling me this?"

His face blanked. "I don't know. I suppose because you seemed interested in us. You're looking for a murderer. You're helping Kesho out." He shrugged. "I don't know really. Maybe because it's dark in a car. Like those Catholic confessionals." Then he looked at the windshield and the streetlight streaming in. He laughed, knocking the glass with his knuckles. "Who the hell knows, huh? Well, I still think the pater makes a great murderer. Now he doesn't have to pay Elisabeth's way anymore."

"Pay her way?"

Chuck got out of the car. I did the same.

"Walter left her with practically nothing," he said as he walked me to the small gray building. An icy wind whipped words away, leaving our faces raw. "He never practiced law. Was in love with architecture." He raised his voice. "He was always talking big projects, malls, housing developments, but getting very little done." I moved closer to the wall for protection. Chuck moved with me. "Mother thinks Dad got moronic around Elisabeth."

I huddled in the doorway, arms wrapped tight around me. "Were they lovers?" Winter in Rome was never like this.

"God, I hope she had better taste than that." Chuck smirked. "Want me to wait to make sure your car's ready?"

"Thanks, I'm OK." I shook his hand, a European habit that surprised him. He smiled and pumped back like a kid learning a new game. The image of the gawky goose came back, and I couldn't help wonder why Elisabeth had turned against him.

"There's something I don't understand," I said. Why was I freezing to death? I took Chuck's pumping hand and pulled him into the office. Warmth and fluorescent light hit me hard.

"What?"

I released him. "Why did your father give you back the check?"

"He didn't need it anymore."

I raised a hand. "*Aspetta!* Let me make sense of this." The Hertz employee looked at me suspiciously. I smiled back and huddled closer to Chuck, lowering my voice. "Your father holds the"—I mouthed the words *forged check*—"he's going to use to get the house you expect to inherit."

"Correct."

"Christmas morning. Elisabeth's dead, the sale to Kesho and Richard is off and your father thinks the house is yours."

"That's why he gave the check back!" He was losing patience with me.

"But the will hasn't been read yet, processed, probated or whatever they do with wills. Your father isn't so stupid he's going to hand over that check before he's sure."

"Can I help you?" The employee had a glossy pink smile and hair as yellow as the Hertz sign.

I waved cheerfully at her. "I'm here to pick up a substitute car. I'll be with you in a minute."

Chuck tapped my shoulder. "What are you getting at?"

"He must have known Elisabeth had changed the will. The check was useless. That's why he gave it back."

"What's the name?" the employee asked. "I'm about to close up."

"Sorry. Greenhouse, Stanley."

"Oh, you're the one who got vandalized. First time that's happened around here."

"I know, I have all the luck."

Chuck tugged at my sleeve like a kid. "You're right! Elisabeth must have told him when she called Friday night. He didn't know before that because right before that dinner, I got my usual telephone lecture about not screwing up in front of Elisabeth. I guess he *was* worried she'd change her mind."

"Listen, Chuck, if Elisabeth told your father she wasn't selling and she'd changed the will, then he had no reason to kill her, did he?"

A funny expression crossed Chuck's face. I couldn't tell if it was disappointment or relief.

What about Chuck though? Was that blackmailing story he'd just told me true? Everyone had a loaded history connected to that house, to Walter and Elisabeth. Even the librarian had her story. I juggled the key to a Ford Taurus from hand to hand. Chuck had left. The Hertz employee applied a new coat of baby pink to her lips and shook out her hair, eager for me to leave. The office window shook with the wind. Outside, the dark was lit by the glow of neon beer ads hanging from the windows of the tavern across the street.

Kesho and Richard. I had to talk to them both, convince them to tell me the truth about Friday evening. What had Elisabeth told Richard? Why had she left the house to Kesho? Why had she changed her mind about the sale? Was Elisabeth's change of heart the pivotal point of this story? Did Richard kill her to correct what the *Ledger* had dubbed An American Injustice?

"Can I use your phone?"

"Huh?"

I pointed.

She jiggled her keys. "A fast one. Local only."

I dialed.

Henry Holmes answered the phone. I explained I wouldn't be able to come over that night and could I speak to his wife to make another appointment?

"She's dead," he said. Then he hung up.

CHAPTER

23

An electric candle shone solemnly in every window of the white clapboard colonial. The front door of the Holmes house, flanked by double columns, was ajar, the red ribbon of its wreath barely lifting. Here the wind was gentler, held back by a thicket of trees. The yellow light of a lantern spilled onto the driveway where a blue police car boasted Protection and Service on its fender. Behind it was Myrna's black vintage Lincoln. Both cars were empty. So was the hallway.

I tiptoed down an oriental runner, scanning for the sound of voices, ready to act like those intrusive reporters who shove microphones into a hapless face and ask, "What are you feeling now, Mr. Holmes?" and hating myself for it, yet too caught up to stop.

"Now come on, Henry, I know you're upset, but there's no way anyone killed Edith." Charles Dobson's voice gnawed down the corridor from the back of the house. I passed the narrow staircase with its electric seat waiting to take Edith back upstairs.

"Her room's been touched. The books have been shifted, drawers opened." Henry's voice was raspy, hesitant, as if not used to speaking. "I can tell."

"It looked as neat as an army barrack to me. You go spreading rumors she's been killed, people are going to think you did it."

I plunged in the direction of the voices. "How can you say that?" I blurted as I turned into an open doorway. Copper George's tall frame blocked me.

"You got a death radar or something, Miss Griffo?" He was huge in his sheepskin jacket and he wasn't pleased. Neither was I.

"Mrs. Holmes asked me to come over."

Charles nodded, looking suitably bereaved. Since I'd last seen him, he had changed into a worn brown tweed coat and brown corduroy slacks. The thin red stripe of his club tie was the only bright note.

"Thank you for coming." Henry shuffled out from behind Copper George, his black knotted eyebrows raised. "Thank you." He clasped my hand with both of his. They were dry and blistered.

"I'm sorry, Mr. Holmes."

"I thought she was sleeping, you see. We ate dinner at six as usual. Then she took her nap. We were going to play pool later." Hazel eyes flickered over my face. "I went to the supermarket. Edith had made a list. I bought everything." His eyes never stopped. "I got to talking to Kathy, the checkout girl. I went to the drugstore. I wasted time." I tried to look kind, to give those eyes a place to rest.

"Someone killed her, but they won't listen." He stopped and everything about him drooped—jowls, eyes, shoulders, brown cardigan. His khakis bagged at the knees. Except his eyebrows. Black in contrast to the sparse white hair on his head. He kept them raised, as if to signal some kind of hope.

"You're the one who's not listening, Henry." Copper George dropped a heavy hand on Henry's shoulder. "Dr. Gordon's just finished telling us she died of a heart attack.

Now if you got any reason to doubt his diagnosis, we can order an autopsy. Is that what you want?"

"No. She wouldn't like being cut up. Can't you tell by just looking?"

Copper George leaned over. "Henry, the doctor looked, I looked. She went in her sleep. Not a scratch on her."

"I was supposed to go first," Henry said. "I wouldn't kill her."

"No one said you did." Charles pointed his well-shaved, powerful chin at me. "Miss Griffo, perhaps you can come back another time?"

"Yes, of course," I slipped out of Henry's clasp. Much better to talk to Henry when these two weren't around. "I am so sorry, Mr. Holmes."

"Wait!" Henry winced at his own loud voice. "Kesho's wedding present. You mustn't forget that. It's out here in the coat closet."

"What's Edith giving that girl a present for?" Charles asked. Copper George followed Henry, his boots heavy on the floor, like a sheriff treading a saloon floor. Henry, in his slippers, walked with silent, surprising quickness. Jowly Charles and his heavy chest stayed put in the center of the den, crowded with yellow stacks of *National Geographic* vying for space with piles of *The New Yorker*. The dirty chintz sofa was partially covered by jigsaw puzzle boxes. At one end, a chipped wooden swan sported a rain hat. On the coffee table, the *New York Times* Sunday crossword puzzle, which had been worked on in ink, was only half-filled.

Charles stood as motionless as a statue in the middle of that messy room, as if still guarding a privilege that had slipped away.

"Too bad about Chuck's shed," I said, hoping for who-knows-what reaction.

"He's a bad carpenter." Only his lips moved.

"You think he's bad at everything, don't you?"

I got no answer.

"He looks happier now," I said.

Charles lowered his chin, doubt clouding those clear eyes.

For a moment I overcame my dislike for this man. "Talk to me." I wanted to hear his version of the story.

"What for?" he asked.

"The good thing about talking to strangers is you don't have to face them for the rest of your life. They listen, then they leave and take your words with them."

"Not with Kesho arrested for murder."

"True, I'm almost as biased as you are, but you have nothing to lose by talking to me. Unless you're the murderer."

"Here you are," Henry said, stepping back into the room, a tremolo in his voice. Copper George hulked behind him, unblinking. Chuck followed, his face as gray as yesterday's snow.

"Jean just told me." His voice was breathless.

"I'll call you," I said to Charles.

"Kesho's mother embroidered that tablecloth for Edith." Henry handed me a shopping bag, knotted eyebrows still high. "It's only right Kesho get it back."

"Thank you." I took the bag.

Henry pressed a finger against pursed lips, his eyes wide. What was going on?

"If this is possibly the scene of a crime," Charles said, "should anything be leaving the house?"

Henry spun around. "Then you do believe me?"

"Crime?" Chuck asked. "What crime? Jean said a heart attack!"

Copper George shook his big heavy head. "Now, Charles, I know how to conduct police business." He waved to me. "What you got there?"

I dropped my hand in the bag and came up with a

folded yellow tablecloth, embroidered in bright flowers. With something hard in the middle. I snuck a glance at Henry. He raised his eyebrows even higher.

"This is gorgeous," I said. "Kesho will love it!"

Copper George made a face at Charles. "What do you think, that Edith was smothered with this?" He slapped the bottom of the empty bag.

"What's going on?" Chuck's voice cracked. "What crime?"

Copper George reached for his eye drops. "The only crime in this scene is in Henry's head."

"We're going back to New York!"

Willy looked up, unfazed, pencil sticking out of his teeth like a giant toothpick. He was on his stomach, spread out on the bed, his school notebook open to a lot of doodles. *Julius Caesar* was scrunched under his elbow. I explained about Edith, about being scared this might be another murder. "It's gotten too ugly here." The realization had come to me after I'd left Edith's house, with its eerie candles in the windows as if already prepared for the funeral. It was the dark drive to the inn, up the narrow lane curving under overbearing, black trees that had done it. I got scared. I called Kesho at the hospital, told her about Edith, the tablecloth Henry was returning, explained that I had to get Willy out of there. She'd just come back from a romantic, expensive dinner with Richard, ecstatic that her spleen was not ruptured. "Go! Don't worry about me. We're going to be just fine." I knew then the baby was safe. "Give the tablecloth to Richard. The bum dumped me back here and took off. Send him over *now*. I want to check out of this place before *I* get stuck with something lethal."

I didn't find Richard, but I told Jean. "Don't worry, I'll tell him," she said, shuffling to the refrigerator and offering me some leftover pasta. I handed her the tablecloth and turned her down.

"'Something lethal!' Lord, that woman was eighty-four! Hearts wear out!" She'd picked up a cold *rigatoni* and stuffed it in my mouth.

Why hadn't I eaten more? Pasta might have given me the strength to deal with Willy still sprawled on his bed.

"Come on, Willy! Maybe the crime *is* in Henry's mind, but I can't take any chances." New York first, then I'd deal with the hard object I'd left in Henry's shopping bag, tucked safely under the front seat of my locked car.

"I won't sleep at your dad's apartment if you don't want me to." I remembered his "Mom would die" only too well. "I'll just make sure you're all right, listen to you lock behind me, and come wake you up in the morning."

I'd tried to call Greenhouse the minute I'd gotten back to the inn, but there had been no answer in his mother's apartment and no answering machine. I'd called his mother at the hospital.

"Why are you calling? What's happened?" she asked over the phone, instantly alarmed. "Something's wrong with Willy? I told Stan he should have brought the boy. He can sit still in a hospital room just as well as anybody else. What's wrong? Are you taking good care of him?"

I reassured her, wished her well, and asked that Greenhouse call the inn as soon as he could.

She sighed. "He's out at a fancy restaurant with two of my old girlfriends and I wish I were with them. Tell Willy to remember his grandmother and call sometime. And take good care of him."

I was trying to. "By the way, your grandma said to call her sometime."

"I did already twice today." Willy didn't budge from his position on the bed.

"We'll come back for the wedding. Now I need you to pack." He still didn't move.

"Please, Willy."

He reared up in slow motion. "I'll stay at David's."

"Who's David?"

His shoulders slumped. "I told you, the guy with the big apartment."

"That's right, on Park Avenue! I thought he was skiing in Aspen."

"They came back. His parents decided to separate."

"I'm sorry. You sure you want to stay there?"

"Yeah, I can help." He kicked his duffel bag out from under the bed.

"I'm sure you can. I'll go pack too." I stopped at the door. "How did you know they were back?"

"I kept calling."

"It's been that bad for you here?"

He looked at me then, eyes facing eyes. "You dumped me."

I went to call David's mother.

It began to rain as Willy and I approached Manhattan, the city lights breaking into drops across the windshield. We began to talk.

"It's like I was in the way." He knew I'd kept on sleuthing and felt betrayed.

"I wanted to protect you." The darkness of the car was giving us both courage.

"You wanted to get all the credit."

"I'm not that selfish, Willy. I try not to be, at least." And then, on the slick black asphalt of the FDR Drive at Ninety-sixth Street, where the tall buildings of the city begin, it dawned on me. Even if I had been blameless, he had to find fault in me. To like me would be to betray his mother. His loyalty had to be fierce and true to both his parents, split, living on opposite sides of the city. There was no room for girlfriends and boyfriends. In his eyes, each hurt the other parent, threatened his and her role. He was holding on to both as best he could. I admired and respected him for that loyalty. My heart went out to him. It was time for complete honesty on my part.

I explained about the Go Home scratched on the rented Buick, about the ice balls that my shoulder and rear end were still feeling. I glanced at the sky blue parka he was wearing, the one I'd thought I'd seen between the trees.

"Did you do that, Willy?"

A car behind me honked angrily. I had slowed, waiting for his answer.

Willy was looking at me, I couldn't tell with what expression.

"If you did, I think I can understand."

"I don't believe you," he said slowly.

I laughed, relief bubbling out. "We're not doing a very good job of trusting each other." I raised my palm, hoping to meet his. "Truce? We talk things out? What we don't like, we say right away?" The hand went down to help turn the steering wheel at the Seventy-first Street exit.

At the red light on Second Avenue, I tried again. "Let's try to think of each other as Willy and Simona, not son and girlfriend?" This time I held out my hand like a beggar's. "I don't think your mom would mind that."

He slapped my palm just as the light changed.

"Thanks, Willy."

I stopped in front of a green awning at the corner of Sixty-eighth and Park. A watery swath of white-lit trees ran down the center of the avenue. Despite the rain, streams of taillights added to the festive air. Behind the glass door of David's apartment building, a gold-buttoned doorman peered at me. The tip of a lighted tree seemed to grow out of his head.

Willy lifted the door handle of the car.

"Wait, I need your help," I found myself saying, suddenly not wanting him to leave me. I reached under my seat and tugged at Henry's shopping bag. I pulled out what looked very much like a calculator.

"What's this?" I said, pointing to a rectangular, black object with a small screen and numbered buttons. Except that this had a flexible antenna about eight inches long.

Willy picked it up, fitting it neatly into his fourteen-year-old palm. "It's a scanner, a wide-band receiver."

"What's that?"

"It picks up calls made on cellular phones, you know, in cars. This has a computer that picks up the frequencies. Once you get the one you want, you can punch in the number and get it every time without having to scan. Some sleaze guys at school are always bragging about how they pick up these sex phone calls. Like some married guy, you know, talking to his girlfriend. Gays making dates. It's like a spy radio."

"Henry Holmes gave it to me. I don't think he wanted the police to find it."

"It's illegal. The government had a fit when the Japanese came up with this thing. They tried to stop it from coming in."

I was impressed. "You know so much."

He shrugged. "I read about it. It's real powerful, with a one mile range. It can go from submarine transmissions straight up to microwaves." Willy flicked long, blond lashes at me. "Not the oven." He was smiling.

"Too bad, you could listen in on my pasta reheating." Which reminded me I hadn't eaten since lunch. It was now ten-thirty. "What are these three buttons for?" I asked, pointing to the top of the scanner.

"The middle one's to plug in a tape recorder. I don't know about the other two."

"Taping the wrong phone call could have gotten Edith killed," I said. "Now I have to find out who has a car phone in Fieldston."

"It works with cordless phones too, you know. And that's illegal only in New York and California."

"Ah." I pictured a large oak desk, an antique enamel and gilt clock, a silver pen and pencil set still in its open box. "My last gift to Walter," Elisabeth had said. Next to the box a black cordless phone.

"I'm going back tonight, Willy. I'd love to have you with me, but I can't. Sleuthing can be dangerous, morally reprehensible . . . " I glanced at him, checking.

"Yeah, I know. Like those sleaze guys at school."

"Right."

He was halfway out the door. "You watch it though. Someone doesn't like you too much."

I got out and helped him pull his duffel bag out of the back seat. "I'm just glad it's not you. Can I give you a hug?"

He looked back at the doorman.

"Too sissy?"

Willy jerked a thumb. "He knows me."

And his mom probably. I flashed him a smile. "I hope David's going to be OK."

"Yeah, sure." Only five feet apart, we waved at each other awkwardly through the rain.

It was only after I had gotten back on the FDR Drive, a slice of Ray's pizza in my stomach, that I noticed Willy had left me his baseball cap. Good protection.

CHAPTER

24

Half a mile from the inn I got rear-ended. Nothing major, a slight jolt to the car that barely yanked my neck. I glanced at the rearview mirror as I unbuckled my seat belt and met a glare of headlights. Then those lights dropped. For a fraction of a second the word *carjacking* flickered in my brain, but I was too happy after having made peace with Willy, too tired after a long day.

I stepped out of the car, glad that at least it had stopped raining. "I bet there isn't even a scratch," I said, looking for the driver. Swift arms clamped down on my mouth and my chest. I was dragged back down the road, away from my headlights, my head held high so that I couldn't even see the color of his coat. I tried twisting and bending but couldn't match his strength. Several good Griffo kicks, donkey style, found only shins and ankles. Nothing vital like a pair of balls. This is a man, I told myself, and he doesn't want me, he can't want me. It's that brand-new Ford Taurus I was driving. Something tapped my skull. My muscles relaxed, my bones melted. Why wasn't I wearing Willy's cap? Then the night fell over my head.

When I came to, it was still dark. Something large, dry,

and unswallowable was testing the size of my mouth. One half of my face was cold, the other half wet and frozen. I didn't budge, waiting for the swirling in my head to slow down and shape itself into thoughts. One shoulder ached and I realized I was lying on my side. Always willing to gratify the senses first, I sniffed. Mud. Sap. Pine trees. The leftover scent of wood burned hours ago. I raised my head and I tried to lift the rest of me. My arms pulled. I tried stretching my legs and my chest jerked against my thighs, pain gripping my wrists and ankles. I was tied up, my arms embracing my thighs, my hands against my heels. A trussed-up pig. I coughed in an attempt to spit out what was in my mouth. The effort made me choke. I panicked, my esophagus twitching. I tried breathing through my nose, but couldn't stop my lungs from heaving, expelling what little oxygen they had left.

Calma, Griffo. Dare tempo al tempo. My nose is the center of the universe, breathing in the beauty of the woods, the smell of Christmas, of hot chocolate by an open fire, warm strudel floating in cream.

I relaxed. Oxygen streamed from my nose into my swelling lungs. Forget my mouth, that only allowed me to scream. I had to get up and get back to the inn where I could warm up and bemoan my fate, and be cuddled and coddled and maybe make sense of this. I had the feeling I hadn't been out for long. For one thing my head didn't hurt that much. It felt awkward and heavy, with a dull throb on the right side, above my ear. No information to be gained by that fact, except that I was thick-headed and my assailant was right-handed like most of the world and everyone I'd met here.

I tried to assess my corporal situation without being able to see much. It was still sometime in the middle of the night. The moon was nowhere in sight. I couldn't see any telltale gray of dawn, at least not from this gutter where I'd been ignominiously dumped, next to a prickly bush ready to gouge my eyes out. I dropped my head back, lifted my knees, gave a twisting heave with one shoulder and managed to roll myself onto my spine. I felt something wet ooze into the small of my back, now exposed. I could see sky. It was still black, purple, dark, blind, clouded; a swath unrolling between even blacker swaying tree tips. The pines I'd smelled.

The assessment I came up with after not too much thinking was that it was a shame I'd left my coat in the car because it was *freddo da morire*—cold to die—out there, the wind glazing me with ice, and there was no way I was going to cut myself out of my bonds without taking all night trying to find that miraculous piece of glass or sawed-off piping movie scripts always come up with. I decided my MO would be to roll over onto Bishop's Lane which was only a few inches above my left shoulder, heave myself up on my ass, and . . . Where the hell was the car? No shimmering white car hulked over the road.

What did you expect, Griffo? The car waiting, door open so you could make your way up to the seat and lean on the horn? Hey, you're alive, with all your clothes on! No car? That's just fine. Think positive, the American way. Don't burst into tears; women aren't allowed to do that anymore. Well, maybe here where no one can see you. No! Use your wits. Your ass is well-cushioned. If you try climbing the road to the inn, you'll probably roll back down like an avalanche, but you can always inch down those three hundred feet to the main road and wait in the middle of the asphalt like a raccoon asking to be flattened.

I got lucky. Romans call that *avere culo*—having ass— which seemed appropriate. I did roll onto Bishop's Lane after a few tries. I heaved myself up on the first try, the throb on the side of my head escalating to the crash of cymbals. And I slowly made my way down, cheek by

padded cheek, my brand-new flannel slacks bought especially for this idyllic country vacation tearing along the
salt and rocks of the road.

I hit the end of Bishop's Lane, where I found a big old
willow swooping down over my newly rented very white
car. Sweet friend, I thought, then noticed that the Taurus
was lopsided, its nose raised on one side, still facing the
climb to the inn. The car had slid down, I guessed, gear
conveniently slipped into reverse by the same hand that
knocked me out. No accomplice had been needed. Only
the ditch, curving with the road at the bottom of the hill,
had stopped the car from swinging into the main road and
maybe colliding into some luckless driver. Bobbing by, I
prayed the car, unlike certain of my parts, would show up
scratchless in the light of day. Greenhouse was never going
to believe this latest fiasco. Neither would Hertz.

My assailant must have been after the scanner. That
obvious thought finally found its way into my dented
brain. No, the scanner was useless. He was after the tape.
He thought I had the tape. Where was that tape? Did
Henry have it? Was he in danger? I stopped at the inter-
section and tried to straighten the curve of my aching
back. Wrong move. I tipped over just as two headlights cut
across me. The car, the size and shape of one of those
whale-backed boulders that kept popping up across this
land, thunked to a stop, backed up until the headlights
picked up my elegant persona, blinding me totally. I
smiled, mud from one side of my nose dripping onto my
lips, tasting sweet in the presence of this savior.

A door cracked open. The scrunch of feet. "Owl-hunt-
ing?" Myrna's bittersweet voice asked.

I soaked in a tub while the wind knocked at the window. Once Myrna had freed my mouth and cut the duct
tape from my ankles and wrists, I'd hobbled over to the

car, found it empty of scanner, donned Willy's baseball cap, and managed to creak out three words, "Jean . . . the inn." Thinking I was accusing Jean of attacking me, she'd rushed me off, groaning in the backseat of her dinosaur, to her guest cottage in the woods. Dripping mud and melted snow, practically bare-assed, I guessed I wasn't fit to enter her pristine mansion. Not that the guest house was slumming exactly. What I'd quickly seen of the large room was ceiling beams, a fireplace, and English country-style comfort marred only by a computer and a lifetime supply of paper stacked in one corner. In the bathroom, tiled in beige and brown, two Tylenols were already beginning to work; the water was hot; the bath salts smelled of freshly cut apples; the tub was long enough for me to gingerly stretch my legs; the towels were thick and soft. *Paradiso*. I banished murder, assailants, tapeless scanners from my head as I swished fresh water around my tongue. Myrna had unraveled my own scarf from my mouth. Yards and yards of it, it seemed, leaving my mouth as dry as old skin. I remembered Henry Holmes.

I popped out of the bathtub, wrapped a towel over my head, shrugged into a large terry-cloth bathrobe and opened the door.

Myrna looked up from a corner of a worn chesterfield sofa, a cup of tea steaming from her hand. She was still wearing the black cloche hat I'd seen her drive by in that morning. "I thought you planned to drown in there." She twisted her mouth. "I know. Bad joke. I'm humorless even in good times."

"I need to use your phone."

"Be my guest." She indicated the other corner of the sofa with her cup where a black rotary phone sat on a folded mohair plaid.

"It's urgent, but it's private, too." Myrna was too petite to be my assailant, but she was certainly related to possible suspects.

200 CAMILLA T. CRESPI

"There's a plug in the bathroom," she said, for a moment leveling her gaze at me above the blue-patterned teacup. She looked elegant in that velvet cloche. An aging Coco Chanel, with the same impenetrable expression.

"Thank you." I retrieved the phone and the phone book. I'd forgotten Edith's number. Myrna went back to the book on her lap.

"He's stolen the scanner," I whispered after identifying myself. Henry had answered after the first ring, as if expecting a call.

"Who's 'he'?"

"I don't know. The murderer. Listen, Mr. Holmes, you might be in danger. I think the killer is looking for a tape your wife had. Have you got it?"

"What tape? No, no. There's no tape."

"Mr. Holmes, Henry," I was practically swallowing the phone, my mouth dry, my jaw sore. "You could be in danger. If you kept that tape, call the police now and give it to them."

"Young lady, what are you talking about?" He hung up. I dropped the receiver on my shoulder. If there was no tape, why give me the scanner? He was lying, that's why.

I riffled through the slim phone book. There were only two Pertinis—G. Pertini and Joseph Pertini.

I woke him up. It took a while for him to catch on as to who I was. My raspy whisper didn't help.

I explained what had happened to me, about Henry, the scanner and the tape, how I thought he was in danger.

"OK, Simone, I'll call the station house and get someone to go over there. What about you? Are you at the inn?"

I made a choking sound. "No. I can't talk yet. In the morning, OK?" I was doing a frog-croaking-her-last, but I didn't want Copper George and his gang barging in on my intimate moment with Myrna. She could clear up a lot of doubts.

"Simone?" I heard Roxanne rumble. "What the hell . . . "

"Don't mention the scanner yet," I rasped quickly. "I don't want to get Henry into trouble. Just mention there's a tape around."

"How'd Simone know your number, huh?"

"I know what to tell them," Joey grumbled at me.

Roxanne's rumble got louder. "Will you tell me that, Joey?"

"She looked it up, I don't know! Come on, Rox!"

"What are you going to tell them?" Roxanne roared. "J-e-e-sus, it's two o'clock in the morning!"

"Just make sure Henry's safe," I said. "And the name's Simon . . . " The phone went dead before I got the *a* out.

"The strongest liquid I can offer is tea," Myrna said when I brought the phone back. She'd taken off the hat.

"Thanks." I sat down on a dark rose flowered wing chair next to the fire blazing in a carved granite fireplace.

With a tight-lipped smile, Myrna pointed to the book now closed on her lap—Virginia Woolf's *A Room of One's Own*. "This place is my own detox center. No alcohol allowed and almost no people."

"Thanks again then." I accepted the cup she offered. "I'm grateful."

From her expression she didn't quite believe me. Close up she looked tired, sad, the usual disdain gone from her face. Except for the pearl choker, she was dressed in the same outfit she had worn on Christmas Eve: a dull dark blue knit suit with tiny moth bites on one sleeve and matching blue vintage Ferragamos on her narrow feet. Her salt-and-pepper hair was neatly brushed back, her face bare of makeup except for a lick of lipstick in one corner of her thin mouth.

"If the police are coming," she said, "we'll go up to the house."

"They're not." I dripped honey into my cup and

glanced at the past issues of the *Prudent Times* stacked next to the computer. She obviously used this place as an office too.

"Jean didn't tie me up," I said.

"Who did?"

"The murderer." I gulped some tea, the hot liquid instantly soothing. "I ask too many questions," I added in response to her mildly quizzical look. "I only wish I knew the question that hit his raw nerve. You know that Edith Holmes is dead?"

She didn't. I filled her in on what details I knew, including Henry being convinced it was murder. As I spoke I wondered where she had been until two A.M.

"Edith would have liked to die murdered," Myrna said with surprising kindness in her voice. "She always wanted center stage."

Putting my cup down, I said nothing of the incriminating tape I was sure existed. "I saw you drive off this morning." In the afternoon Charles had mentioned her still being away. "It's been a long day for you, too."

"Yes, it has," she answered. "That's all I'm going to say about it."

"I need to ask more questions if I'm going to make any sense of Elisabeth's death. And maybe Edith's." I shifted my weight forward, to the back of my thighs, to give my rear end a break. "Why did Elisabeth leave Kesho that house? You must know."

Disdain slipped back on her face. "You're not the police. You have no authority to ask anything of me. You're not even some private investigator."

I found myself laughing, my throat aching from the effort. "Italians don't care about authority. We figure it's never brought us anything good in the past, so 'rule made, rule broken', which, I'll admit, doesn't make for progress or justice." I stopped laughing. "I'm sorry. You surprised me. I didn't think you'd believe in vested authority. Think

of past presidents! Politicians in general, the Hill-Thomas
hearings, the Rodney King verdict, that New York judge
blackmailing his lover! Authority screws up all the time."
Myrna had put her teacup down and was listening to me,
her arms now wrapped around an orange paisley pillow.
Her attention spurred me on, made me feel as if suddenly
I were on a podium.

"Women have never waited for authority, have we? We
just go ahead and do whatever has to be done century
after century. Even when we don't get recognition or a
share of the authority, we still keep doing what needs to be
done." I sat back and sipped more honeyed tea, feeling
good. I had just justified my sleuthing, stood up to my
own doubts, to Greenhouse's skepticism. "And what I have
to do, even though you might not like it, is help Kesho.
She's another victim of authority gone stupid. I'm asking
for your help."

"All I can give you is a good motive for murder."

CHAPTER

25

What are you talking about?"
Myrna stood up and walked over to a small paint-ing propped against a shelf above the desk. Draped in a long black cape, a woman sat in the same rose flowered wing chair I was on. I recognized Elisabeth by the telltale wisps of hair around her cheeks, the long neck. Under that cape, she appeared tall and large-framed, but her head was incongruously small.

"My son did that painting," Myrna said. "It's a study for a companion piece to that horror portrait of Walter that's over the fireplace at RockPerch. Chuck never got around to it, thank God."

"What motive?"

Myrna slipped a hand behind the painting, coming up with a photograph that she tossed in my lap. It showed an unsmiling tall handsome black woman with a baby in her arms. Next to her was a much younger Elisabeth, holding shears and a basket of cut flowers, her mouth spread in a tight-lipped smile. They both looked unhappy.

"I took that picture," Myrna said. "That's Kesho and her mother Shirley." She sat back down in her corner of the sofa, at the very edge so her feet could touch the floor. "Two weeks after that picture was taken, Elisabeth handed Shirley two thousand dollars and a one-way ticket to Accra, Ghana." She dropped her head to pour some more tea.

"You mean Kesho's mother never stole that money!"

"No."

"Elisabeth let everyone think Shirley was a thief? That's horrible! Why?" Then I remembered. "My God, and you called Kesho 'thieving servant seed.' What is the matter with you people?"

"Many things." She held out my refilled cup. I hesitated, then took the cup and put it down on the mahogany tray that acted as a coffee table. I did not feel like sharing tea.

Myrna's face remained expressionless, her brown eyes glassed over. "I called Kesho Friday night, after that frightening dinner. I wanted to apologize for that unfortunate remark. I wanted to explain why she shouldn't stay here. She needed to know what Elisabeth had done to her family. I asked her to come over."

"If you knew Shirley hadn't taken the money, you're just as guilty. And why this sudden need to confess?"

Myrna's freckled hand searched her neck, as if she were missing something. "I realize you dislike me, Miss Griffo, and I'm not in the least bit interested in justifying myself. I am answering you only because your little speech about the strengths of women showed me how hopelessly naive you are. Somehow that moves me. Actually it reminds me of Elisabeth when she first came to Fieldston." Her hand dropped onto her lap, upturned. She stared at it, fingers splayed. "I'll correct that. It reminds me of how I first thought of Elisabeth. It took me a while to discover she had a way of spawning expectations she never met. Everyone fell in love with her. Anyway, that doesn't matter anymore." She wiped air with that same hand, her face soft. "Kesho came over about an hour after the dinner. Charles was out. I told her about her mother being innocent. She became enraged, storming up and down my living room, punching chairs, slapping tables. For a few minutes I thought she might start smashing up the house. Then she ran out. Half an hour later Charles saw her up at Elisabeth's. I believe him." Myrna's eyes met mine.

I was angry. At her for letting Kesho be ashamed of her mother for thirty years, for allowing a man to die thinking his wife had wanted to leave so badly she had stolen to do it. I was angry at Elisabeth, at the situation, at the very real possibility that a furious and vengeful Kesho had stormed up to RockPerch.

"Why tell her now?" I asked, trying to stop myself from sneering. "Was it because you didn't want Kesho as a neighbor? Because Chuck would lose the house? Why now?"

"To hurt Elisabeth," she said flatly.

Enough to drown her? Instead I asked, "Was Kesho wearing the Paco Rabanne earrings when she came to your house?"

"Yes, they're so gaudy I couldn't help but notice. But she left with both of them on. You'll have to believe me, although that might be hard for you under the circumstances." Myrna reached for the photograph on the tray and slipped it inside the pages of Virginia Woolf. "Elisabeth left Kesho the house to right a wrong. She was ashamed of what she had done to Kesho's family. I knew her well enough to be sure of that."

"And then she was so nice as to want to sell Kesho the house for three million dollars."

Myrna leaned forward, intensity animating her face. "You've just made your pretty little speech about women not waiting to be given authority to do what they must. That's easy to say, but what about those women who want to get out and can't, who are held down? That money would have gotten Elisabeth out of here! She hated this place! She was miserable under Walter's thumb. He controlled everything she did, gave her a pittance of an allowance, bought her long black clothing she detested, forced her to take acting lessons. When he finally understood she had no talent, he called in a painter to give her lessons with Walter presiding over every brush stroke. He wanted her to be grand and glorious, a beautiful artist he could show off. He filled my son's head with the same absurdities! Walter was jealous, convinced someone would steal his prize away. Then he disappeared and left her with practically nothing."

"Charles took over, whirring incessantly about his generosity, about how wrong she'd been to marry Walter. My husband didn't like his younger brother. Walter refused the concept of hard work. He was too flamboyant, too dramatic. He was Daddy's favorite. He stole Chuck's affection. He stole the catch of the high school, the beautiful Elisabeth." Bitterness had whipped up in her voice. "Charles and I got stuck with each other."

"She could have left, so could you."

Myrna's eyes flickered to her door. "Yes, I know. There's the front door just waiting. But I didn't want to be poor. Not after my father drank away all his money by the time I was eighteen. I grew up well-to-do, you see, and money is like smoking: it leaves you with a spreading cancer. Elisabeth grew up poor, and was afraid to go back to one-room apartments and the rest. We were both caught." Myrna gave a short laugh, cocking her head. "The irony is that now the Dobsons are bankrupt." She looked genuinely amused.

"Did Elisabeth have a lover?" I asked.

Myrna's face tightened.

"There are rumors around," I said. "She had a lover and Walter found out and drowned himself in Lake Ontario. That's one. Edith Holmes's take is that Elisabeth killed Walter."

"Leave it to Edith to come up with something ridiculous." Myrna rose as she spoke, dodging the coffee table to go over to her pile of old *Prudent Times*, stacked underneath the paned window. "They made a book of the *Tightwad Gazette* this year. In three years that paper built up a subscriber base of a hundred thousand. I consider myself lucky with fourteen thousand." She started leafing through the top paper. "I have to get back to work. After the funeral. I need to." Her hands were trembling. Outside, a branch knocked against the window repeatedly.

I stood up and hobbled to her, all my muscles stiff. "If she had a lover and you know who he is, at least tell the police."

She turned to me, her eyes wary.

"He could be another suspect."

"Why does it have to be a 'he'?" Myrna asked, suddenly angry. "Why are men the only ones we're allowed to love? Why do you look surprised?"

"Only because I had assumed—"

"Where's your female freedom, your courage, your defiance of authority now? Yes, Elisabeth had a lover. A woman, who loved her more than all those stupid dicks put together. A woman who didn't make demands, who didn't tell her how she had to be, a woman who just loved Elisabeth until that woman was sick from the pain of loving her too much, of having to hide that feeling." The pain was all there, on Myrna's face, welling in her eyes, embedded in the grooves of her skin. "In this room I did not hide. Within these walls she loved me back for a brief time. Then Shirley saw us through this window." Myrna flattened both her hands on the panes as if to cover the view. It was the first time I noticed she wasn't wearing a wedding ring. "Elisabeth was so ashamed of being found out, she gave Shirley the two thousand dollars and sent her to Ghana. And I, ashamed of her shame, rejected, made to feel like a thief myself, watched as Walter thundered about the missing money and Elisabeth pointed the finger."

"I'm not ashamed of my love. It's as good as any man's love. Better than most. It produced one lovely memory that I consume sparingly, tightwad that I am." She squeezed her eyes shut. I expected those welling tears to drop down, but nothing came. "I do, however, regret I did not have the courage to defend Kesho's family."

I fished into my sweater pocket and offered her a crumpled tissue. "You had the courage to tell me you're a lesbian."

Myrna blew hard into the tissue. "Anger got the better of me." She wiped her nose, looking at me with grieving eyes. "Besides your little speech told me I was safe with you."

"Thanks." I was grateful for her trust. And embarrassed. Not by her sexual orientation, but by the rawness of her pain.

"Just before Walter disappeared"—Myrna rammed the tissue up her jacket sleeve—"Elisabeth started to write me a letter reminiscing about our affair. She must have been feeling very lonely, I don't know, but she mentioned some physical details. Walter found the letter in a drawer, didn't realize in his dumb anger that it was something that had happened years ago. They had a fight, she told him she never loved him and he drove off." She looked up, dry-eyed, her face hardening into the protective mask I had mistaken for disdain. "After that Elisabeth no longer even pretended to be a friend or a sister-in-law. But I refuse the burden of Walter's death. I married Charles to be close to Elisabeth. When she discovered she couldn't bear children, I had Chuck so she could have a child to play with. Those are burdens enough."

"Thank you again for your honesty," I said, extending my arm.

"Honesty should be a must among women," she answered as we shook hands.

After helping me wrap myself up in her mohair throw, Myrna drove me back to my car. She had enough foresight to bring a couple of logs which we dropped down in front of the back tire to help me drive out of the ditch. By now it was four o'clock in the morning. Myrna watched over me while I bumped out onto the road after a few timid tries. Not only honesty among women, solidarity too, I thought, as I looked at her standing in the middle of Bishop's Lane in her old Ferragamo pumps, her dull brown parka over her knit suit, the wind swooshing through her hair and dropping the temperature down into the teens. I started to get out of the car to give back the throw and thank her. Myrna blocked the door with her hip.

"Keep it for now," she said as I rolled down the window. "It's too cold. Just tell Kesho she'll be miserable. It's all right to be a lush in this town, but not a lesbian or a black."

"Does Copper George know you told Kesho about her mother?"

"Charles told him. He overheard Kesho yelling at Elisabeth about the two thousand dollars that wasn't stolen. That's how I know Charles did see Kesho up at Rock-Perch."

"No," I insisted. "She told me she wasn't there."

"Charles had no way of knowing the money wasn't stolen. All these years I never told him the truth about Shirley."

I was trying to help Kesho. She wouldn't lie to me. "Elisabeth could have told him."

"Never," Myrna said and turned away.

I opened the car door. "Please, one more question."

She pivoted on those narrow feet. "You're pushing your luck."

"My last, I promise. Do you think Walter could have been killed?"

"By Elisabeth?"

"By anyone."

"I don't know and I don't care. Good night. Don't forget to tell Kesho what I said."

"She's too stubborn, she won't back out," I called out after her. "That's how you get things to change."

She turned one more time. "Kesho, the Rosa Parks of Fieldston?"

"Why not? *Ciao e grazie!*" I waved goodbye.

The big white Holmes house looked stark and handsome in the dark with only those eerie electric lights flickering from all those swagged windows. The front lantern was still dropping soft yellow light onto the Christmas wreath of the door. The wind seemed to have hit that barrier of tall trees and stopped. A postcard small town scene, looking deceptively safe.

I circled into the driveway, expecting to find a blue "Protection and Service" police car manned with two policemen guarding frail old Henry. Instead I found a beat-up Chevy parked at the other end of the driveway. The windows were so fogged up I could barely make out Joe slumped down behind the wheel.

"Didn't they believe you at the police station?" I asked, getting in the front seat and feeling my body creak at that simple movement. A dark shape popped up from the back seat.

"Hi, Simone!" Roxanne said. Her voice sounded sleepy.

"Hi. It's Simona. With an *a*."

"You OK?" Roxanne asked. "You got any idea who bopped you? You look kinda shaky."

"I'm all right. Just a bit dented and stiff. But what are you two doing here? Where's the police?"

Roxanne shook her head, spraying hair on my face. "I thought we should scoop the police. Maybe the killer would come and Joe would catch him, make the papers, the raise, the marriage, you know."

Joey sat up and began sweeping the windshield with one of his gloves, each sweep revealing more of Henry and Edith's house. "I *am* the police!"

"Yeah I know," Roxanne countered, "but you're Santinelli police, not Copper George police. You follow me, Joey. I'll take you to the top."

"You'll take him to the unemployment line," I said. "Did anyone show up here?"

Roxanne's hair hit my face again. "No one. If he was Italian, he'd be up to his hairline in lasagne and family."

"The phone rang a lot, though," Joe said. "And Henry spotted us and came out. Wanted to know what we were doing in his driveway. He was all wired up, carried a shotgun."

"You should have shown him your badge," Roxanne said, arms flapping over the front seat like laundry on a line. "We're lucky he didn't call Copper George. Rich people always go for the top brass."

"He saw Rox and took us for lovers."

"Which we are."

"Didn't he recognize you?" I asked.

Joe laughed. "Didn't seem to. Told us we could do our loving in his driveway any time. Said in his day, the Depression, he didn't even have a car. He made do with a quick kiss behind a tree. Can you imagine?"

"Sure he recognized Joey," Roxanne said. "Everyone knows him. Henry was just pretending. Makes it easier on him. I do that sometimes, when I don't want to handle something right away. I mean, I sure wouldn't like to think I'm in danger. And he was scared."

Joe ran a hand over Roxanne's forearm. "I don't know about that, Rox. I think he was just confused. I mean his wife just died."

Roxanne's arms went limp as Joe caressed her. "We're lucky to have each other, huh?"

"Yeah," Joey said.

My eyes closed and my head fell back against the seat.

"Henry kept talking and talking." Roxanne's voice was low. "I bet he hasn't spit so many words since the day he married that woman. I'm going to get Mama to invite him over for dinner. He's too old for her, but she sure could use the company. Hey, you asleep, Simone? Simona?"

"You got it." I said, unable to open my eyes. "With an *a*."

"You go to sleep," Joe said, suddenly sounding very paternal. "We'll watch the old man."

"Charles was out," I said, finally registering what Myrna had said.

"Out when?" Roxanne asked.

I sat up. "After that dinner Friday night, he went somewhere. I don't mean RockPerch. Before that. Kesho was still at Myrna's house. Joe, you've got to find out where he went. He could have gone to a neighbor, a friend. Ask around."

Joe had gone back to clearing the windshield again.

"Please. It could be important."

"We'll look into it," Roxanne said.

"And thanks for watching Henry for me. Both of you."

"Sure." Roxanne's arms went back into motion. "His back door's locked. We made sure of that. He's safe with us. You go on to the inn and get to bed."

I opened the car door and slowly extended a leg. "I need a favor from you, too, Roxanne."

"What?" She sounded suspicious.

I stretched the other leg out of the car and edged myself to the end of the seat. "Your brother works at the local bank, doesn't he?"

"You bet. Assistant branch manager."

"I need to know if Walter Dobson really left no money when he disappeared."

"Rox, that's illegal," Joe protested.

"So's murder!" Roxanne took the words right out of my mouth. "I'll get right on it."

"Thanks." I lifted myself up and slowly got out of the car. I was getting stiffer and sleepier by the second.

Roxanne's arm came after me. "Are you going to make it back OK?"

The temperature out there hadn't gotten any warmer. "I'll be fine."

"That's good," Roxanne said, "but there's one thing I don't get, Simone. How did you get—"

"In the Fieldston phone book. It was real easy. There was only one Joseph Pertini listed."

"How'd you know I was going to ask that?"

"It's the first assumption I've gotten right since this story started. Thanks for asking, Roxanne. You made my night."

CHAPTER

26

❄

Except my night wasn't over yet. I wanted to check the back of Henry's house, maybe look for broken windows, a door left ajar, a trampled flower bed. My tires scrunched on more gravel as I circled to the back. My headlights picked up a wide trellis entwined by bare rose branches, grazed across more white clapboard, a couple of dark windows, a blue door. All seemed quiet.

Trampled flower beds! In the middle of December? I laughed at my illusions of detective grandeur, realizing I was punchy with fatigue, humbled by my talk with Myrna, and upset that Kesho had lied to me. It was time for bed.

I swung in front of the garage and started to back out when the garage door swung open and Henry appeared in the headlights, one arm hooked under a shotgun aimed right at me.

"It's me, Mr. Holmes! Simona Griffo!" I fumbled out of the car and stood by the car door. "I was just checking that everything's OK. I hope you don't mind my trespassing." I did not get closer.

Neither did he. In that glaring patch of light, Henry looked cross, tangled eyebrows hovering over his eyes, the barrel of the gun still pointed at me. "Did you send that policeman over here?" His voice had lost the hesitancy he'd had earlier.

"I was worried about you."

"The girlfriend with all the hair, too?"

"They're a team. Look, if you've got that tape, Mr. Holmes, please give it to Joe. He's still parked out front. We don't want anything to happen to you."

He looked at me for a moment, his shoulders curved, his jowls and eyes heavy. Underneath a plush camel bathrobe that still showed its gift box creases, he was fully dressed, his feet in running shoes.

"I didn't mean to scare you about the killer," I said, pointing to the gun. "I just wanted you to be careful. If Edith was killed, as you say . . . "

"She was killed," Henry confirmed. "Smothered with her pillow most likely. There was nothing wrong with her heart."

"She knew something she wasn't supposed to, isn't that why you think she didn't die a natural death? What did she know? Did she record an incriminating phone call with that scanner you gave me? Let me help you, Mr. Holmes."

The gun lowered. "The name's Henry. You play pool?"

"No, I don't."

He closed the garage door behind him and walked out of the headlights. "Come on, it's cold, Miss Griffo."

"The name's Simona."

After he unlocked the blue back door and turned up the thermostat behind the door, I followed him across a long kitchen with warped, stained wood cabinets and a wide-plank floor. He moved quickly on those sneakered feet. Behind the rounded refrigerator, Henry opened a door and pressed a light switch. "Watch the steps."

I looked down a steep incline of painted white steps

ending in a square of blue industrial carpeting. Not sure my legs would carry me down and then back up, I hesitated. "Did you hide the tape in the basement?"

"No, I don't want to talk about the tape. I want to show you where Edith and I played pool. Every night, we played." He raised his knotted eyebrows. "You look surprised. What is it? Am I too casual after my wife's death or is it our playing pool? You young people think someone hits seventy, the carpenter should start hammering up a box."

"I don't know what I think, Henry. Except that I'm very tired."

"Edith and I talked about death, when one of us would be left alone. Of course, I was supposed to go first. Men always are and I wish those feminists would remember that." He forced a smile, his whole face lifting with the effort. "What we decided was to celebrate the living moments." He swept his arm out. "Are you going down or not?" That's when his voice quavered.

"I'd love to, Henry. I'll just have to take it slow."

"That'll be two of us."

We made it down into a large space painted light blue, its walls stacked with a lifetime of books, magazines, and antique bric-a-brac. Under a coned lamp, the pool table, with its multicolored balls gathered in a wooden triangle, glowed shamrock green in the middle of the room. Four cue sticks lined up against the far wall.

Tired as I was, I didn't care about pool, but I liked Henry and understood his loneliness. "It's a beautiful table." I ran my hand along the carved mahogany. I wasn't being entirely selfless. I wanted information, too.

"When Edith's legs couldn't hold her up long, she learned to play from a wheelchair. She'd bet me and beat me." He jutted out his chin. "My wife enjoyed her little victories." Something in his pleased, proud expression told me those victories had been his to give.

"Another hobby was antique fairs," Henry said, his arm sweeping across a metal shelf crowded with porcelain cups of all shapes, colors and sizes. He'd left the shotgun upstairs. "I think Edith possesses more than a thousand cups and saucers." He walked over. "Take your pick."

"Thank you, I couldn't."

He raised his eyebrows, exposing gentle hazel eyes. "Please, for your help."

"What did Edith find out? Does a tape exist or am I making one of my stupid assumptions again?"

Henry began picking up one cup after another, blowing dust out of their bowls.

"Mr. Holmes, please. There's a killer out there. He's already zonked me on the head, tied me up and left me to freeze just to get the scanner. Even if there is no tape he's going to think there is. You yourself said you could tell someone had been through your wife's things."

Henry held up a flowered, sea green cup rimmed in gold and a blue and gold saucer. "A tape of what?" He wasn't good at lying.

"The killer's phone call to Elisabeth maybe. At eight o'clock Christmas Eve Elisabeth announced she was selling RockPerch. Two hours later she changed her mind. Why? Maybe someone called her, threatened her, and your wife recorded the call. Your property abuts Elisabeth's land."

The cup and saucer stayed in front of his chin. "Why would anyone want to threaten that lovely woman?"

"Come on, Henry, I know it's been an awful night for you. You've lost your wife and that must be devastating. But please be honest with me. There's no reason you would think your wife was killed unless you know there was a reason to kill her. Nor would you hide all night in your garage in the company of a shotgun if you weren't scared that the killer was coming back."

"The policeman is watching the front. I'm watching the back."

"Why didn't you tell Copper George about the scanner?"

"He'd ask too many questions. I need to sit down, Simona, with a cup of caffeine." He lifted his chin above the cup, his eyes filled with sleep. "I would enjoy your company."

"I'm not leaving you yet."

"Good." He smiled sadly and slipped the cup and saucer into the pockets of his bathrobe.

Back upstairs in the warm kitchen, he took off his bathrobe and prepared the coffee. I kept my black coat on to cover my tattered backside and washed the sea green cup and mismatched saucer that he insisted was now mine.

"Let's start with the scanner, Henry," I said, after we sleepily settled into the coziness of a bay window banquette. I gulped strong black coffee from my new cup, hoping it would unclog my head. "Why did you give it to me?"

"I didn't want Charles to think she listened in on him. He's a neighbor and a friend. Copper George would have made a joke of it and told the whole town."

"You wanted to protect her memory."

He cast a surprised look at me. "Yes, I did. Edith thrived on knowing about other people. Even as a young woman, when we were dating, she was always filling me up with tidbits about everyone else. Rich or poor, she had to have a ringside seat on their lives." He took a long sip of coffee from a Schlitz beer mug. "She was an insecure woman. I never managed to turn that around."

"What did you do with the tape recorder?"

"It's in the upstairs bathroom. Doubles as a radio. I put it in there before Copper George and Charles came over. We've got radios in every room." He pointed with his chin.

A black plastic model sat above the old refrigerator like a fat tomcat.

"She had to have something going on around her all the time." Henry stopped, his head slightly cocked, as if listening to the new silence in his life.

"Edith claimed Elisabeth killed her husband," I said after a few beats. "Was there any truth to that?"

"I don't know. It was something new. She started telling everybody after Elisabeth died. I don't know if there was any truth to anything she said." His sadness made me want to hold his hand.

"The newspaper accounts of Walter's disappearance mentioned that you both saw him that Sunday before he went off. Did you?"

"Edith did. She wasn't lying this time. We were both cleaning up the garden. We do it every year at the end of March, beginning of April, depending on the weather." He lowered his head. "Well, we did. She said, 'Look, Henry, there's Walter.' She called out to him and waved. She said he waved back with his hat."

"You didn't see him?"

"No, I was probably on my hands and knees. I don't remember much of that day except that it was awfully warm." He rubbed his hand over the back of his neck. "I even got sunburned. When the police asked us about Walter she told them I had seen him too. I backed her up, of course."

"That's what people who love each other do," I said. Richard had backed Kesho in her lie. I would have done the same for Greenhouse.

"Edith meant no harm. She just couldn't help herself." Henry sat back on the banquette and took another sip from his beer mug. "Maybe someone should start an Overcurious Anonymous."

"Where's the tape, Henry?"

He looked away. "In Goose Lake."

"Henry!"

"After everybody left tonight, I went down to the lake and sank it in the same hole Elisabeth drowned in."

I shook his arm in frustration. "Did you at least listen to it? Do you know what it said?"

"No!"

"Didn't your wife tell you anything?" I wanted to scream at him in anger. How could he be so dumb?

"No."

"How did you know about the tape then?"

"She rattled it under my nose, happy as can be. 'Oh, Henry. This is the best yet.' I walked out and went grocery shopping."

"When? Last night, just before she died?"

"Yesterday morning."

"How did the killer know she had the tape?" I could hear my voice rising, but I couldn't stop myself. "Did she call anyone, see anyone? How could you throw that tape away? That was evidence in a murder case!"

"I didn't want to know!" he yelled back, his face twisted in pain.

I sucked in my breath, mortified. "I'm so sorry, Henry. Please forgive me."

He dropped his head in his hands, covering his ears. "I don't want to know anything about anyone for the rest of my life!"

We had little to say to each other after that. I apologized again and thanked him for the lovely cup and saucer. He followed me out.

"Copper George needs to know what happened," I said as gently as I could.

"He never believed a word Edith said. He won't believe me."

"Try him." Maybe the tape had gotten stuck on the same ledge that had held Elisabeth from sinking to the bottom. Maybe it could be dried out and still listened to.

Maybe it would help Kesho and keep this sweet man safe. I raised tired arms. "I am sorry about all of this," that "all" now including two deaths and the mired lives I had learned about during this holiday season. Over Henry's shoulder, in the dim light from the garage lamp, I could see a palisade of bare, bristled trees, behind which hunkered the dark mass of RockPerch.

"Be careful." I kissed his worn, still warm cheek, and watched him re-enter the safety of his house. Then I drove to the front, warned Joe that Copper George might soon be on his way, asked him to find out what phone calls Edith had made from the house yesterday and got a no for an answer.

"I'm a policeman," Joe protested in a whisper. "I can't go telling you things like that."

"*Dai*, be a pal," I whispered back. "You gave Roxanne the information about Elisabeth's phone calls."

"No, I didn't." We both looked at the backseat where Roxanne was curled up, fast asleep, a mound of black hair covering her face. "Darn her and her cousin! They're as thick as thieves."

"Watch it!" the hair growled. "That cousin's gonna be the next chief of police!" The body didn't move. "And don't stereotype Italians, Joe. We're not thieves!"

"Did I say that? I didn't say that. I just said you were thick . . . "

Roxanne let out a loud snore. At five-twenty in the morning, I took that as a cue to go back to the inn and a bed.

CHAPTER
27

The bed was rocking and a deep, warm voice was telling me something. I cranked open an eye. A green arm wavered into sight, a white-toothed smile. "Rise and shine, girl!"

"Kesho," I mumbled, hugging my pillow. She was shaking my shoulder, giving me nausea. Then a dark furry head jumped into my face and all I saw was a black nose twitching between blue slivered eyes.

"Wake up, lazybones!" Kesho said. "I thought you were staying in New York. Now that you're here, you've got to come too!"

"I'm fine right here." The cat rasped my nose with his tongue and settled under the tuck of my chin. I shifted sight to my other eye and got Kesho's green shoulder and the handle of a wheelchair sticking out of her back like a dagger. How morbid, I thought.

"Welcome back," I muttered and turned over. Premi did a protest croak. His tail lashed at the back of my neck. Kesho started stroking my hair with a soft hand.

"This my lucky day, Simona! My day to make peace. I need my friends around me."

I groaned.

"Come on!" she cajoled in a rippling whisper that tickled my ear. "Richard's going to drive us to Candlewood Lake. It's beautiful up there, a great way to meet the day."

"Meet the day?" I turned back over, both eyes wide. Premi took refuge under the pillow. "What time is it?"

It was seven thirty, late for her, she said.

"Are you OK?" I asked, blinking at the glare of happiness coming from her face. I was vaguely thinking of painkillers and their doping effect.

She grinned back, catching Premi's paw. "I will be. I really think I will be."

I sat up. "You're no longer under arrest!" My head popped, releasing a slow, dull ache.

Kesho laughed as Premi sidled into her secure lap. "Copper George doesn't give up that easy! But maybe by Friday, when I'm supposed to go before that judge, maybe by then I'll be out of this mess. Hurry up and get dressed or it'll be too late. Here!" She threw last night's clothes at me and noticed the torn slacks. "What happened?"

"I forgot to use a sled."

"What are you talking about? If Stan were here, I'd think you two got a little flustered with zippers and buttons."

"I wish."

"Tell me later. We'll be out in the car with coffee and carrot cake. Jean's up at the Holmes house, making sure Henry doesn't starve to death." She wheeled herself and Premi out of the room.

I rolled out of bed, stumbled to the shower where I sat over the drain hole, letting water pour over me and climb to the tip of the shower rim. I pulled myself up in time to avoid flooding the bathroom and got dressed in black tights, a black skirt and a violently purple sweater that I hoped would help me stay awake. Sometime during the dressing process, I remembered today was operation day for Greenhouse's mother. I called her Florida apartment, called the hospital. No answer anywhere. I mentally wished her good luck, blew Greenhouse a kiss and staggered out the back door. Richard's rented white Mercedes straddled the driveway, muffler puffing out smoke like an arrogant cigar.

"Hi, Richard," I said, throwing myself into the tan leather front seat that smelled of pure money. "I see Kesho found you."

Richard gave a slight shake to his ponytail, a puzzled look on his face. The cold air had colored his face rugged and wiped away some of the city slick. "She never lost me."

"She was looking for you last night." The memory had come to me in the shower, as cold water streamed a tunnel to my brain. A thought produced itself. Lovers backing up each other, one lying for the other. How far could that protection go?

I slipped two more Tylenol into my mouth. A hand appeared over my shoulder, holding a paper cup of steaming coffee. "Thanks, Kesho. I need this."

Kesho was stretched out across the back seat, thermos in her lap, her bad leg in a flesh-colored brace and looking like a one-hump camel. The rest of her was covered in a black mini skirt, black combat boots, green socks and her signature green sweatshirt with Ruffy sequined over her chest. Her usual handwoven red-and-ocher cloth wrapped her neck.

Richard shifted into gear, and the Mercedes wound down Bishop's Lane as smoothly as silk. The swath of sky between the flanking row of trees had turned pearl gray since I last looked up from the vantage point of the ditch. I toyed with telling Kesho and Richard my adventure, then decided I was too tired. Fighting not to sink back and close my eyes, I veered to more comfortable thoughts.

"*Allora*, Kesho, why are you so happy?"

"They're going to autopsy Edith Holmes," Richard answered.

"Good!" Henry had come through. I drank the coffee in one searing gulp, instantly feeling better.

"Jean went up about an hour ago," Kesho said, "with coffee and a pie and some leftover pasta. Copper George was there, talking on the phone with the Medical Examiner, I guess. Anyway, Jean overheard him and called us the minute he left. Jean wasn't sure exactly what was going on, Henry wouldn't talk, but Edith apparently knew something about Elisabeth's death and may have been killed for that information."

"If she was killed," I said, handing her my cup for more coffee, "you'll be in the clear. You were still in the hospital last night."

"Well, Richard did take me to Auberge Louis for an early dinner. Five o'clock! I couldn't wait. I was ravenous." She smiled, probably thinking of the baby, and instead of coffee, dropped a slice of carrot cake in my hand. Fine by me.

"We have witnesses to that," Richard said.

"*Fantastico!*" I nibbled, crumbs spreading over my lap. We had just left Fieldston and were driving up Route 7, the road of Kesho's accident.

"The maitre d', the waiter," Richard went on. He looked good in a burnt brown turtleneck and a shearling jacket of the same color. Even his corduroy slacks matched. "Just as we were leaving, that loud woman who always eats at my Bistro West stopped us. Plenty of witnesses."

"With this leg, it's not as if I could slip out with the excuse of going to the ladies room and run over to throttle Edith." Kesho waved as we passed the copper beech she'd smashed into. "I'm just as tough as you!" she called out.

Richard laughed. "The car wasn't."

I contemplated my hand, bare of cake except for a sparrow's breakfast. Edith had eaten her last supper at six. "When did you get to the hospital?"

Richard snapped his head in my direction, his laugh gone. "You don't think Kesho has anything to do with Edith's death?"

"No, I don't," I said defensively, instantly annoyed by his accusation. "But Copper George isn't going to let go of his case that easily. Unless she has an airtight alibi." I was wary of both of them. I didn't like the fact they'd lied to me about Kesho not being up at RockPerch.

"Well, that moosehead will have to give up," Kesho said, weariness coming into her voice. "Richard dropped me off at the hospital just after seven. The woman in the next room was watching 'Jeopardy' and shouting out all the answers. She got every one of them wrong, too. By the time you called, Simona, I was ready to get out of there for good, so I got Richard to take me back to the inn. I'm sure the head nurse would love to tell Copper George just how pleased she was about my leaving without bothering to check out. I wasn't about to wait until morning."

I gave Richard a quick sideways glance. Where had he gone after dropping Kesho off? "I read about your connection to RockPerch," I said, quickly explaining about the article Nell the librarian had sent over. I also told them about Sarah Bishop having died on that ledge. I wasn't sure I knew what I was trying to get at.

"Everyone seems to have a claim to that house," I added.

"My mother's claim was a little stronger than a ghost's from Revolutionary times."

"Well, now it's yours, Rich," Kesho said.

"Ours," he corrected. He grinned, looking up in the rearview mirror. "That's why I'm marrying you, baby. For your gorgeous bod and your bricks."

Kesho's laugh would have burst a balloon. I recalled what I wanted to ask Richard. "You used to weekend in these parts, didn't you?"

"Yeah, about five miles out of Ridgefield."

"Do you remember anything about Walter's disappearance?"

He glanced my way for a second, then went back to the road ahead of him. "A lot of gossip. Why do you ask?"

"Because there are people around who think Elisabeth's killing is connected. In fact, Edith thought all along Elisabeth killed Walter. She went public only after Elisabeth's death."

"Which means there was some good in her after all." Kesho tapped my shoulder. "Quit worrying, Simona. It's going to be fine. I heard a mockingbird sing just five minutes before Jean called." Her voice began to lilt. "In my books Ruffy always tells the other homeless animals, 'if you hear a mockingbird sing, know it's not you he's mocking, but all those mighty-highty-tighty animals out there who think they're better than you.' " She laughed. "Aunt Rose taught me that one. She'd say, 'you hear 'im trillin', you start singin'.' Well, this morning I heard him loud and clear."

Her optimism held us quiet as we drove through Danbury and skirted one side of Candlewood Lake, past neat, modest homes painted smoky blue and barn red and looking like Monopoly houses forgotten in the woods. In the luxury of my padded leather seat, with the car gliding over the road, I wished my suspicions would go away. I didn't like Richard much, hadn't really forgiven him for treating Willy so badly. Now my feelings colored my reasoning. *Che c'è di nuovo, Simona?* So what's new?

At the top of a hill, Richard swung the car into Bear Mountain Reservation and parked. We were surrounded by pines, naked trees, and the usual boulders lying on the leaf-strewn ground like sleeping baby elephants. An occasional streak of snow brightened the brown-gray tapestry. Above us the sky was still a leaden dome with a slit near the horizon showing a sun turned white from cold.

"What now, hon?" Richard asked, frowning as he looked at the wooded slope that presumably led down to the lake.

"We're walking down to the lake," Kesho said, pointing to the J. F. Kennedy hiking trails. "There's a lookout ledge with a beautiful view."

"The wheelchair won't make it," Richard protested. "It poured yesterday. It's going to be a mud bath out there." In back of us, a man started sawing wood.

I would have been just as comfortable doing my clouded thinking in the warmth of that fancy car, the buzz of the saw lulling me to sleep, but Kesho insisted. No wheelchair, just her crutches. Crazy as the idea was, Richard easily gave up the fight. Either they had run through this argument before or he knew the power of Kesho's will.

Slowly we made it down the slope, Kesho now covered in a red fake fur coat, swinging her crutches with the strength of an athlete. Richard hovered next to her, one arm outstretched ready to catch her, while I slipped and slid down the narrow path, grabbing one branch after another, smelling the pine sap, waking to the cold air, spying glimpses of ice-blue lake, listening to the buzz of the saw soften.

"Here we are," Kesho said finally, using one crutch to indicate a cluster of gray birches. She hopped inside the circle of trees and let Richard lower her on a flat rock ledge the size of a two-seater sofa. I followed and was taken aback by the sudden sight of the long half-frozen Candlewood Lake.

"You win, hon," Richard said. "Great view."

"A place to make peace," Kesho said as we wedged in beside her on the ledge. "The Ewe people of Ghana believe that forgiveness must be sought and given at dawn." Her lips stretched into a smile. "A little late for dawn, but maybe they'll give me leeway for being a lost city woman."

Richard dropped an arm on her shoulder. They bent heads together, Kesho's face turning sad.

"I used to think the Ewe people had to be gods," she said, "for my mother to choose them over me. I grew up hating her for it." She reached for Richard's hand. "You see, I didn't know anything about the early sixties, the back-to-Africa movement, the claiming of our heritage. We were the only blacks in Fieldston, and my father was too angry at my mother to explain anything. I remember Jean trying a couple of times, but I guess I didn't want to hear any excuses. My mother had left me and she'd stolen to do it too. That was more than enough knowledge for me. I even threw out the letters she sent me." As Kesho spoke to us, her forehead still touching Richard's, she kept her eyes on the lake where ribbons of water rippled their way around broken and melting ice.

"The brothers and sisters I met in New York opened my mind. So did Aunt Rose." Kesho lifted her head. "My mother didn't leave me. Not knowing where she came from exactly, she went to Africa and chose Ghana as her home, the Ewe as her people. To bring me back my ancestry. That's why she went. She was in Accra only three months when she died. She was always going to come back."

Kesho unwrapped the red-and-ocher cloth from her neck and flattened it out over her stomach. "This Kente cloth, woven by the Ewes, is the only thing I own of hers. A friend sent it back." Kesho took Richard's hand and wrapped the cloth around their clasped hands. She turned and spoke to Richard in a low voice. "Aunt Rose is coming to the wedding. She called me this morning. Cousins, friends, grandchildren, the whole wonderful black clan is coming. I'm forgiven and you're on, white baby."

Surprise beamed on Richard's face. "Christ, Kesho, that's wonderful!" He hugged her hard.

I looked on that intensely private moment without shame, happy for them, all my suspicions vanishing. They broke apart, hands still wrapped in the Kente cloth. Kesho closed her eyes, and I could almost hear her ask her mother's forgiveness for hating her all those years, maybe even for marrying a white man. Richard looked up at the trees, his eyes blurry. Maybe he was forgiving the bank that had foreclosed on his mother. To my surprise, taking my thoughts to my ex-husband, I discovered I had already forgiven him. The buzz of the saw stopped and for a fraction of a second there seemed to be perfect quiet in our world.

Then Kesho turned to me, her face settled into beauty and peace. "Shirley Larson, my mother, never stole a cent from those Dobsons."

I nodded. "Myrna told me the truth."

"But *I* didn't tell you the truth, so here I am seeking forgiveness for that, too. The whole world came crashing down on me that night. I was up at Elisabeth's all right. Ready to do her in, I was so upset. I was shaking her so hard I lost my earring. She kept yelling back, 'You should be happy. I've given you the truth. You know now. You're on firm ground.'"

"And what she was saying came through the anger after a while. Now I could be proud of my mother, be proud of me, of what I've done with myself, of my white man, of the white-and-black baby coming. That woman, that whole family could do me no more harm!" She fixed her gaze on the lake again, as if the water breaking through the ice gave her strength.

"The Ewe people also believe," she said after a moment, "that morning dew makes children grow." Her voice was light again.

Richard chuckled. "I guess there was a lot of dew the morning you crashed the car."

Kesho turned to me and smiled. "I'm pregnant, you

see, and we thought we were going to lose the baby."

"Congratulations." I kissed her. "I'm happy you're both well." I said nothing about having known all along.

"Thanks." Kesho tucked her arm in Richard's and stretched out her good leg. "If Shirley had known the Ewe language, my name would have been *Ami*, Saturday, the day I was born. That's how the Ewe name their children." Kesho swept her free hand under Richard's chin. "I like *Ami*. What do you think, Rich? Saturday's the best day of the week. I sleep all day."

Richard kissed her nose. "*Ami* it is, even if she's born on depressing Monday."

"If it's a he, we'll shift the accent to the last syllable."

"It's a great name," I piped in, feeling as if I should sneak away and get lost in the woods. "It also means 'friend' in French." Guilt at having doubted these two lovers was climbing up my boots along with the mud. "Its Latin root is love. You're getting the multicultural best." They kissed, paying no attention to my nonsense. "Maybe I should wait up in the car."

"No, stay." Kesho broke away and held me back with a hand. "You're a friend now. I want to thank you."

"Me too," Richard said, looking nicer with lipstick across his mouth. "I've been kind of an asshole."

"It's too early to thank me," I said, standing and wiggling around as if to generate some heat. Actually I was embarrassed. "All I've come up with to clear you is a bump on the head and a sore behind." And then I told them about my past night, leaving out Myrna's love for Elisabeth and Henry's despair at his wife's snooping.

"You mean, the man threw the tape in the lake?" Richard asked. He was pacing between the birches, cracking twigs with his cowboy boots.

"That's what he maintains," I said, "and I have no reason to disbelieve him."

"Mockingbird, what are you doing to me?" Kesho

asked the tip of a pine tree. "The killer on a tape. That would have been great! Dial 1-900-KILLER for the thrill of your lifetime. What happens to tape once it's been in water?"

"I don't know," I said.

Richard picked up Kesho's crutches. "That lake's eight feet deep. They'll never find it." He held out his hand for her.

"Maybe they will. Elisabeth got stuck on that ledge." I held Kesho's elbow as she lifted herself up from the ledge with Richard's help.

"I don't want to think about it." As Kesho tucked her crutches under her arms, she looked across at the wooded ridge on the other side of the water. "My dad used to bring me out here from Fieldston in his pickup truck, hoes and rakes and tool box rattling in the back so loud, it was kind of a riff. Hewley'd slap his hands on the dashboard, trying to catch the upbeat. I'd start singing." Kesho threw her head back and let out a shout. "We were so lousy, we'd break up laughing. Hewley'd tell anyone who cared to listen, 'Hers and my black bones, they ain't got one beat of rhythm!' He loved breaking stereotypes. Only time that man would laugh." She turned around, "Well, friends!" and looked at the steep upward path that would take us back to the car. "I'm still going to believe that mockingbird's song is aiming at the mighty-highty-tighty of this world, which is not me."

"Even with a three-million-dollar house?" Richard asked, rubbing her neck, possessive and happy. "And four books selling like McFries, you're not?"

"Damn right." She started to wag up the hill in her red fake fur, her sculpted shorn black head aiming for the top of the hill. Richard followed, full of love for her, ready to catch her. I trudged after them both, certain Kesho would not fall.

CHAPTER

28

I slept on the way back, vaguely remembering Richard lifting me out of the car like a kid and dropping me on my bed. I slept deeply, with dreams I didn't remember upon waking. Garlic got me stirring finally, the smell of it sizzling in olive oil, a much more festive aroma than Christmas potpourri, I thought, as I stretched out on the bed and discovered I was in pretty good shape. I lifted my head and felt no protesting throb.

Kesho twisted her head in my direction as I walked into the kitchen. "Hey! Welcome back to the land of the living." She tossed a head of garlic at me. I miss balls tossed to me, keys, magazines. Garlic I catch.

"How can vampires not like this stuff?" I said, crackling the garlic head and dropping its paper thin skin on the floor. Premi extended a paw from Kesho's lap. "Even the cat likes it." He looked up at me, empty-pawed, and meowed.

Chuck was bent over the stove, a sandy hank of hair practically dripping into the frying pan. Next to him a covered pot of water was boiling over.

"Hi, Chuck." I quickly stepped up and lifted the lid, scalding my fingers in the process. "What are you cooking?"

He didn't look up. "Spaghetti with something unpronounceable. Richard taught me."

"You just missed him," Kesho said. She was sitting in her wheelchair, her bad leg propped up on a needlepoint footstool. "He went into the city to get more food for Saturday. More flowers. Instead of a hush-hush wedding, we're going to have us a blowout." A smile spanned the width of her face.

"Your aunt's approval means a lot."

"You bet. For a while I felt like I'd been dropped in a tub of bleach. She gave me my nice toasty skin back. And wait till you see the cake Rich designed. It's big enough for one of those Moonie mass weddings." She cast me a sly sideways look. "Maybe you and Stan want to join us in the 'I do'?"

"Sure," I said, shrugging the thought off. I sucked my fingertips and watched the garlic popping in the oil. Chuck needed to stir it around, to make sure all the oil got the flavor. And he had the flame too high.

"Wouldn't be a bad idea." Kesho wasn't going to shut up. "I think you've got something good going. Stan's got that glitter in his eye."

There had been moments when I'd thought of having a fat little baby with Greenhouse, usually when I was lonely and dreaming up someone to play with. Or when I was incredibly horny and wanted something to show for it. Immature thoughts that flitted through the brain and then evaporated. I'd never actually pondered a full-time commitment with this man.

"Too soon to tell," I said, my fingers itching to stir that garlic, to lower that flame. Wait a minute. I was lying. Of course I'd thought of commitment. Going to bed at night in my tight loft bed, wondering what it would be like to wake up to him every morning, his kind face scrunched with sleep. Lots of times I'd thought it would be wonderful. Then I would visualize his holster lying on my coffee table with the gun nestled inside or I would see Willy's freckled face frowning at me.

"We're still discovering things about each other."

Kesho flapped eyelids at me. "I aim to keep discovering Richard my whole life. If not, I'd die of boredom!"

I couldn't hold back anymore. "Garlic shouldn't burn. It leaves a bitter taste."

"Yeah," Chuck admitted, looking at four blackened cloves. "Richard told me to watch that. It went so fast." He looked chagrined.

"Come on, don't worry about it. Lower the flame, toss two fresh cloves in and it's going to be fine. That's *aglio, olio e peperoncino*, you're making. Garlic, oil and hot pepper. You throw the spaghetti in the boiling water, I'll chop parsley."

"I got the spaghetti," Kesho said. Chuck grabbed it before she could fling it at us.

"A year from now, I'm taking over as cook at this inn," he said. "I know Jean can always use a handyman in a creaky old place like this, but what she really needs is a cook. Richard's agreed to let me apprentice in one of his restaurants."

Kesho and I sang out our approval. I proceeded to chop while Chuck stirred and straightened his back, trying to look the chef. Kesho took out a box of place cards and started drawing a miniature Ruffy decked in tails and a top hat.

It was fun being in that steaming kitchen, smells that had been with me since childhood reassuring me, making me forget about Elisabeth and Edith dead, about Greenhouse pacing a hospital floor and Willy comforting another bewildered boy about parents splitting up. Besides it was one o'clock and I was starving.

"Is Jean still at Henry's?" I asked as I nudged Chuck to check the pasta. He was following directions on the label and waiting for the timer to go off, which can have gummy results.

"No, she just went to buy something," Kesho said, her head bent over the table. "Henry's gone up to Litchfield until the funeral. A niece came to pick him up."

The back door swung open, and Jean appeared, wiping her feet. Behind her was Copper George, holding two fat bags of kitty litter against his chest.

"Chuck, it smells wonderful," Jean said, opening the storm door and coming inside. "You're going to be so good at this. I just know it!" She popped open her coat.

Copper George stepped out from behind her, big in his sheepskin jacket and hat. "Where there's garlic, there's an Italian," he growled with his customary friendliness.

"Lovely smell, isn't it?" Kesho said, maintaining her smile despite his sudden presence. "What's the news on the autopsy?"

He dropped the bags on the table, over Kesho's place cards. "If Edith's death isn't natural"—he pointed a finger at her nose—"I'm going to want your exact whereabouts. You and that hippy boyfriend of yours."

"Stop treating me like shit!" Kesho swung at the bag in front of her with a clenched fist. "I didn't touch her! I've got witnesses!" The bag splashed on the floor, flooding the linoleum with kitty litter.

"Oh, Lord," Jean said and rushed to get her broom. I dropped down and started gathering the kernels with my hands.

"I'll do it," Kesho yelled, stretching out an arm and nearly falling out of her wheelchair. Premi dropped to the floor.

"Don't move," I said. She straightened herself up with a "damn."

"Jean and I'll take care of it." Premi sniffed at his litter and looked bewildered. I wanted to take the broom and hit that lug of a policeman right between his eyes.

"Miss Griffo, you and I have some talking to do." Copper George's boots scrunched as they approached me. "I hear someone attacked you last night."

"Not now," I said as I gathered fistfuls. I could see Chuck draining the spaghetti. "After lunch, I'll come down to headquarters." Jean's broom swept past me.

"You should have reported it right away."

"I was sleepy." I stood up. Thanks to Jean, the floor was clean again. Chuck was now swirling the pasta in the frying pan.

"That's not what I hear. Let's go into the living room." He took my elbow. I resisted. In two seconds the spaghetti would be ready to eat.

"The door," I said, glad for the excuse of Charles standing in the doorway in his black-and-white jacket. "Hello Mr. Dobson. I'd love to talk to you."

"What for?" He looked like an empty crossword puzzle.

"Your viewpoint of the last few days." I jostled my elbow against Copper George, still watching the pasta progress out of the corner of my eye. "After lunch. All right with you?"

"No. I'm looking for Myrna. Jean, you see her?"

Jean shook her head. "Sorry." She hooked the broom back behind the cellar door.

"Hi, Dad." Chuck put the bowl of spaghetti on the table. My mouth was building up a saliva sweat just at the sight of that garlic-embedded steam. I gave Copper George a pleading look.

"I've got to eat."

"Mother's gone over to the church for the funeral arrangements," Chuck said. He held up a plate. "Want to taste, Dad?"

Charles looked swiftly about the room as if his petite wife might really be there. Then he looked at the plate Chuck was proffering. "I can't eat garlic."

Kesho tossed me a look, her composure regained.

"Do you like garlic?" I asked Copper George who was still hanging on to me, maybe mistaking my elbow for a banister.

"Can't stand the odor," he confessed.

I threw Kesho back her look. We were dealing with vampires.

Copper George tugged. "Let's go to the living room. The food will keep for five minutes. I know most of the story from Pertini anyway."

The phone rang.

"That's for me!" I shouted. Greenhouse from the hospital. It had to be. Just in time a voice crackled on Copper George's two-way radio. He let go of my elbow to answer, and I started for the phone.

"Oh, Lord, Simona," Jean called after me. "I forgot Willy called. He was so excited I could hardly understand him. Richard told me you were fast asleep so I didn't wake you."

I stopped, panic closing my throat. "What? His grandmother. Something happened to his grandmother?"

"Lord no!" The phone kept ringing. "He's getting something for you that'll blow your mind." Her forehead crumbled. "I think that's what he said. He's coming on the 4:59 train to Danbury. Wants you to pick him up. Real important, I know he said that. I should have left you a note." She patted her curls. "I'm sorry. Edith's death has gotten me all—"

"The phone," I said, and made a dash for the entrance hall.

It was for me. I'd gotten that right. Not Greenhouse though. Roxanne, who had spoken to her brother. Walter had left Elisabeth some money after all.

"Not gobs, but enough to live on in grand style for a few years," she said. "That's all my brother would say. He didn't like doing this. But I twisted his arm."

"Thanks." My mind was focused on Willy. What was he getting me that would blow my mind?

"Listen to this," Roxanne said. "A month after Walter was reported missing, there was no more money." She held her mouth so close to the phone, her words came out wet. "What'd she do with it, huh?"

A spending spree was a possibility. So was blackmail. "Listen, I've got to go. Copper George wants me to tell him about being left to freeze in that ditch. Joe isn't in trouble because of me, is he?"

"He got an official reprimand. He wasn't supposed to go out on his own like that. Good thing Copper George has no idea I was with Joey the whole time. I got out of that car the minute you drove off."

I thanked her again, realizing I didn't really know what I was going to do with her information. That drowned tape seemed the important evidence. And what was Willy getting for me?

I called him at his friend David's house. There was no answer. I called his mother's house—no answer. I tried Greenhouse's apartment and got the answering machine. His wonderfully calm, warm voice asked me to leave a message. "I miss you," I said and hung up.

The phone bleeped for half a ring.

"Hello?" I slammed the receiver against my ear. It was him, this time. Same warm voice, without the calm.

"Jean, can I take this in your bedroom?" I yelled to the kitchen.

"It's all yours!"

"Kiss him for me," Kesho shouted.

"How's your mother?" I stretched out on Jean's bed. The phone clicked as someone put the receiver down in the entrance hall.

"She's still in Intensive Care. She hasn't come out of

anesthesia yet. She's going to be fine. I know she is. The doctors are sure, too. It's just taking a little longer. They won't let me see her." Greenhouse stopped, silence hanging heavy on the line.

"I wish I could be with you," I said.

"I'm calling from her room." More silence.

So I told him about the second death, about taking Willy to stay with David, how on the way we'd talked. I didn't mention my encounter with the murderer, only that Edith's body was being autopsied and that Kesho might be cleared before her case was heard by the judge on Friday. How her leg was much better and the baby was fine. I told him about my morning at Candlewood Lake. About Kesho's Aunt Rose.

"We're all in a euphoric mood. Chuck's even learning how to cook. I can't tell how good he is yet. I only got to smell it."

There was another pause. Greenhouse took a long breath. "Simona, I'm grateful I have you."

I flipped over on my stomach.

"I talk," he said, "and you listen."

"You don't do it very often so I hang on your every word."

"No, that's not what I mean. I . . . ." In the short silence that followed I heard the rustle of clothes, the shifting of position and I imagined him hunching over, tugging at the phone line in that nervous way he adopted when speaking to Willy.

"Sim, I'm trying to say that here's my mother getting a hip replacement at the age of eighty-three, and you're there for me to call and talk about it. I know I haven't said much in the three years we've known each other, but all of a sudden I want to make up for it." A rasp got caught in his throat, like a laugh that took a wrong turn. "If you were here we could be corny and hold hands."

I dug my head into the pillow and missed the feel of him. "I'd like that."

"I planned to go it alone after the divorce. I was going to have dates, occasionally zero in on one for a couple of months. Willy was going to be my pal, the only one I needed."

"That's a heavy-duty burden to put on any kid."

A barely heard breath. "Yes, it is, but that's not the issue here."

I changed ears, shifted position on the bed. Why was I sounding like a therapist all of a sudden?

"The issue is that you're important," Greenhouse said. The more confident he sounded, the more nervous I was getting. "In a different way, but just as important. Listen, I knew I loved you, but I didn't know how much until these past three days, when the only other woman in my life is having a hard time. Does that make sense?"

"I don't know." What was he telling me?

"I missed Willy, but I thought of you and what I would be telling you if you were here with me. You should see my mother's apartment, Sim. She's got all this stuff from my childhood."

I changed position again, this time swinging my legs down to the floor.

"If you were here, I'd tell you about my father. How he wouldn't let religion into our house, so my mother stuck a mezuzah behind the chest of drawers in my room. How they loved each other even though they didn't agree on anything. How—" He stopped, his breath becoming hot air blowing in my ear.

"God, Sim, I finally realized I can love you and love Willy and not take anything away from either of you. Do you know what a relief that is?"

"Yes, yes, I do." I was overwhelmed. "Maybe not from your point of view. From mine, yes." A mountain had been moved and I could see sky all the way down my life. Clear frightening sky that brought tears to my eyes.

"I want you to move in with me."

I rubbed the back of my hand against my nose and tried to get some sense of perspective back. "Let's talk about that when you get back."

"You don't want to?"

"I don't know. On the phone it's hard." What about Willy? What would he say? "Right now you think your mother isn't going to come out of the anesthesia. That doesn't make for reliable declarations."

He started to protest then said, "Hold it a sec," his voice screwed tight. "They're wheeling her in." I heard crackling sounds, the sibilance of whispers, a moan, the swoosh of sheets. More crackling, a thud, then Greenhouse. "She's OK. I'll call you back later. I meant what I said." He hung up before hearing my "I love you."

I held on to the receiver as if it still contained him. I swept my eyes over the surrounding pictures of Jean and Bill hugging each other and beaming into the camera. Move in with Greenhouse? Open up the gates and let love flow? And if we failed in this game? What country would I run to this time?

29

I went back to the kitchen, now empty of men. "What happened? Garlic got to be too much for them?"

"I was just getting ready to thrust their hearts with a wooden stake," Kesho pushed her empty plate aside, "but Copper George drove off to solve the problem of over-turned Christmas trees on Main Street."

"He wants you to go to headquarters before the end of the day," Jean said. Her plate was empty too. "I got rid of Charles by saying I was sure I heard Myrna's car going up the lane." She lifted her fork. "He took off in a pigeon strut."

"And Chuck's gone to the shed to work off the weight of Dad's love," Kesho added as Jean slurped the last strand of spaghetti from the bowl.

I lashed Jean with a starved look. "That must have been tasty," I said, emphasizing the past tense.

Jean widened her eyes. "I couldn't stop it was so good. Besides, worrying makes me hungry."

"When are we going to know the results of the autopsy?" I shuffled around the table, fidgeting with the tableware.

"By tonight," Jean said.

"How's Stan the Man?" Kesho asked, sitting up in her wheelchair, her eyes scanning my face and understanding something was wrong. "His mom OK?"

"Yes, thank God."

She cocked her head and flashed me the warmth of her round brown eyes. "You're lucky. He's a great guy."

A great guy who thought love took a back seat to work. A great dad with a son I still had to understand. A great cop who could get killed any instant.

"I know he's wonderful." I was lucky, but I was scared too. And hungry.

Jean stood up with the empty bowl in her hand. "Henry loved your Comfort Pasta, Simona," she said, as if that would help. "It hit the spot this morning."

"Thanks, but there's none of that either, right?"

"There's some leftover turkey."

"No, *grazie*. If I have any more, I'll grow a wattle."

"Pasta for breakfast?" Kesho made a face. "I'd throw up."

Jean snorted. "You'd probably throw up at anything these days."

Kesho laughed. "Come on, Simona, drive baby and me over to the Danbury Mall. You can eat all you want. I can buy more place cards, then we can both pick up Willy at the train station."

In that crowded, monstrous structure, every store was offering after-Christmas sales. The sound system still churned out carols. The holiday decor was garlands of leafless white sprayed twigs, fuchsia bows and white fake pines, around which senior citizens wandered clutching rolls of holiday wrappings, and mothers pushed strollers stuffed with babies and next year's presents. Teenagers whooped by in packs, showing off new earrings, jackets, sweaters, talking movies and CDs, having a grand time, school a distant future in their minds. I wheeled Kesho between bodies and talked.

With a regenerating slice of pizza in my stomach, I told Kesho about Greenhouse's live-together proposal, about my marriage and divorce, "my fear of loss," sounding, at moments, like a TV talk show therapist. At others, I reverted to being a child, dumbfounded to discover that love was as breakable as a toy.

"I don't know why I'm sounding off about my hesitations," I said, stopping to look at a white castle of twigs half-buried in fake snow and surrounded by white trolls and reindeer. "Deciding to marry Richard couldn't have been easy."

"What's this?" Kesho asked, her eyes taking in the fuchsia-clad prince and princess mannequins, with their pink complexions and arms upraised in a royal salute.

"I think the management was aiming for a snowy winter fairyland scene."

"Yeah, no black." She wheeled herself away with strong arm strokes and plunged into Record World. I followed, chagrined for her.

"I guess they've never seen New York snow, huh?" Kesho said, her optimism bouncing back as she picked up a Wynton Marsalis CD of trumpet concertos. I asked a clerk to get me the latest Guns 'n' Roses tape for Willy.

"I think marrying a white man is going to be OK," Kesho said as we lined up to pay. "I think loving Richard is going to be enough. In our group—artists, writers—it can even be perceived as an 'in' thing. I think it's fine. I tell myself I'm hip and he's the man I love. Why should I care what color he is? Sometimes I even have this ego-swelling fantasy that I might help promote some future harmony between races. Then there's the me that comes from my parents' experience, from Aunt Rose and her friends, from looking in a mirror and instantly knowing

I've got a very different heritage from that white man I love to touch and share with. That's when I realize I'm only guessing that it's going to be OK." She paid for her CD.

"What happens to this tape if I throw it in water?" I asked the cashier, handing over my credit card when it was my turn.

"You buy another one." He was a tall blond teen who looked like he'd stopped eating at birth. "And you sign the back of your card."

"*Dio*, I'm always forgetting. I just got it in the mail." I signed the new card and handed over my driver's license as proof of identity. "The tape gets warped?"

"Beyond recognition."

"Shit!" Kesho said.

He bobbed his head at her. "Yeah."

"You've got to take a leap of faith," Kesho said, as we left the store, taking a last look at that tacky Christmas centerpiece. "With Richard I've done a jump that should win the gold it's so long."

"And you're pregnant now, too."

She spun herself around, almost hitting me with her bad leg. "Hey, that wasn't some irresponsible mistake! We planned it. I wasn't going to wait until I was forty like my mom did."

"You're a lot surer of your feelings than I am of mine. You're willing to have a baby together. That's all I was trying to say."

"Sorry, I get touchy about that black-and-pregnant crap I hear all the time." She wheeled herself away with me following, feeling suddenly as if I were walking on eggs. She stopped in front of an elevator and gave her head a shake.

"For 350 years, assertive got blacks dead. Now we can't have enough of it." She broke into a laugh. "It drives Richard nuts. It turns him on, too."

"You're awfully happy for—" I stopped, wishing I could push the replay button.

"For someone facing a murder rap?" Kesho finished for me. "I got two choices. Scream at the injustice, which would only get me a sore throat, or take it slow and easy." Her chocolate sweet eyes hit me with a hot wave of reassurance. "Stop worrying, Simona. No jail. I promise on that mockingbird I heard this morning.

"As for Richard and me, we're going to make it. So will you two. The operative word is trust." She tugged at my arm as an elevator opened. "Now come on, let's clog our sorrows with food."

"No tape. That's a bitch." Kesho sucked on a milkshake, her eyes locked on the pastel-colored carousel spinning in front of a glass wall. We were on the second floor of the mall, sitting in a wide patch of low sun, being regaled by a salsa rendition of "White Christmas." All around, a forest of tables was filled with shoppers, empty trays, crushed paper cups, stray french fries. Fast food booths crowded each other out behind us. An ideal place to talk murder.

"We went butterfly hunting on that one." I poured garlic salt on the second slice of pizza for the day.

"We did what?"

"*Andare a caccia di farfalle*. It means wasting your time—no offense intended to the lepidopterologists of the world. The chance of recouping that tape from the lake was about zero." My mouth clamped down on the tip of a slice.

"Do you at least have any idea who attacked you?"

"A man. Someone who knew . . . " I swallowed and then fanned my mouth.

"If you'd wait a bit, the slice'll cool down."

"I'm too hungry, and like Jean, too nervous."

"Worrying isn't going to get you anywhere good."

"I've tried thinking, which didn't give me the slightest clue as to who killed Elisabeth."

The carousel stopped, spewing reluctant children. The kids waiting in line screeched with joy. Behind them, through the glass wall, I could see the two top levels of the parking hive.

"My attacker had to be someone who knew that Henry had given me the tablecloth and thought he'd slipped the tape in with it. That means Chuck, Charles, Copper George and whoever they told."

"You told me. I told Richard and Jean."

"I wasn't attacked by Jean!" That was about the only thing I was sure of. I took another hot bite to hide my discomfort and looked away. A lone Santa Claus was staring at the plastic carousel horses as if they might take him back to the North Pole.

Kesho slapped her empty cup on the table. "Copper George wants me to be the murderer so bad, his teeth are rotting from the taste of it."

"Why does he dislike you so much? It's too personal to be just racism." I took a cooler bite, enjoying a thin, crisp crust.

"Look over there." Kesho's straw dripped chocolate and pointed to the left of the carousel. Santa Claus had moved away.

"That shop, DiRusso T's," Kesho said. "Verna DiRusso owns it. She's making the T-shirts for the wedding."

"What's Verna DiRusso got to do with Copper George?" The name was familiar.

"Verna is his ex-wife. The first one."

"That's right! Roxanne mentioned her. She's the reason he hates Italians."

"She's the one that kept his heart as part of the alimony settlement. Verna doesn't know it, but I'm the one who ratted on her. Copper George stopped my dad's truck one day, I was about ten or eleven at the time, and he started giving Dad a hard time about getting the truck inspected. Then he said something about how Dad shouldn't lose what little brains he had just because my mom up and left him."

Something pinched behind my eyes. A thought or a memory was blurring my brain, as shapeless and pale as the melted mozzarella I was eating.

"That's when I told him Verna was going to do the same thing to him," Kesho said. "I'd seen her up at the Bear Mountain Reservation smooching with another man more than once." She twisted her mouth. "He's been on my ass from that day on."

Willy was coming! That's what was pinching my brain. He had something that was going to blow my mind! I peeked at my watch. Three o'clock. Plenty of time. I pushed what was left of my pizza away and gave Kesho an admiring look. "You've got guts to come and live in Field-ston, with the chief of police after you."

Kesho swung her wheelchair around, barely skimming the chairs. "Rich says I could walk around the world on my guts. I say I'm just not into giving anything up. Not for the Dobsons and not for that pea brain. Let's go see Verna. I've got to quadruple my T-shirt order."

I started to weave her wheelchair through the obstacle course of tables and chairs. The Santa Claus caught my eye again, bright red in a crowd of pastel-clad kids. What was he doing here? Christmas was over. Then I saw more red. Beyond him, in the window of a video games arcade. Red and blue. A jacket worn by a tow-haired boy hunched over a video game. A Rangers jacket!

"That's Willy!" I called out, feeling a quick surge of warmth. "That's the jacket I gave him for Christmas! Hey, Willy!" I started waving. "Over here." I propelled Kesho across the floor. "He's wearing my jacket!" The arcade was a hundred feet and dozens of tables away. "What's he doing here so early?"

Kesho cupped her hands over her mouth. "William, son of Stan the Man!" she shouted. "Get that handsome face of yours over here!"

He looked up from behind the window, tossing his hair back and breaking into a grin of recognition. We flurried arms at him like frantic mothers. He ducked behind the door and walked quickly toward us.

"Wait till you see this," he called out, fifty feet away, his excited face as red as his jacket. As red as the Santa suit behind him.

Kesho's wheelchair caught on the leg of a table. I backed her up.

Willy reached in his pocket and then stopped abruptly. Santa Claus bumped into his back. The boy's face went from red to snow white.

"Ouch," Kesho said, as her bad leg hit the back of a chair.

"Sorry." I looked up. "Willy?"

He started to run behind the carousel, skimming the glass wall, with Santa glued to his back.

"Willy!" The sight wrenched my stomach. *"Aspetta!"* I ran after them as they headed for the glass door at one end of that long wall.

"Security!" Kesho yelled behind me. Santa Claus ran fast, half-lifting Willy, who tried hanging limp as a puppet, his feet dragging. They were only twenty feet ahead of me now. "Wait for me," I cried helplessly, knowing that Willy had no choice. One red arm was opening the door, the other thrusting Willy out onto the ramp that led to the parking garage. I saw a gun in the white gloved hand.

I careened after them, dodging people who stopped to stare, shoving open the double doors, tearing up the ramp, ducking into the concrete darkness of the garage. A gleam-

252   CAMILLA T. CRESPI

ing new silver van drove up, blocking my view for precious seconds. My lungs pushed against my throat, my stomach and chest heaved. Fear told me I would never breathe again. Then I dashed behind the van and caught sight of Santa and Willy out in the open sun, beyond the overhang, running up another ramp to the floor above. For a moment they faced me, but Santa had too much beard and false eyebrows for me to recognize him. Willy looked terrified.

"I'm coming," I yelled after him as if I could save him from that gun. The van honked and passed me. Kids giggled at me as their mother slipped into the first free spot on that uncovered top floor. Opposite the van, wedged between two cars, Santa was pushing Willy against the railing. Forty, fifty feet below them, I could see a gray band of skull-crushing tarmac.

"I've got it!" I yelled, stopping by the bumper of the van. Willy looked back. Santa's beard jerked in my direction. "The tape." I plunged my hand in my pocket. "That's what you want, isn't it?" I showed a corner of my tape, careful to cover the Guns 'n' Roses label with my hand. I had Santa's full attention now, but his gun stayed embedded in Willy's new jacket, aimed at his waist.

"Henry gave it to me after all," I said, keeping my voice steady, light. Hey, I was an old hand at this. "I just didn't take it with me in the car." I rattled the tape. "Willy's got nothing that has to do with the murder."

"Nothing," Willy said, between lung-splitting breaths. Santa thrust his hands into Willy's pockets, jerking them inside out. A paper floated down between cars. A photo. I caught a glimpse of a pearl necklace. Myrna's necklace.

I waved the tape. "Let him go!"

Willy kicked the photo under the car, a look of triumph on his face. Santa held on to him, but fixed his gaze on me. I had what he wanted. Or so he thought.

"Let him go and I'll throw you the tape."

"My dad's a policeman." Santa straightened up but the gun stayed where it was.

"If we do anything funny you can always shoot us." The gun was in the man's right hand which meant he was right-handed, which meant his left hand was going to have a hard time catching anything.

Behind me a van door opened. I heard something being dropped. "I'd stay in the van," I said in a low voice. "That Santa has a gun." The door slammed shut.

Santa started to blink, undecided what to do.

"If you're worried I've played the tape, I haven't. You could say it's still in its wrapper." I was praying he couldn't see the glint of cellophane. "Make up your mind. It's getting cold out here." Something hit my ankle. Out of the corner of my eye I saw an empty baby stroller parked next to my feet. "I'm not lying about not having listened to it. Scout's honor. Yes, even Italy has scouts." Not that I'd ever belonged, but I was trying to give him time to realize that shooting a boy and a woman in front of a big family of kids and one mom wasn't going to get him anywhere pleasant like the Caribbean.

"I was going to take the tape to the police this afternoon," I lied, throwing the tape up in the air. His right hand dropped an inch.

I caught the tape and lobbed it high in Santa's direction. "Run," I yelled at Willy, grabbing the stroller. Santa looked up, raising both his hands and the gun in the air, waiting to catch the tape. Willy leaped, rolling over the hood of the car to his left. I ran in for the kill just as a white gloved hand caught the tape. I smashed the stroller against Santa's knees, my head going for his stomach. The gun dropped. I fell backwards on impact, landing on the gun. He lunged for it, kicking me in the process, dripping spit on my face with the effort. I kicked back, my arm sweeping the gun which slithered toward the van. My thigh got another bruising kick and those gloved hands grabbed my neck.

"Get your hands up, Santa Claus!"

Unmistakable blinking eyes widened in surprise. Copper George straightened up and raised his hands. I twisted my neck to see Willy standing with his legs spread, both arms raised at chest level with the police chief's gun firmly clasped in his hands.

"You're a disgrace to Christmas," Willy said, managing to sound as old as his dad.

Kesho's head surged above the edge of the ramp, leading a parade of seven security men, all black, all strong, guns in hand.

From the rear window of the van, our audience of four kids and one mom cheered. I looked back at Copper George, hands up, blinking his way to years of jail.

"*Allora*, what don't you like about Italians, eh?"

30

W hat did I tell you guys?" Kesho said the following
night. "That was some mockingbird I heard, huh?"

"I should have known it was Copper George by the
way he stuffed that scarf in my mouth." I bit into a slurpy
rigatone. "He doesn't like me."

We were sitting around Jean's dining room table once
again, this time gobbling bowls of Comfort Pasta. Jean,
Chuck—who had done the cooking under my guidance—
Richard, Kesho, Willy, and Greenhouse.

"Your son saved the day," I said, spooning out a third
helping for Willy.

"No, you did," Willy said. "Dad, you should have seen
her with that stroller. I mean, lethal stuff."

I laughed along with the others, happy to be made fun
of. "You did save the day, though, Willy. If you hadn't
called in saying you were coming back with something to
blow my mind, Copper George would never have come
after you."

"I think I deserve a little credit here," Jean said, offering French bread.

"That's right," Kesho jumped in. "She's the one who

forgot Willy called and gave Simona the message in front of that bastard."

We gave Jean a round of applause.

"Wait a minute." Richard raised his Missoni-clad arm. "How did Copper George know Willy was at the mall?"

"That's my doing again." Jean's face puckered with chagrin. "I bumped into him out on Main Street and I started telling him how worried I was about poor Henry when this nice green Jaguar drove by. 'Why, that's Willy,' I called out." She waved a hand in imitation of her gesture. "Copper George flagged the car down. I thought he was doing it for me so I hurried over and told Willy and this nice-looking woman that Simona was at the mall with Kesho. The chief let them turn around on the spot, in front of my eyes. Even stopped traffic for them. I guess he couldn't very well yank Willy out of the car right there on Main Street!"

"He followed them," I said. "I guess that Santa suit he told me about the night of the murder was still in the trunk of his car."

"I looked for you by the food counters," Willy said. Sauce dotted his chin. "But then I saw that video arcade, you know. I got a little distracted."

"I'm lost," Greenhouse said. He looked tired, his eyes softened by past worry. "All I know is my son and the woman I love almost got killed." He clings to reality a lot.

"They didn't, though." Kesho raised a finger. "Elisabeth did and Edith, too."

"Copper George smothered the old lady." Richard stole a rigatone from Kesho's plate. His own plate was empty. "Autopsy showed waterlogged lungs, dilation of the right side of the heart, a lot of oxygen in the blood—"

"Rich, enough!" Kesho tugged at his sleeve. "Some of us are still eating."

"I don't believe I cooked this," Chuck said, looking up from his plate for the first time. "It's so good."

"Lord, yes." Jean said with an eager smile. "You have found your art."

"Lucky you!" Kesho twirled a fork in the air. "I can't cook beans. That's why I'm forced to marry a restaurateur." Richard threw a roll at her.

I took a long gulp of water and reached over to hold Willy's hand. "This morning the police smashed open the pool deck at RockPerch. What Roxanne's dad had suspected was true. They found what was left of Walter."

"The chief of police killed him?" Greenhouse asked, with a quick look at his son.

"No," Richard said. "He buried him."

"It's all right, Dad," Willy said, doing his deep voice. "I'm a big guy, you know."

"Damn big." I gave Willy a hug. We were fast friends now, at least as long as the afterglow of shared danger lasted.

"The cops aren't all as good as you, Stan," Kesho said. "I never thought that man would break down, though."

"Verna," Jean threw in. "That's Copper George's first wife. She got him to confess. Clever guy, Santinelli. He knew what would open George up."

"Who's Santinelli?" Greenhouse asked.

"He's going to be the new chief of police," Jean said.

"And his cousin Roxanne filled me in," I added.

Greenhouse turned to look at me expectantly in that quiet way I love. I gulped wine this time. "Elisabeth killed Walter. According to Copper George, it was an accident. Walter was in a rage, slapping her around. She shoved him away, he slipped and hit his head against the concrete corner of his desk."

"If she didn't kill him on purpose," Willy asked, "why did she bury the body?"

"Elisabeth called Copper George right away. When he came over she was hysterical, blaming herself. He played into her hysteria and convinced her she was in real trouble, that no one would believe it was an accident."

"Yeah," Richard said, "I remember something about her having a lover at the time. That would make it tough for her."

Chuck looked up from his plate, anger clear on his face. "That's horseshit Edith was shoveling out." Did he know about his mother?

"Elisabeth's love life doesn't matter at this point," I said. "What is important is that Copper George admitted he offered to get rid of Walter's body for money. He was building a big house he couldn't afford and trying to hold onto his second wife by buying her things."

"He didn't care two cents for that woman," Jean said with an assertive shake of her curls. "He was spending all that money to show Verna what a rich husband she'd lost."

"Maybe. Anyway, Elisabeth agreed, and they both tucked Walter under the pool deck in the middle of the night. This was a Friday night. Roxanne's father had just laid in the deck that day so the grouting was still fresh. Then Copper George made Elisabeth wait several days to announce that Walter drove off Monday morning, which just happened to be April Fool's Day. A cute little touch on his part."

"Clever," Richard said. "If Walter disappears three days later, no one's going to unearth the new deck."

"That Sunday Copper George went to the house, donned Walter's cape and hat, and paraded up and down the edge of the property, hoping that busybody Edith would see him while she did her annual garden clean-up and mistake him for Walter. Which she did. At least until a few days before her death. The following Wednesday Elisabeth finally told Charles that her husband had left her."

"Dad was so scared the precious Dobson name might be smirched," Chuck said. "He waited days to tell the police."

"In the meantime," I scooped up the last of the sauce

from my plate, "Copper George flew to Toronto with Walter's suitcase, clothes and credit card, checked into a fancy hotel, set up the scene, came back the same day. He could pass for Walter if no one looked too close. He'd fooled Edith. Both men were tall and big. Copper George admitted he kept Walter's hat on during check-in to cover his red hair, even pretended to go to the bathroom while the concierge went through the paperwork. The concierge apparently forgot to mention the hat to the FBI."

"The misguided protective instinct," Richard said. "I've done it in my bistros when someone asks for a customer over the phone. Especially if I think it's a wife."

Kesho bared teeth.

Greenhouse dropped elbows on the table. "The FBI didn't compare signatures on credit card and registration slip?"

I released the fork from my mouth. "They matched. Copper George got lucky. Walter hadn't signed his new card yet. It happened to me yesterday at the mall. I know, I'm sloppy," I said, countering his look. "Anyway, a few months later Elisabeth gave Copper George what Walter had left in their joint bank account—sixty-two thousand dollars."

"Then Kesho and Richard come along," Greenhouse said, "dying to buy the house. Elisabeth decides it's time to get out from under the Dobson thumb, throws an exorbitant price at them. They accept. When Copper George finds out, he calls Elisabeth to stop her, afraid new owners will dig up the pool area."

I nodded. "Charles told him right after the dinner."

"That sounds like the pater," Chuck said, hair falling over his glasses. "He was probably hoping there was some ancient town ordinance that would stop a black from owning Dobson property."

"That's the famous phone call Edith taped," I said. "Lucky for us, Henry didn't take my advice. He never told the police he'd thrown the tape in the lake. I'd gotten him too upset about tampering with evidence in a murder case."

"Bless his heart," Jean said, picking up a heaping bowl of salad off the buffet.

Kesho clapped her hands. "Amen."

Richard leaned over to skate his hand down her back. "Elisabeth did what she was told. She canceled the sale. I'm witness to that. I almost socked her one for it, too. So why'd he kill her? He didn't trust her anymore?"

"She turned on him," I said. "She agreed not to sell, but he had to come up with a lot of money—steal it if he had to—or else she was going to go to Santinelli—"

"Who's Santinelli again?" Greenhouse asked.

"D-a-a-ad!"

I liked the sound of that D-a-a-ad. "Santinelli's the new police chief. Elisabeth was going to show him where Walter was buried. She was also going to say that Copper George was her lover at the time and that he killed Walter in a jealous rage."

Chuck looked sad for a moment. "She was good at distorting things."

"It was only her word against his," Jean said.

Greenhouse knocked a fork against his plate. "He was the chief of police. I would have believed him."

"Stan!" Kesho's eyes widened with disbelief. "You believe Darryl Gates?"

Greenhouse looked muddled.

I pawed his foot under the table. "The police would have gone over the whole case, maybe found a missing clue that would point to him."

Jean broke a roll in half. "Poor George has been on edge a lot lately. Santinelli's been nipping at his heels for the chief's job. Wife number three was getting restless. Verna was back with her DiRusso T's at the mall where everybody could see her." She started to wipe her salad plate with the bread, then dropped the roll as if it were too heavy for her hand. "He's been in bad shape for some time."

"DiRusso!" I finally made the connection. "That's the clue! DiRusso's the name he used on the airline ticket. William DiRusso. Same initials as Walter Dobson. Why am I so dumb?"

"Beats me," Willy said, spreading out his hands.

Greenhouse laughed.

"Thanks, you two." I shoved the salad bowl their way.

"Greed got Copper George," Chuck decreed. "It's always greed."

"I think it was love," Jean said. "Loving Verna made him crazy."

"No way," Willy said. "It's anger. Shakespeare would call that his tragic flaw."

I cocked my head. "Why anger?"

"He was real angry at Kesho because she told him his wife was playing around, right?"

Kesho did a slow nod. "You can say that again, baby."

"You see, it's love," Jean insisted.

"He's angry twenty years. So he arrests her. Big mistake. Dictated by anger. That's when Simona and I team up, to help her out. And we nail him."

"You get an A-plus on that paper." Kesho was so happy she was giving off heat. "God bless both of you. Now, what's black-and-white and loved all over?"

Greenhouse slumped back in his chair, his eyes finally grinning. "That one's easy."

"It is?" I wanted to love him so badly, my thighs were trembling.

Kesho looped a hand in the air. "If it's so easy, Stan the Man, what are you waiting for? Let's have it. What's black-and-white and loved all over?"

"You and Richard, who else?"

"Well, I'm black-and-blue and haven't been loved in eons." I was in bed now. After dinner, Willy had given me a sneaky look and said he was off to the movies with the ice-skating sisters. The minute he was out of the door, I'd developed aches and pains that forced me to my room, Greenhouse following.

"Look," I pushed aside the quilt to show off a splotched blue thigh where Copper George had kicked me. My rear end looked like a baboon's so I kept that hidden. "Thanks for telling the murderer I interfere with police work."

"I wanted him to keep an eye out for you and Willy." Greenhouse sat on the edge of the bed, fully dressed. My hand cupped his knee.

"I had a nasty revenge planned, but that meant being deprived of your best body part."

His knee shuddered. "I won't ask. What did Willy have to blow your mind?"

"A Polaroid of Myrna's pearl choker, the one she wore Christmas Eve. Remember, I took him back to New York after Edith died?"

"Sure, he stayed with David, whose parents are getting a divorce."

"That's right. Well, David's mother took the boys into Harry Winston's yesterday morning to get her engagement ring appraised, and there was the choker Myrna had worn Christmas Eve, up for sale."

"Willy recognized it?"

"Remember Willy asking you about rich ancestors?"

"Yes, what was that about?"

"The choker. Myrna showed him portraits of gracious ladies all wearing that necklace. Willy thought that if Myrna and Charles needed money badly enough to sell a family heirloom, one of them or both killed Elisabeth to get RockPerch. So he went back to David's, called the inn and left the message for me, got a Polaroid camera, went back to Winston's and asked to photograph the necklace for a school project." I hit the pillow, laughing. "Same convincing charm his old man has." I blew him a kiss. "Then David's mother didn't like the idea of Willy taking a train to Danbury by himself so she drove him here. The rest you know."

"Willy's got a lot of determination," Greenhouse said, still fully dressed. "He'll make quite a career for himself at whatever he chooses. Now I wish he'd just be a boy."

"He is. He forgot his mission completely in front of an Addams Family pinball machine." I kissed the fingers of his hand. "I never meant to put him in any danger."

Greenhouse's expression relaxed. "You should carry a warning sign: Ignites When Curious."

"Which is always."

"You bet." He raked fingers down my hip.

"I'm igniting right now," I said, feeling my bones go spongy.

"What do you think? Should we?"

"Make love?" I sank down.

"Live together."

"Oh." I opened my eyes. "What will Willy say?"

"You looked pretty chummy down there."

"We're both on a high."

"He likes you and he's the one who said he's a big boy." His hand was warm on my stomach.

I stroked his lips. "I talk better with you in bed. Naked."

"You mean you moan better."

"That too."

"I want to talk with my head."

I sat up and covered my breasts with the quilt. "This sounds serious."

"You know it is and you're avoiding the issue."

"I've gotten used to feeling marginal."

"What are you getting at?" Impatience crept into his voice.

"I've been so busy wanting you, I think I got lost in the desire."

He retreated his hand. "You mean the waiting is more exciting than the event."

"No!" I took his hand right back. "That sounds terrible. I'm emotionally muddled, is what I mean. You didn't prepare me in any way."

"I didn't know it was coming either."

"Do you really mean it?" That hand felt too good. What if what I called love was only good sex? "You probably don't know. A lot's happened in five days. Willy catching us making love for one. Maybe you're just trying to legitimize that. Then your mom's operation scared you and you reached out to me. Are you asking me to live with you because you love me or because I happened to be around during a bad moment?"

"I'm getting the third degree?"

I squeezed his thigh. "Doesn't feel too good, does it?"

"No." I heard a shoe drop.

"Look, Greenhouse, we've seen each other for clumps of hours at a time. A few weekends when you're not on call and Willy is off with his mom. We need days together."

"I did try this time." The other shoe dropped. "A whole week we were going to be together."

"We may discover we can't take it." His hand was beginning to wander.

"That's right, you won't let me get in a word edgewise. Who knows, you might even overcook the pasta. That's why we should test it out first."

I lay back, letting go of the quilt. "And if it doesn't work? Will you guarantee me another studio for six hundred dollars a month?"

"I'd help out." Fingers tiptoed over my breast.

"Oh, God." I pulled him down. "I'm scared. I don't know why I'm so scared."

He wrapped himself around me. "I love you."

I nestled my nose in the opening of his shirt. "I love you too, but please give me time."

"Yes," he said simply, holding me until my heart quieted down. I lifted up my head to kiss him.

"About my being Jewish," he started to say.

"What about it?" Instead I licked his chin.

"I think we need to talk about that, too."

"Hm, hm." I bit into his neck. "A must." I reached down and pulled at his shirt. "Lots of talking. But before all that—"

I glanced down at the heave of his stomach, at the gray tail of hair feathering out of his belt.

"What?" His breath warmed my ear.

"I want to make love to you till the cock crows."

And I did, although the cock turned out to be Willy, crowing "Jingle Bells," in the driveway loud enough to wake the dead.

EPILOGUE

I'm back at the office. The Christmas tinsel and holly have been swept away, and my desk is piled high with comps of children. HH&H is looking for a spokeskid for a new client who retails children's clothing. After sorting through endless smiling faces, I keep looking back at my bulletin board where I've pinned the place card Kesho so carefully drew for her wedding. Ruffy, in his top hat and tails, almost winks back at me. Wouldn't he make a perfect spokesquirrel?

The New Year's Eve wedding was moving. Greenhouse held my hand while I cried and Willy handed me tissues. Jean leaned into Chuck, nodding her approval. Chuck lost the gawky goose look. Premi swept between our legs like a broom gathering affection. Kesho and Richard beamed when the judge pronounced them man and wife. Their artist friends clapped. Aunt Rose and her entourage held serious faces.

After the newlyweds handed out the "Who's black-and-white and loved all over?" T-shirt to all their guests, the DJ spun the first record. Premi rocketed out of the living room and the party got loud and gay. Roxanne and Joe showed up, invited as a thank-you for their help. So did

Nell, the librarian. I apologized to her for passing myself off as a journalist. She didn't mind, saying she was only too happy to be at the wedding. Later I saw her huddled in a corner with Kesho's black art professor, trying, over the music, to discuss the importance of Zora Neale Hurston in women's literature.

Willy asked me to dance once, then decided that Aunt Rose's sixteen-year-old niece was more his style. Greenhouse teamed up with seventy-year-old Aunt Rose to win the boogie-woogie contest. I kicked off my heels and danced with Joe *and* Roxanne. In that living room, cleared of Shaker tables and flea market furniture, with the window glass shaking with music and the century-old floor creaking under our feet, I like to think we forgot racial differences.

I went outside to gulp some cold air. While Premi peered at me from the doorstep, tail curled over his paws in a noncommittal stance, I thought of Elisabeth. "What am I?" she had asked me. I didn't know. Neither did Myrna or Jean or Chuck, I suspected, each one fitting Elisabeth into a cutout of their own expectations. Expectation was a dangerous word, I decided, as the outdoors rubbed the party heat off. It was so often based on assumptions borne of our own desires. Dangerous and frightening, I thought, the marriage vows still ringing in my ear.

Aunt Rose appeared at the back door, peering at me in concert with Premi, her orchid corsage flicking at her chin.

"It doesn't fit right," she muttered to the cat. Since she was a dressmaker, I assumed she didn't accept Kesho's store-bought dress, a long sheath of embroidered white tulle over a mini satin shift that I thought gorgeous.

"Kesho can wear anything," I assured her.

She looked up at me, head crouched in a flowered red hat. "I'm not talkin' about what she was wearing. I sure did like that Kente cloth hugging her head like that, made her look like a flower." It had taken the place of the veil.

"My Kente cloth's doing it all," Kesho had said, getting dressed. I had just offered to lend her my pearls for the "borrowed" part of the wedding musts. "It's something old. It belonged to my mother so it's borrowed." She grabbed both my hands, the brown of her eyes deeply warm. "It's new because my mother's story is new, new to me. And wonderful."

"What about 'something blue'?"

A disappointed look came over Kesho's face. She dropped my hands and began to wrap the red-and-ocher cloth around her head. "This piece of cotton is so blue, it's wet."

"Kesho says it's a matter of trust," I told Aunt Rose, finally understanding her worry.

Aunt Rose bobbed her hat. "At least with all those restaurants that man's gonna keep her in food, if nothing else." With that she went back inside. I stopped to pick up Premi. He rubbed his head under my chin and gave me his Rolls-Royce purr.

At midnight, we toasted the New Year. Aunt Rose sidled up to me and clinked her champagne glass against mine.

"When's Kesho goin' to tell the Dobsons and the rest of this town about this trust business?"

"I think she already has." In the afternoon Myrna had come by to leave a silver stuffing spoon as a wedding present and to tell Kesho that Charles was not going to contest the will.

"Thanks for convincing Dad," Chuck said, placing a hand on her arm. It was the only time I saw them touch. She gave Chuck a shaky smile, declined Kesho's invitation to come to the wedding party saying, "I'm in mourning" and slipped out.

The dancing continued until six in the morning when

Kesho threw her bouquet. Roxanne lunged for it, then showed it around as if it were a diamond ring. Then those of us who were still awake tramped up to RockPerch to watch the bride and groom pick the spot where the traditional sugar maple would be planted in warmer weather. Kesho promised Nell to honor her homeless ancestor Sarah Bishop with a plaque on the ledge where she died. Nell gave everyone a horsey smile.

Finally, with orange lining the horizon to the east, we all threw birdseed as the new couple ran to the white Mercedes.

"The birds choke on rice," Willy explained, laughing when the car was stopped by a rope he had tied to the back bumper and a two-foot-thick tree.

The wedding and the vacation were over. In the afternoon, after we exchanged hugs with Jean and Chuck, and I rubbed my nose against Premi's sweet-smelling head, we drove back to the city. I never did get another look at the fawn I tugged out of the water, although I didn't stop trying until we hit the Hutch.

Henry and I have been exchanging short how-are-you notes since I've been back in the city. He's often at Jean's, and next week he's off to Roxanne's house for her mother's baba ghannoush. This morning I went to the post office to send him a picture book of Rome I hope he'll enjoy. Now I always have my morning coffee in his mismatched cup and saucer. I feel it reflects my life in some way.

Greenhouse hasn't mentioned living together again. I think about it all the time, but don't tell him. Sometimes, especially at night, I wish him always with me. Then in the morning, when I look at my tiny apartment, filled with my things the way I want them, I turn into the teenager that doesn't want her precarious space invaded.

Last Sunday night the fear of loving him came back, as heavy as the rain outside. I was watching Miss Marple on

TV and remembered, in the midst of those clipped accents, my first soul friend, Judy Akroyd. She left Rome to go back to England when I was seven years old, and had written me a note. "I'm gone. I love you." I looked up "gone," a new English word for me. The dictionary gave me three words for Judy's one. "Dead, lost, ruined." Missing her, I started putting "gone" and "love" together.

Greenhouse and I have talked about religion. His father thundered that the suffering in the world proved there was no God. His mother slipped a yarmulke on his head whenever Dad wasn't around. He grew up ambivalent. When his father got killed, Greenhouse didn't want to betray his atheism. Marrying a gentile was easy, even though his mother wasn't happy. His ex-wife was religious so letting Willy grow up Episcopalian seemed the right choice.

"No regrets?" I asked him after we took Willy home after a movie last night.

"It's a great heritage."

We skipped down the subway steps. "You could start with a seder where the history is read out loud."

"What do you know about seders?"

"I live in New York. I've got connections."

He dropped tokens in the turnstile. "We'll see."

"Willy would be fascinated. It's part of him. He should know."

"We'll see."

"I could make an Italian-Jewish meal. *Carciofi alla guidea*. Artichokes fried in liters of oil. Not very good for you, but delicious. If you insist on matzoh balls I'll put some parsley in them. You need that little bit of flavor."

"Simona . . ."

"I'll make them small. They're prettier that way. They won't stick in my throat. The gefilte fish is always much too bland and the haro. . ."

"Simona!"

The train screeched into the station. "What, honey?" I automatically stepped up to a closed door.

He grinned, wise to me. "I think that's one dinner I'll make."

I wished him, "Mazel tov," and hooked my arm in his. For once, both train doors slid open to welcome us inside.

COMFORT PASTA

4 tbsps. olive oil
1 large carrot, minced
1 celery stalk, minced
1 large onion, chopped
4 garlic cloves, peeled
2 lbs. beef chuck, cut into bite-sized pieces
2 cups flour
2 cups white wine (optional)
1 tbsp. tomato paste
5 plum tomatoes, quartered
½ tsp. red pepper flakes
3 cups low-sodium chicken broth
1½ lbs. rigatoni
½ cup grated Parmesan cheese
¾ lb. fresh spinach

Select a heavy-bottomed pan with lid in which all ingredients can fit. Sauté garlic cloves in oil until lightly browned, stirring well. Put flour in a paper bag. Discard cloves and raise the flame to high. In batches drop meat in the paper bag and shake. Flour meat right before adding to pan or else it will get gummy. Add meat to hot oil in batches and brown well on all sides. Add the wine and cook over high heat until almost evaporated. Remove browned meat and set aside. Lower flame and add onion, scraping the bottom of the pan. Sauté onion until translucent. Add tomato paste, stir and cook 2 minutes. Add a tablespoon of broth if onions are too dry. Add celery and carrot, stir and cook 3 minutes more. Add browned meat and accumulated juices. Add tomatoes, red pepper flakes, salt, and pepper. Stir. Add broth. When broth starts to boil, lower flame, partially cover pan, and simmer meat for 1½ hours.

Up to this point can be prepared ahead of time. Stew can be frozen.

Bring a large pot of salted water to a boil.

Cook stew ½ hour more at a low boil before serving. Wash and stem spinach.

Add rigatoni to boiling water. When al dente, drain. Add spinach to stew and stir. Spinach will wilt with the heat. Pour half of the stew into a big pasta bowl. Add half the Parmesan. Stir. Add the drained rigatoni. Stir. Add rest of stew and Parmesan. Stir again and serve. *Buon appetito!*

Serves six hungry stomachs.

Born in Prague to an American mother and an Italian diplomat father, Camilla T. Crespi came to the United States as a teenager and did not go back to Italy until she graduated from Barnard College. In Rome, she dubbed films for leading filmmakers such as Federico Fellini, Luchino Visconti, and Lina Wertmüller. Thirteen years ago—not an unlucky number for Italians—she returned to New York, got married, and found work in an advertising agency. Wanting to write, she enrolled in Columbia's Graduate Writing Program. The first Simona Griffo mystery, *The Trouble with a Small Raise*, was published in 1991, a year after Crespi received her MFA.

She is currently at work on her fifth mystery, *The Trouble with Going Home*.